The Whispering Wall

The Whispering Wall

Patricia Carlon

This edition published
by arrangement with Wakefield Press, Australia

First published in Great Britain by Hodder and Stoughton, 1969;
first published in the United States of America in 1996

Published by
Soho Press, Inc.
853 Broadway
New York, NY 10003

Library of Congress Cataloging-in-Publication Data

Carlon, Patricia, 1927–
        The whispering wall / Patricia Carlon.
            p.   cm.
        ISBN 1-56947-111-8 (alk. paper)
        I. Title.
    PR 9619.3.C37W48   1996
    823—dc20
                                    96-20040
                                        CIP

10 9 8 7 6 5 4 3 2 1

CHAPTER I

———

Sometimes Sarah imagined that death was behind the heavy dark doors of the corner wardrobe, watching her with one bright, knowing, watchful eye. That was in the nights, when light struck through an unprotected corner of the window, on to the big round keyhole, sparking it into brightness, a round bright circle winking at her from the dark.

Then she would wonder what Bragg would say to the imagining, and she was glad there was no chance that in some unguarded, lonely moment she would let out her fears of the night and see the pale eyes reflect the pity in the oozing voice.

Lying there with nothing to do but think, she would remember odd snatches from her life and from the lives of others; trifles she had never remembered before – like a tartan sash lost and grieved over when she was four; the death of a canary; a school lesson forgotten; hot summer Sundays and a young clergyman stammering over his sermons, conscious his audience was weighing him against his predecessor and finding him wanting. Hot summer Sundays, Sarah remembered, and remembered, too, her resentment at being cooped up in the crowded church with all of summer – the open paddocks, the song of cicadas, the cool velvet of brown creek waters – waiting for her outside, while she had to sit in a starched cotton frock listening to a stammering voice.

Lying there, fifty years and a thousand miles from the paddocks and the child of ten, Sarah remembered odd bits and pieces of the sermons. She didn't want to because remembrance made her uncomfortable as she heard again the stammering youthful voice speaking of people and hatred and sin.

It had made her feel guilty, that remembrance, because she hated Bragg so badly, from the soft oozing voice to the plump hands, and it wasn't fair or just that hate, Sarah knew. It was actually a terrible sin to hate Bragg, who was competent and thought herself kind and comforting and a credit to the nursing profession.

Yet how, Sarah fretted, could one feel anything but hate for a person who invaded every privacy, who knew all about you, or thought she did, and discussed that knowledge over your recumbent quiet body; who called you 'poor dear' and referred to you over and over again as being laid out like a fish on a slab.

It was at those moments that Sarah acutely regretted her lost voice. She would have liked to have told Bragg concisely and quite crudely, what she, Sarah, thought of that beastly phrase; but at other times, in the lonely dark times, she was glad she could no longer speak, or it would all tumble out to Bragg's receptive ear, to be later repeated to the doctor and old friends – about the wardrobe and the bright knowing watching eye in the night, and a hundred and one other things better unsaid.

Sarah could never think of the woman except as simply Bragg. Not even as Sister Bragg, or Nurse Bragg, and certainly not as Cornelia, though on that first morning that Sarah had become aware of the world again Bragg had smiled down at her, plump hand patting Sarah's own, and had said, 'Hello, dear. Isn't that nice that you're awake at last. I'm Cornelia Bragg, dear. Just think of me as Cornelia. All my friends do.' And then pity had clouded the pale eyes and she had turned to the doctor and oozed in her thick, syrupy tones, 'Not a blink, doctor. Do you think she hears? She's laid out like a fish on a slab, with as much life to her, poor dear.'

Sarah hated remembering that, the first time she had heard

that phrase. It reminded her how the knowledge had crept on her, then burst on her, like a terrifying flood, that she could no longer speak or move – that her mind was a prisoner in something inert, that was no longer her possession to use as she willed; that she was, as Bragg claimed, a mere lifeless fish on a slab, laid out for inspection and probing by anyone who chose to come.

There was only the book to cling to. Sarah couldn't remember how long ago it had been that she had read it, but it had been about a person in her own condition – paralysed of body and voice by one savage unheralded stroke.

It had spoken of the victim's body as feeling heavy as lead. Sarah would have liked to have written to the author of that and told him he didn't know what he had been talking about, because in her particular state there was a thistledown light-ness about her body. You couldn't make thistledown butter bread, or spoon up cereal or do high kicks. Sometimes Sarah amused herself with the idea of Bragg's expression if her patient in some way managed a sudden high kick in the bed, but thistledown didn't do anything except lie and wait for something or someone to move it somewhere else.

There was something else Sarah remembered about that book – remembered and clung to in desperate hope. The vic-tim of that unheralded stroke had recovered in the end. Oh, not completely, but enough. She couldn't remember if it had been a leg or an arm that had continued to fail him, but what-ever it was it had been a trifle beside the main point – that the rest of him came back to movement and living.

Whenever Bragg, or one of the visitors who came and peered at Sarah and clucked over her, had been particularly trying, Sarah would remember the book and think only of the pleasant time when she was once again Mrs Sarah Oatland, and not just a fish on a slab, to be peered at by every comer and labelled as worthless, or worse, a nuisance.

She was a nuisance to Gwenyth. She knew that, because there were no subterfuges about Gwenyth. The plump, neatly dressed figure never condescended to sit by the bed, as old friends did, and pretend, even for a little, that Sarah was still a living creature and might understand the words they said, even if she didn't acknowledge them. Gwenyth's visits were brief. She came, Sarah realised, and knew by Bragg's expression and voice that the nurse knew it too, solely to keep an eye on Bragg. She made no bones about it. Her visits were always unheralded, and she would stand in the doorway of Sarah's room, dark eyes probing round it, noting the position of every ornament, every trifle. There had been one day one of the shepherdess candlesticks from the mantelpiece had been moved to another room for some reason or other. Gwenyth's always rigidly high chin – an insurance against the onset of double chin – tilted further aloft. Her thin voice knifed through the warm still air of Sarah's room, accusing, 'Nurse, what have you done with my aunt's shepherdess?'

Sarah had found amusement in what had followed. Bragg had thrust up an equally rigid chin and had said crudely, 'I haven't run round to the nearest pop shop with it, Mrs Oatland. You've a nasty suspicious mind, haven't you?' And then triumphantly, in the face of Gwenyth's astounded ragings she had added, 'You can sack me if you like – or if the doctor lets you – but if you do you'll be nursing the old dear yourself. It's not one nurse in a hundred wants this sort of case. Too much heavy lifting and round the clock watching.'

Gwenyth's rage had died to an icy prod. 'This is a ridiculous scene. You've been offensive, for no reason. I have a duty to my aunt. She is incapable of caring for her own property. I've accused you of nothing, but people are in and out of here all the time and my aunt's possessions . . .' Bragg had smiled maliciously. There was no backing down in her brief. '. . . are going to be yours one day, and you're keeping an eye on them. Rightio. That's fine by me, so long as you don't expect me to account for them all. If you're scared they'll all be gone before you get your hands on them, you can always shift in here and give a hand with the old dear.'

Sarah had known, and was grateful for it, that there was no danger of that. In her middle-aged widowhood, Gwenyth had her own small apartment and comforts she would never give up, certainly not for an aunt by marriage who was now merely a nuisance, a hindrance to Gwenyth's taking over the big old house on Parkland Avenue. Her watchful unheralded visits had continued though, and her enmity towards Bragg had grown. It was partly that enmity, Sarah thought sometimes, that made Gwenyth speak her mind so much, thrusting aside Bragg's hushed, 'You oughtn't to speak like that in front of the old dear. She might understand every word and think how you'd feel yourself if . . .'

'Don't be ridiculous,' Gwenyth had retorted once. 'My aunt is no more than a vegetable.'

For once Sarah had warmed to Bragg. 'Plenty've vegetables have sent out shoots all of a sudden,' she retorted swiftly. 'Look at onions – brown dried up things – and all of a sudden there are green shoots bursting out the top of them, and they're back to life.'

Gwenyth hadn't laughed, but Sarah had wished the gift of laughter was still hers. In darkness, alone, with just that bright keyhole watching her, she had found there was no amusement at all in being a mixture of fish and onion. It had become revolting. She could still remember the sickness of despair and frustration she had felt that morning, because that day had been the day Gwenyth had decided the house must be divided.

She had stood by the bed as usual, never once looking at Sarah as she spoke – perhaps, Sarah had thought bitterly, fearing that in the depths of the faded eyes there would be protest and panic and dismay – and had said crisply, 'Nurse, I have been speaking to the doctor. It appears no one can say how long my aunt will survive like this. It's six weeks – over six – since she had the stroke and . . .'

Bragg had sounded startled and upset. 'You mean, you're going to sell the house over the poor dear's head? Where's she going to go then? Your place?'

'Don't be ridiculous.' Gwenyth had sounded tired. 'I couldn't sell the house. I haven't any authority, but her solicitors say part of it can be rented. There's that little flat at the back downstairs, for a start. My uncle put that in years ago to tempt a domestic to stay on. You know how it is – to get anyone to do a bit of scrubbing you have to offer the earth.' Her plump shoulders moved impatiently. 'But that finished when uncle died. There wasn't money for help in the house. Anyway, my aunt said there was no work for anyone, and she preferred looking after her own things. She wouldn't even share the house.' Exasperation creased the smooth white forehead for a minute. 'She could have been getting an income from that flat for years if she'd rented it. It's quite self-contained, and then the front part downstairs only needs a stove. There's that little room with a sink. Put a stove there – it's only a matter of extending the gas piping, I'm certain, and it wouldn't cost much – and that's a kitchen. There's already that shower room down there. And the door at the top of the stairs can be locked. It will mean two flats downstairs to bring in some money. She's going to need it. She could be like this for years. Couldn't she?'

Sarah wanted to scream a protest. She wanted to cry out that she wouldn't share the house, wouldn't have strangers roaming through her beloved rooms, have them touching the old furniture she kept polished with love and constant care; and most of all she wanted to protest at that last challenge to Bragg. She waited for the woman to deny it, but Bragg only shook her head and whispered, 'You oughtn't to talk like that. The poor dear might understand every word.'

'Oh, stop being a fool!' Gwenyth had turned away impatiently. 'If there was any life in her it would have shown in her eyes when I spoke about the house. The house,' there was suddenly sheer temper in the thin voice, 'is the only thing she's cared about since my uncle died. She wouldn't sell it, she wouldn't rent it, she wouldn't part with a stick of the furniture because it belonged to this wretched house, and she couldn't bear a corner of it empty . . .'

Bragg had laughed then. To Sarah's mind, it was the nicest thing about Bragg. The woman's laugh was gay and youthful, even when it mocked, as it did when she said, 'Asked her for some of the furniture to furnish up your own place, did you? And she put you in your place?'

Gwenyth had kept her temper. She had said only, 'My husband was in foreign service. We had no chance to accumulate things of our own. When he died and I came back here the furniture was my uncle's – my husband's uncle . . . a lot of it . . .' she had pressed on ' . . . belonged to uncle's parents.'

'That makes the old dear closer to Granny and Grandpa than you, doesn't it, when it comes down to brass tacks? And evidently he left the lot to the old dear, so . . .'

Gwenyth had turned away, throwing over her shoulder, 'There'll be someone here today to see about the stove downstairs. I'm advertising the back flat in tomorrow's papers. I'll be here tomorrow to show any callers round.'

She had let herself out, as she always did, and Bragg had come back to Sarah's bedside, to ease herself into the big cane chair and say to Sarah, 'There's one mercy, dear, that one will never let anyone in the place who isn't just so. You'll have people down there so respectable they never eat chips out of newspaper. They'll be a prissy lot, you'll see, but it's all to the good. You won't need to worry about them making off with your things and spoiling the place, not of course that you can worry, can you?' The long face bent over the bed, the pale eyes searching Sarah's features. 'I wish I knew if you could worry.' There had been uncertainty in the oozing treacle of her voice, which had slowed, spacing each word carefully. 'If you understand, what she said, what I'm saying, you're not to worry. She'll get someone in who'll take care of your things. She won't let anything happen to them. Not ever.'

The long features had drawn back. Unspoken between them lay the knowledge that Gwenyth was only waiting for the vegetable, the fish on the slab, to die, before she claimed all the furniture and the house as her own, so she would certainly see that any tenants took care of everything.

So it had been a surprise when the child had come. Sarah had never expected that. She had thought a child would have been the last thing Gwenyth would have had in the place. She had no children of her own, was impatient with the children of friends, yet two days later she came upstairs, with the child and her mother in her wake and had stood beside the bed. 'Nurse, I have arranged that Mrs Abcons and Rose will live in the flat at the back of the house. They will be moving in tomorrow,' she said.

Bragg had echoed Sarah's own surprise in her questioning. 'A child? You've let to a kiddie?'

'Yes. Rose is eleven. She will be at school all day, of course, but Mrs Abcons has agreed that after school Rose will do any messages for you. It will save the expense of phone calls – the phone bill is ridiculous for these last weeks – and it will mean Mrs Furlong can go earlier. It's unnecessary to have her hanging around in case you need a prescription made up, and to bring you tea. Rose will do that.'

Sarah saw her own contemptuous cynicism echoed in Bragg's long face. Saw pity too, as Bragg eyed the child and her too-tall, too-skinny frame. Blue-rimmed glasses over the blue eyes gave her a too-adult look, too, and the close-cropped short brown hair took away any feminine grace the child might have possessed. To Sarah's eyes she was a child without childishness as she gazed gravely round the circle of adults. She longed to cry, 'Run away, my dear. Right out of here. Bragg might be sorry for you, but she'll use you ruthlessly. She's lazy, about things outside nursing me, at least. She'll send you to the shops and forget half a dozen things and have you trotting back and forth every afternoon. And as for tea – the woman nearly drowns herself in it. It won't be one cup. It will be tray after tray you'll be bringing in. Mrs Furlong wouldn't play along with that. She's grown-up. Older than

Bragg. But you're a child. You'll be running after her till you're asleep on your feet.'

She was furiously angry – with Bragg for the cynicism and the amusement in the long face, with Gwenyth for her cupidity in saving a few dollars a week at the child's expense; and with the child's mother, for allowing it.

Doesn't the woman see what will happen, she wondered? Or does she see, and doesn't care, so long as she has a roof over her head? She wondered if that were it, if the woman had been turned away from plenty of flats because there was a child who might be a nuisance, if she couldn't pay the high rents of places where she might be accepted. But then Gwenyth was saying, 'Mrs Abcons is a fitter at Carper's Bridal Salon, Nurse. She has a very good position.'

'I'm sure,' Bragg said dryly with a nod of her head to the younger woman. For a moment Sarah thought she was going to add crudely, I bet she has, or you wouldn't have let her in for fear she couldn't pay the rent.

But Sarah had gone on fretting, not even listening to Gwenyth going on talking, as she worried about the child, and wondered why, if the woman had a good-paying job, she was putting the child in a place like this where she'd become a drudge if it was allowed.

Only when Gwenyth had gone did she realise why. As Gwenyth's footsteps receded down the stairs, the child's mother crossed to the bed to stand looking down at Sarah. Sarah, gazing back, saw a slim, blank-faced woman who could have been any age from thirty to forty. Her brown hair was as boyishly cut as the child's, and the eyes were the same blue. She was, Sarah realised, what the child would be in another quarter of a century, though – oh, I hope so, Sarah fretted – the child's eyes would surely have a happier, younger expression.

Still looking at Sarah the woman said, her voice low, almost flat in cadence, reminding Sarah oddly of the breath of wind through long grass, 'I'm Josie Abcons, Mrs Oatland.

Perhaps you can't hear me. I hope you can, because I want you to know we shan't be any trouble to you. We'll take good care of your things down there, too.'

For a little moment she stood silent, still gazing at Sarah as though she was hoping for some acknowledgment, then Bragg said almost aggressively, 'She can't answer you, so why bother her. She can't . . .'

Gazing still on Sarah, Josie Abcons nodded. 'I know. Mrs Oatland junior explained. I had an aunt who had a stroke. She got better. Partly better. After a long time. She went on a cruise then. To Sumatra, Thailand, places like that. She said she felt completely at home. She was left, you see, with a jerk in her neck. She used to tell us about the native dancing – when they jerked their necks back and forth, hers jerked too. Afterwards, if anyone looked at her pityingly she used to say she was doing her eastern dancing exercises.'

Bragg laughed, but the eyes and the face watching Sarah didn't change their blank expression. It was, Sarah thought uneasily, almost as though the woman had forgotten what amusement was.

Still gazing at Sarah, Josie Abcons said, 'I'm grateful for getting this flat. Because of Rose. I'm often at the salon till well after closing time. Rose has to be on her own a lot. It's been . . .' Sarah saw the slim hands slowly clenching at the woman's side '. . . worrying' and she knew that Josie Abcons hadn't been worried. She had been frantic. Then, rapidly, Josie added, 'In one place we were, the caretaker wouldn't leave her alone. I found her in the street one evening, too frightened to go home without me. In another there were older children in the block. Rose was too young then to understand, till too late, what they were up to. She nearly fell foul of the police. It's . . . I've been getting terrified all the time she's alone, but I can't leave my job. I have to work at something, and everything seems to take me away . . .' She finished in a rush. 'I'm grateful for this. She'll be under your eye . . .' With an abrupt change she asked, 'Hasn't Mrs Oatland senior any other family?'

'Than *her*?' Bragg's jerk of her sleek dark head towards the stairs was eloquent. 'No. That's why *she* has the say-so about everything. Mind you, you could be out on your ear double-quick any time,' she added. 'You never know with these stroke cases. She could get her voice or her wits or anything back any tick of the clock and then she'd chase you out if . . .'

The flat voice held surprise, 'I thought she couldn't show any life? How can you tell how she'd feel?'

Bragg's plump hand smoothed the sheet almost posses-sively, Sarah thought shrinkingly. 'Oh, the old dear and I understand one another. No, she can't talk or anything, but somehow . . . you can't explain things sometimes, but with a patient like this you can guess, after being with them for a while, when they're liking something or when they're upset. She hasn't been so well this last couple of days –since *she* spoke out there were tenants coming downstairs. There's really no signs to cling to – physical signs, I mean – it's just a sense of knowing something's up with her, that she's not happy. Well, I know that sounds a bit cuckoo. Who'd be happy laid out like a fish on a slab? But *more* unhappy, "uneasy", maybe is the word I want. It's all just guesswork, and maybe I'm a bit odd, going crackers in my old age.' Her laugh was cut short. 'But I still . . . you know, I think she hears all right. I try to shut her up. She talks about the poor dear being a vegetable, as much as though she can't wait to shovel her up and stick her in the garbage can!' The plump hand smoothed possessively over the sheet beneath Sarah's chin again.

'It's just things I feel when I'm with her that make me think her wits are still there, knowing what we're saying. Things like, well, she likes the windows. When I shift the bed over there, see, by the fireplace, I feel she's happier. Odd, isn't it? Because with her laid out like that you'd think she'd loathe the sight of the outside world and people hurrying about, but, no, I get the idea she's happier there.'

'But can she see them?' Josie asked. 'Perhaps it's just the air on her skin or . . .'

Bragg shook her dark head. 'She can tell the difference between light and dark. The doctors do all the tests possible, you know. Hold a light close to her eyes, and she'll shut them all right. She can tell the difference.'

For the first time expression came into the blank face watching Sarah. It was only a trace, a thoughtful frown, but Sarah was glad of it. She was finding it unnerving seeing that blankness staring down at her.

Then Josie Abcons asked sharply, 'If she can close her eyes why don't you get her to close them – winking signs, I mean – for "yes", and "no". If you question . . .'

Bragg's tone of contempt was from the professional to the ignorant as she scorned, 'Of course we've tried that. Goodness, that's the first thing you think of with cases like this – can they wink, or lift a finger for "yes" or "no". We tried. Over and over. But nothing happened.'

But you wouldn't let it, Sarah wanted to cry in protest. It's only in the last week I've managed it at all, and I need time. I'm tense and terribly, desperately eager to get through to you and everything goes wrong. You won't wait! If you'd only wait, give me time to relax, to force my lids up and down, but you go too fast. If I don't respond in a matter of seconds, you're all shaking your heads and saying that after all I couldn't hear and wasn't that sad, but the sad bit was you were wrong. It wasn't true. Not true at all. I can hear and if you'd only give me time I'll get through to you now. Ask me a question and tell me, as you did before, 'One blink for "yes" and two for "no"' and then wait – wait till I do it. I'll reach you and I won't be cut off any more.

She felt she was actually saying, screaming the words, but she wasn't, because they were going on talking earnestly about her – Bragg saying that in spite of Sarah's failing to acknowledge the doctor's questions she felt that Sarah sometimes could hear what was being said; and Josie Abcons talking about the aunt who went to Sumatra with her head nodding and jerking like an eastern dance.

After a little Sarah closed her eyes. She was desperately tired and frightened – of the future and even the present – and annoyed at the thought of the woman and the child among her possessions downstairs.

When she opened her eyes again the child was beside the bed. Sarah could hear the mutter of voices from the other side of the room. She couldn't turn her head to see, but knew Bragg and the child's mother had moved to the far corner of the room.

The child was gazing at her curiously, lips slightly parted to show small, irregular-looking teeth, her tall, skinny body bent as she peered down at the old face on the bed. As Sarah's eyes opened, the thin body jerked upright, the blue eyes behind the blue-rimmed glasses widening in fright. The thin body took a step backwards, then the child was still again, gazing at her. Sarah felt like crying. It was the final cruelty to have become such an oddity that she was a thing of terror to a child.

Rose took a step forward again. Her body arched over the bed. She whispered, 'Mrs Oatland, can you hear? Blink . . . blink once for "yes" and two for "no". Like great aunty did when she was sick. Can you hear?'

She was going to get through, Sarah thought exultantly. She was going to get through. She could feel her eyelids starting to close, then abruptly Bragg was there, her big plump hands moving the child aside. 'Now, you mustn't worry the old dear, Rose. Look, she's closed her eyes. Wants to go to sleep, poor dear.' The plump hand smoothed possessively at the white sheet again. 'You run along with your mother, Rose.'

The next day the others came. Sarah couldn't know how long she had been lying there asleep while they stood around her bed watching her. She only woke to the knowledge that there were strangers in her room who'd been peering at her and talking about her while she slept. She woke to rage and the frustration of not being able to voice her resentment at all the invasions of privacy she was having to endure.

She disliked the man as soon as she saw him, and that had nothing to do with her anger or frustration. It was a dislike as swift, as divorced from anything else, as had been her liking for the child and her mother. The man's looks had nothing to do with it either, because Sarah would have frankly admitted he was the type of which her own mother might have said with comfortable relief, 'Such a respectable, prosperous-looking man, my dear.' It was something utterly apart from looks or a voice hinting at a little too much self-assurance. It wasn't even dislike of the slight nicotine staining of the long fingers, or the way his dark hair was formed in a pronounced widow's peak on his narrow forehead. It wasn't even the expression in his brown eyes, because they were expressionless in the narrow face that smiled down at Sarah. It was something apart. Something to which she couldn't put a name, till suddenly out of the blue, to her utter astonishment, she thought, I'm afraid of him. Afraid! and that was ridiculous. She was lost in astonishment and bewilderment and couldn't concentrate on what they were all saying over her still body.

Gradually, because unless she concentrated firmly on voices, even the sense of hearing seemed to desert her, Sarah became aware that the self-assured voice was saying, as though the matter were fully settled – though later on she knew it wasn't, that Gwenyth hadn't then given her approval to his coming to the house – 'We'll be here merely a few months, Sister Bragg. Just till we've had a look round and settled on a home to buy.'

'A-ah?' Bragg's interest and curiosity broke out. 'You're just married, then?'

'Why, no.' Even his laugh, Sarah thought, lost again in amazement at her reaction to him, had that respectable, prosperous ring to its depths. 'What made you think Valma was a blushing bride, Sister?' There was faint mockery in the voice as it spoke the name.

The woman was just outside the range of Sarah's sight, and she didn't speak. Bragg said, 'Well, taking a furnished place, you see? I just naturally thought – why, they're just married and going to set up house for the first . . .'

'I'm afraid not. We've been married years. Four years. Five next autumn. Right, Valma?' But the woman still didn't speak and the assured voice went on. 'We've been moving around – my work, you know. There's no chance, or sense, in buying furniture when you live that way. It's only now we're settling for a time. Perhaps for good. So this place will be ideal for us for a while.'

Tartly Bragg asked, 'And does Mrs Oatland reckon on you being ideal for the flat?'

He laughed and said, comfortably assured, 'Oh, she'll agree. I'm paying her for two months in advance to start with. I'm quite respectable . . .' there was a hint of mockery again in the voice '. . . and I have a most respectable father-in-law, who'll probably come and stay with me for a week soon.'

How odd, Sarah reflected. Or was the man so ego-ridden he always thought in the first person? She supposed he was, to speak so, to say, 'I have a most respectable father-in-law. Who'll stay with me.' No mention of his wife. The man spoke as though she didn't exist, either to own her own father, or entertain him, or even to be part of the household, when the father was present.

It annoyed Sarah unreasonably, yet that was absurd, she told herself impatiently. It was none of her business. Let the woman – Valma – stand up for herself. But then she was annoyed at Valma too, for standing there mutely while her husband talked on, full of his own plans, never mentioning her or her preferences or wishes or anything else, though the setting up of a home, the inviting of her father would all be of vital interest, had to be so, to her.

Distracted, her hearing failed her again. Then slowly she began concentrating again, in time to hear the man say, 'Roderick Palmer. Oh, you wouldn't recognise the name, Sister. You wouldn't be old enough now to have been more than a teenager when Rod's name was well known.'

Oh, Bragg, Bragg, Sarah thought in annoyance, don't fall for that. He's laughing at you. For all your dyed black hair you're in your fifties. Twenty-five years ago when Roderick Palmer was singing his way through the concert halls of Europe you were probably listening to him on the radio and doing a private swoon over that mellow voice. Just as I was, she remembered, and knew the excitement of her thirties all over again at the thought that Roderick Palmer might come to her house and meet her.

Excitement died. She pictured him, or rather, the man who'd smiled at her from newspapers all those years ago, entering the warm quiet room and standing looking at her and speaking of her to Bragg as laid out like a fish on a slab, and she felt quite sick.

Impatiently she pushed the thought aside, refusing to think of it, dwelling instead on the past – on her thirties, when Roderick Palmer was young too. How old would he be now, she wondered. Probably older than he admitted. Stage people always took off a few years, she thought. But he'd be a few years older than her, she guessed – say sixty-two or three. And what was he doing now? Not singing. That had been over for . . . for fifteen years surely? One day he was a star. The next he was ill. And the following year the world had moved on and forgotten him.

She was suddenly afraid that if he came she'd find he was a broken creature, shrivelled of body and mind and pocket, feebly grateful for his child's invitation . . . But he hadn't had a daughter, she thought in amazement. She was sure of that.

All those years ago he'd been married, and there had been one son. A son. Who'd later died. There'd been no mention of a daughter, and he couldn't have had one later on in life to be old enough now to have been married for five years come the next autumn.

Bragg remembered that, too, and thrust his mocking compliment into limbo with a brisk, 'I remember him and he had a son I do remember, but never a daughter, surely.'

'Clever Sister to remember.' He didn't sound put out in the least. 'So you're an old fan of his. I must remember to tell him. You're right, of course. He's actually my stepfather-in-law. Unwieldy title, isn't it? My mother-in-law married him three years ago. She died last year, and he's been damn lonely since.'

Again never a mention of his wife, Sarah thought. My stepfather-in-law. My mother-in-law. It grated on her unbearably, that casual – or could it be deliberate, she wondered? – ignoring of his wife, his clutching at everything from her stepfather to her mother as his own particular property.

'I see.'

Bragg, Sarah thought, sounded tired of him. She wondered if Bragg was noting that constant play on himself and was as irritated by it as Sarah herself. She wished she had the tongue and voice to discuss it with Bragg when the pair went away, and the woman . . . and what was the woman like, Sarah fretted. She saw her only in profile as they moved in a group, Bragg leading, towards the door. She was just the sort of person, Sarah thought impatiently, who would stand meekly for a man with an ego like that – a whispy-looking creature, older than Sarah had expected – the mid-thirties so she guessed, though the man looked little older than just on thirty. Her short hair was pale, and so was her skin, faintly freckled on her arms, and when she said, in the doorway, 'Goodbye, Sister Bragg', the voice was whispy and childish and pale of timbre.

'Goodbye, Mrs Phipps, Mr Phipps,' Bragg was saying and then shut the door firmly after them, and crossed, heavy-footed, to the cane chair, and sank into it and peered down at Sarah. Her plump hand smoothed at the already smooth sheet beneath Sarah's chin. 'She'll take them, all right. Two months rent in advance would do it, even if they weren't so respectable, right down to the name. Phipps . . .' she rolled it round on her tongue '. . . you couldn't see a Phipps robbing a bank or even getting drunk on a Saturday night, could you?'

She laughed at her own imaginings, then sobered. 'Poor dear – I wonder if you took it in? About Palmer? You know,' she was shaking her head slowly, her long face mournful, 'I hope he doesn't come. He's probably a cranky old fusspot by this. Those singers always have weak chests and constant colds, it seems to me, and a thousand and other made-up aches and pains. Oh well . . .' slowly she heaved herself out of the chair again, hands gripping the sides of the chair '. . . got to see about my tea, then I'll rub you down.' With unconscious cruelty she added, 'Don't you stir till I run back, dear. Won't be long.'

Sarah wasn't angry, or even hurt, by the words, only amused. She lay there picturing Bragg's gape-mouthed astonishment if she returned to find her patient had disobeyed and really moved. Imagination was about all that was left to her, and day by day it was growing stronger as a shield against pain and weariness and despair. In imagination she could turn hurtful phrases into things of mild amusement that entertained her and filled the motionless hours.

So lost was she in the picture of a frantic Bragg trying to make her patient move and failing, so that she went running round the room, searching in closets and cupboards, demanding to know who'd moved the old fish from her slab that way, that it took a long time to realise there were voices to be concentrated on again, and a longer time before she realised – unable as she was to move her head at all – to know that the voices weren't whispering beside her but speaking in the room below. Interest quickened, because neither whisper belonged to a friend, or Bragg. One, even whispering ghost-like, could only belong to the man called Phipps.

Sarah had ceased to be surprised that Bragg had so swiftly and unerringly guessed her patient's preference for being in one spot in the warm, quiet bedroom. It had become just another violation of her privacy to have her thoughts guessed, just as it had become a small hard core of malicious delight that the other woman at least had failed to find out one secret of

Sarah's. That was the chimney-wall. It wasn't the window that made Sarah prefer that part of the room, but the chimney-wall. With the head of her bed up against it, it became a kind of sounding board. She had found that out years before only by accident, when the bedroom had been redecorated and the bed thrust aside against the wall. For some absurd reason – Sarah couldn't even remember now what it had been – David Oatland had stubbornly refused to be uprooted from his bed, in spite of the redecorating, though she could clearly remember undressing among all the decorator's clutter, with David grumbling away in the bathroom, and then the two of them lying side by side and Gwenyth's voice whispering up behind the wall from below, startling them both.

Sarah had often reflected afterwards how odd it had been that neither she nor David, so swift to share everything, thoughts and all, should never have discussed that midnight talk. On her own side she had known there was embarrassment, a fear to tread on the delicate fabric of family relationships. Perhaps David had felt the same. She only knew that they had never discussed it, but that when David had died his will had been unexpected. She had known there had been a will that had included Gwenyth, as their nephew's wife, but his final will had not made a mention of her. It had been no surprise when Sarah had known the last will had been made a few days after that ghostly voice had whispered up to her and David in the night.

In the face of Gwenyth's unconcealed temper over the will, Sarah had been tempted to tell her, to say bluntly, It was your own fault. David always had a great sense of family. He felt responsible for you as his nephew's widow, till he heard you gloating over his house, his possessions. You were our guest that night, after you were newly widowed – you and that friend of yours who accompanied you home after your widowing – and in the night you gloated to her how the place would soon be yours; that you know the old fool – yes, that was what you called David, Gwenyth, and he was no fool at all – but you told that friend of yours that David, the old fool, had left everything to his nephew and now it would come to you instead. Everything would be yours, so long as you let me live here and cared for me. That was David, a great sense of family, as I said before. He didn't realise how I'd have hated the situation. He was just afraid for me, seeing me growing older and lonelier and more helpless. He wanted to make sure I'd always be comfortable and looked after properly. So he planned on Rob having everything, with the provision that the house wasn't to be sold, that I was to go on living there, with you and Rob caring for me.

David thought he'd planned beautifully for us all, but you had plans, too, Gwenyth. Plans that included an old people's home for me – shunting me out of the way, as you so gracefully put it. It would have been easy enough, according to you, if it could be proved I was gaga – that was your expression, Gwenyth – and needed expert care. You'd even worked out that if I was declared mentally ill I could get free treatment, and that would be another burden taken from you.

David never said a word to me, or I to him, but that will's the result of that gloating little talk you had that night in the sitting room under our bedroom.

Sarah had been tempted to say it all. Only the thought of Gwenyth's open-mouthed gaping, her red-faced attempt to defend herself or to deny the truth of Sarah's words, stopped her in sheer revulsion at the imagined scene. It had seemed far more sensible to let the grievance of the will remain simply that, a grievance, without explanation.

Sarah had remembered the wall, though. Several times in the years that had followed, she had gone to her bedroom to listen to whispers floating up to her from her guests in the sitting room, had been amused and sometimes faintly annoyed at her resultant eavesdropping when her draperies had been criticised, her dress described as dowdy, her afternoon tea cake as too dry and herself as 'getting a bit doddery', but never in those years had she heard anything that, like that first eavesdropping, caused her more than a moment's worry. The listening had been simply a rather wicked game she had played to ease the growing boredom of living alone.

Till her stroke. Then it had opened a lifeline of reality in the midst of confusion, because the doctors, though sure she couldn't hear, had nevertheless spoken in front of her guardedly, and she hadn't had the voice to question and demand intelligent, forthright answers to her questions. Only when they went downstairs to the sitting room, to be given tea and cake by Bragg while they discussed her, did Sarah learn anything about herself. Even when the news was depressing, and once, even frightening, it was still reality, knowing the worst about herself, and she had clung desperately to the fact that she knew, just as well as Bragg did, and better than Gwenyth did, how she was doing.

It had been the thought of losing that lifeline with hard fact that had upset her more than anything when Gwenyth had decided to divide up the house, because the sitting room would no longer be available to the doctors for talks among themselves and with Bragg. She felt now, listening to the whispering wall, that she had a double dislike for the man named Phipps. He was taking from her the one link with frank knowledge about her condition, and he made her feel unreasonably afraid.

She was aware too, in sudden swift disgust, that her boredom-breaking game was over. She wouldn't enjoy listening to the whispers downstairs from now on. There'd be none of her old friends down there any more, taking tea and sherry, dispensed by Bragg, while they gossiped after visiting the old fish on the slab upstairs. No, now there'd be only the visitors to the Phippses. Sarah could imagine it quite clearly. Phipps would nearly always be the sole speaker. That assured, ego-ridden voice would roll over any interruptions, going on and on about himself, his father-in-law, his doings, his everything. It would, Sarah decided, be tiresome and intolerable.

Still she listened now and felt triumphant smugness in the

rightness of how he would sound. He was harping about himself, just as she had known he would, the assured voice whispering through the wall to her, 'I think this is going to suit my plans beautifully.'

The woman's answer was nearly lost to Sarah, it was said so softly. 'What about that nurse, Murray? What about that nurse?'

Murray, Sarah was thinking, and deciding that the combination of Murray and Phipps was so painfully respectable it sounded unreal, when the wall whispered with the man's reply. 'What about the nurse?'

'What's the first thing people do in a crisis? They run for a nurse. And there'll be a nurse right over us. Right over us. We'd be expected to run straight up there where she's sitting with that corpse. Honest, Murray, it's how she seems, that old lady, just a corpse staring up at you – where was I? Oh, I know – I was saying we'd be expected to run straight up there and grab that nurse and . . .'

'Nurses have days off. I've planned it. I planned it all out the minute I walked in there and saw her. She's an asset not a liability to me. I'll get friendly with her. A bit of butter and those old maids purr like tabbies. Soon I'll suggest she needs a breath of air, a trip to Woolworths, or a visit to her Great-aunt Matilda, and my charming wife will be happy to sit with the old lady while nurse is out and . . .'

'Murray, Murr . . . ay, I couldn't! She's like a corpse, that old woman. I just told you . . .'

'You'd better get used to corpses, Val . . .' the wall hummed with the brutality of that assured voice warning crudely '. . . if we're going to turn your stepfather into one.'

———

Astonishment gave way to bewilderment. There was only silence now in the room below. Sarah wished she could have knocked on her wall and called to them, demanding to know what they were talking about. Lying there, fretting with discontent, she tried to make sense of that statement with its absurd phrase, 'You'd better get used to corpses if we're going to turn your stepfather into one.'

Why, Sarah thought in amazement, the man might have been speaking of turning a chicken into paste. She wanted to laugh, and felt further frustration because she couldn't. She could feel, on her motionless body, little prickles of sweat, and bewilderment grew as the knowledge dawned on her that she was frightened. Frightened . . . again, she thought. She'd been afraid of Phipps when he'd stood by her bed, peering down at her and now, because of some stupid bewildering phrase heard through a wall, she was frightened all over again. None of it made sense.

Valma Phipps made it even less sensible, when the wall whispered primly with her voice saying, 'You shouldn't talk that way.'

'Dear, dear, and how else would you like to phrase it? Do we speak in hushed accents of the . . . let's see . . . about-to-be-dear-departed? Or perhaps . . .'

'I meant . . .' there was neither primness or whispiness in the curt response '. . . that someone could easily overhear.'

'There you're wrong. I've done plenty of homework on this particular place. You and I, and dear Palmer, are going to be nicely secluded down here. The nurse is safe enough. An asset even, as I said before. Who's going to suspect anything wrong when we knew there was a nurse in the place?'

'When we've taken pains to get her out of the road right at the right, or wrong, minute? That's . . .'

'We'll be taking no pains. You're becoming a complete whiner. Do you realise that? A whiner. Leave the nurse aside for a minute and think who else is here? That old woman – no better than a corpse as you've said yourself – and a woman and a child out the back. They'll never overhear us. Did you notice the thickness of that wall between this part of the house and that flat? Your old corpse had no intention of letting the servant's noise upset her when she fixed that flat. We won't hear a word from them, or they from us.'

'Kids are nosey. Ever think of that?'

'Not that one. Weren't you listening to the junior Oatland? Lord, there's a woman for you – voice of honey and eyes like a calculating machine.'

It was so true Sarah might have applauded if she'd been able.

Fascinated now, fright – that absurd, unreasoning fright with no sensible basis – forgotten completely, she listened to the assured voice going on. 'Didn't you hear her saying that the brat was scared of men? What type of man would it take to make a pass at a skinny brat like that, I wonder?'

The woman's voice said tightly, 'I wouldn't be surprised at anything a man did,' the voice rose, 'and don't come back at me with what about things a woman'd do, like planning about Palmer! See, just don't say it – or look it,' was the seemingly unreasonable addition. 'If it happened like Mrs Oatland told us, the kid's got a right to be scared of men. Think of her being chased round an empty block of flats by an old creep of a caretaker with a dirty mind and itchy hands? Think . . .'

'I'm merely thinking she'll keep well away from me, and

Palmer, and this flat. Which is what I want. It boils down to a kid who won't come near us and a woman who looks too tired to be interested in anything, an old woman who's only a quarter alive and a nurse . . .'

'Who's just the age and the type to be hanging round Palmer all the time. Thought of that?'

There was no whining in the voice this time, Sarah reflected. It held malicious triumph. Sarah hated it and hated the whole knowledge that the man and the woman below in her old sitting room liked scoring off each other, seemed to detest one another, if the tone of their voices could be believed. Yet that made no more sense than anything else of her morning, she upbraided herself, because why should a pair who detested one another set up house together, plan to invite a visitor, plan to do something . . .

Her thoughts broke in confusion. What did they plan to do with Palmer? She was back to that, to that utterly absurd phrase about turning him into a corpse.

As though echoing Sarah's thought, the man's voice whispered to her from the wall, 'Palmer won't be alive long enough for trouble.' There was silence, then he went on, 'And the nurse will be busy – with the old lady. A pretty broad hint that she's neglecting the old woman, a whisper to the doctor, a suggestion that she pay more heed to her job and where . . .'

'You try that and she'll be out on her ear and we might have a far smarter type under our feet, something young and up to the minute. Anyway . . .' the voice jeered '. . . aren't you forgetting we were going to get all cosy and palsy-walsy so it's suggested she visit Auntie and I sit with the old woman? Your ideas are getting a bit boxed.'

'Whiner.' But the man's retort was absent, disinterested, then impatient. 'Who's to know we spoke to the doctor? Do you think he'd tell her, on my hinting, that she was neglecting the old creature? Not a bit of it. You'll see. It'll be a simple matter of "Nurse . . ." what's her name again? . . . Bragg, well, a simple matter of, "Nurse Bragg . . . I want hourly temperature readings; hourly attempts to raise a response from her – a full record kept." You'll see, it would be something like that. Not a hint about us, but she'll be kept on her toes with the old woman all the time. She'll be more than grateful to be let off the hook, even for an hour. Can't you see how it fits in with everything? For God's sake . . .' the voice rose suddenly to black rage '. . . get that stupid look off your face! You look like a cow at the bails!'

Sarah half expected a childish quarrel, with the woman crying back, 'And you're like a bull at a gate.' But there was silence till the man went on, the whisper quiet and even again. 'A hint to the doctor means Nurse tied down – and cranky. Eager to get off the hook. Isn't that right? If we're friendly by then it would fit in nicely if Nurse is the one to suggest we might do a favour and sit with her old biddy upstairs. Right? Then after it's all over, where are we? Nurse saying that she had to have a breath of air but doctor had ordered constant attention, so she asked kind Mrs Phipps to step up, and wasn't that terrible, because old Mr Palmer was taken queer. Mr Phipps did his best, of course, but he wasn't a nurse to know something was badly wrong, and by the time he'd fetched his wife and the doctor and . . . well there you are.'

I don't believe this, Sarah told herself in astonishment. I don't believe it at all. It's impossible and ridiculous. Fright was back though. She felt sick with the force of it. She wished that Bragg would come back, quickly, though other times when the wall had whispered to her this way, there had been an urgent demand in her that Bragg stay away till the whole conversation was over and Sarah had drained the full of it. Now she wanted Bragg to come, to bend over the bed and hear those voices too . . . and explain them.

That was the really important thing. Sarah knew that now she would never rest comfortably again till those words were explained to her, and in a comforting fashion that would leave her sleepy with relief and content.

Bragg was late. For the one time Sarah wanted her desperately she was late. That was unusual. By the time the bedroom door opened again and Bragg's long face came peering at her, Sarah was in a lather of fright, wondering what had happened.

Bragg knew at once that something was wrong. She was starting to say, as she bent over the bed, 'I'm sorry that I didn't come . . .' and then she stopped, and the long face bent closer towards Sarah. The older woman had often wished the woman wouldn't do that, bring her face close so that her breath touched Sarah's own unmoving flesh, but this time she welcomed the warm breath as easing her own chill.

Bragg said sharply, drawing back, 'What's up, my dear. Something's up, isn't there? Something's wrong. Now what is it?' She stood straight and watchful beside the bed, her plump hands automatically smoothing at the sheet under Sarah's chin.

Sarah could visibly see the other woman thinking, seizing on possibility after possibility, weighing it, discarding it eventually and seeking for some other reason for her patient's distress, while her fingers felt for pulse, checked on the smoothness of undersheet, the comfort of pillows.

All the time she went on talking, too, her voice oozing the syrup of comfort over the motionless human dough below her hands.

'Your pulse is just a little too rapid, dear, just as much as though you'd been up to tricks while I was gone, and I wouldn't really be surprised, because that last specialist – the one with that funny little moustache – said he betted one fine day you'd open your eyes and then your mouth and bawl us all out. You won't do that though, dear, will you? Bawl us out, I mean. Everything's for your own good. Still I wouldn't mind what you said. You say just whatever you feel when you get your voice back, and that won't be long, you mark my words. Why you look right now as though you could tell me a lot of things – bawl me right out for being late back . . .'

The voice stopped. The anxious searching for reasons that had etched lines across the woman's forehead was gone. She said lightly, 'Well now, you're cross and put out I was late, eh? That's it, isn't it? Well, that just shows, dear, you're still ticking over right enough. You can reason all right, and I bet you can hear a lot too. We'll have you trotting round again sooner than you think. But you know, dear, it wasn't my fault I'm late up. Mrs Oatland wanted my signature – a witness you know – on the lease that Mr Phipps is signing. She wasn't going to let him run off and maybe see something better, not when he had the cash in his pocket for two months rent in advance, and then . . .' Abruptly she stopped. A slow, ugly flush rose up from chin to hairline. She said flatly, 'I guess my tongue runs away sometimes. If you can hear, dear, you must be angry, but I really can't like young Mrs Oatland. Oh, well.' She sighed, patted the sheet again and said briskly, 'I think, dear, we'll have the doctor along just the same to check that pulse of yours.' She moved to the window, adjusting the curtains so the light no longer fell across the bed. 'You rest for a bit till he comes. You mustn't get into a fret from now if I'm away a bit too long. I'll never be gone too long, I promise. And then . . .' she laughed richly '. . . there's nothing going on in here to disturb you while I'm gone, is there, dear?'

You're a fool, Bragg, Sarah reproached the long face silently. A fool, but quite a good-hearted fool, and I shouldn't dislike you, but why didn't you come sooner? Why didn't you hear them and tell me what it all means? Her eyes tried to frame the reproach, to warn that something was terribly wrong, but she knew it was no good. Bragg had settled the reason for her patient's distress, and now the doctor would come and peer at Sarah and whisper to Bragg over her.

How, Sarah wondered, did she get through to the doctor that the wall had whispered to her of murder?

A man, Rose's eyes warned her, and instantly she slid down from the window seat where she had been kneeling, and tried to become a shadow below the long draperies on the window's right, clutching at them rigidly as she realised he had already seen her before she'd moved and now he was coming up to the open window, a tall, thin man with fair hair already receding from his forehead. The forehead right then, as he stopped outside the window, was creased in a frown above the blue eyes. She realised he was trying to get a look at her. Then he asked, in a voice that reminded her oddly of elastic, as though the words popped out grudgingly and almost snapped back into his mouth without sounding, 'Did you fall?'

Rose hesitated, decided there was no point, and certainly no dignity, in crouching there under the draperies, and stood up. That way, with herself inside and the man out, their eyes were almost on a level. She said, 'No. No, I didn't fall.' And added quickly, 'Thank you.'

The fair brows frowned. 'Thank me for what?'

Rose blinked, disconcerted. Reddening, she said with dignity, 'Thank you for enquiring whether I was hurt.'

She thought for one second he was going to laugh. Certainly his mouth made a little movement, but there was no smile in voice or face or eyes when he said, 'I didn't. I asked if you'd fallen. Not if you were hurt. That would have come later. If you didn't fall, why did you pop down like a jack in the box?'

Rose's uneasiness was vanishing, which she realised was odd, because snappy people, especially men, made her want to run and hide, but in spite of this man's unsmiling face and his snapped off voice, she was calm enough to retort, 'They pop up, not down, you know.'

'If they pop up, they have to go down or they couldn't pop up again.' Then he added, 'This is a ridiculous conversation and you're wasting my time. You're not hurt. We've settled that. Good.'

She thought he was going to leave. He certainly shifted ground a little, then stopped when she said, 'Thank you for enquiring,' and then added in a rush, 'I popped down because I didn't want you to see me.'

The fair brows went up this time. 'Why not?' He came closer and peered in through the window at her. 'You look respectable enough for visitors.' Then he frowned. 'But you're too thin. What do you have for breakfast?' Without waiting for an answer he said. 'Who are you anyway? A grand-daughter? Niece? Great-niece? Well?'

Rose said doubtfully, 'I've an uncle.'

'Where?'

'Up . . . up there . . . north, right up there on . . .'

'You're pointing to the east.' But now he spoke absently as though his thoughts had gone on to something else. After a moment he added, 'I thought Mrs Oatland had no relatives at all apart from her niece.'

Rose started to explain she didn't belong to the Oatland family, but slowly the words died, because now his frown was growing and growing till it finally became a scowl.

He snapped at her, as though she was some way to blame. 'Why wasn't I told all this before? How long's this been going on behind our backs. No wonder the old lady's upset and lying there in a lather of sweat. Bragg's a fool. Why didn't she explain . . .'

The rest of it was lost, because he had turned on his heel and gone hurrying round the path to the front door of the house.

Leaning out, Rose could see him punching the bell and punching it again quite violently, but for all his impatience the door remained closed long enough for Rose to slide from the window seat, open her own door and go out on to the path, sidling down towards him, stopping when the front door opened to frame Nurse Bragg.

The man demanded, without preamble, 'Why the devil didn't you tell me that wretched niece's turned the place into a rooming house? Mrs Oatland, for a blunt certainty, knows all about it, and you're wondering why she's lying there in a sweating panic for . . .'

Rose could see the woman's long face reddening and her head jerk back, so that her gaze caught sight of Rose on the path. She said sharply, 'Rose, what're you doing . . .'

She was going to be blamed, Rose knew. Called a sticky-beak and a noseyparker and a few other things, and frantic that there might be a complaint about her to the Mrs Oatland who'd let her mother the flat, Rose blurted out, 'The man wanted to know if I was a grand-daughter or . . .'

The woman said sharply, 'She's not, Doctor. No relation at all.' Her tongue flicked its tip round her lips. She said almost hoarsely, 'Rose, you can start being useful right now. You run along up to the kitchen and make tea. Will you have a cup, Doctor?'

'What? Oh, I might as well, but look here . . .'

'Rose, you run along up.' The words were a command, given almost angrily and the child darted past the two on the doorstep, making for the stairs, flicking a glance as she passed down the hall to the door at the right that led, she knew, to the flat that would soon, tomorrow probably, be occupied by the people named Phipps.

She wasn't annoyed at being shooed out of the way. The house intrigued her, with the oddness of the kitchen – the real house kitchen as she thought of it to herself – as distinct from the little kitchenette in her own flat, or the newly made one in the other flat. It had seemed absurd to Rose to have a big, streamlined kitchen mixed up with the bedrooms and bath-rooms upstairs, even when young Mrs Oatland had explained, 'My uncle had this fixed up when the house was modernised and that housekeeper's flat fixed up down there. David – my husband's uncle, David Oatland – used to do a lot of business at home, and they turned the old downstairs kitchen into a sort of office and made the new kitchen up here.

'David said it was commonsense. He liked his breakfast in bed and liked it scalding hot. Why, sometimes he had even had dinner up there in his bed, and my aunt encouraged him in it.

'Everyone . . .' Rose remembered how the woman's face had flushed as though she were angry at the memory '. . . in the district considered him an extremely odd person. Oh, mind you, it made sense in a way. There was really no longer any room for a kitchen down there, what with the flat and then the office; and the business people could talk to him there, then move next door to the dining room – that will be a bedroom now – and then into the sitting room later. It was convenient enough, I admit, but of course there were drawbacks.

'David had that little lift affair put in to have the food sent down from the kitchen to the dining room below, but it kept sticking. It stuck . . .' Rose had nearly laughed outright at the doom-ridden tones '. . . with two roast ducks and everything that went with them the night my husband and I entertained friends here. I've never forgotten it. Everyone laughed and pretended it was all very funny, but it wasn't. Can you imagine sitting there in front of cold tinned tongue, smelling those wretched ducks and knowing they were stuck between upstairs and down? It was terrible, and that wasn't the only occasion, though it was the worst, when things went wrong.'

Rose remembered how Mrs Oatland's tongue had run slowly over her lips, as though savouring something pleasant, before she had added, 'But now it's proved to be all to the good, as the house makes three homes comfortably.'

Rose remembered something else, her mother's soft comment afterwards, which Rose had known was more to herself than her listener. 'That woman likes the taste of the future. You can see her enjoying it – and the poor old thing upstairs is still alive.'

The child had puzzled over the words. They hadn't made sense. Remembering them now, she puzzled again and could still make no sense out of them, not even the bit about the old lady being still alive, because the previous day old Mrs Oatland had looked . . . Rose couldn't think what word would describe it, though perhaps *flattened* was best. That was it, she thought, going slowly upstairs. Mrs Oatland had looked flat – flabby and deflated like an empty balloon; something from which all life and air had gone. She remembered being afraid, there in that big hot quiet room, and how she had bent over the bed and been even more afraid that perhaps the old lady had died and no one had realised it, so that she'd spoken to her, asking her to blink, if she were really alive.

Panic rose in her again as slowly she stepped on to the landing and stood looking at the open doorway facing her – the doorway to that warm, quiet room. She didn't want to go near it at all. She knew where the kitchen lay – to her left – and she tried to turn towards it, but slowly her feet dragged, left right, left right, up to that open doorway, till she was looking into the room.

The bed was near the window this time, with light coming in through the glass and dazzling Rose, so that for a horrible moment she had the idea that the bed was empty, and panic swept over her – the stupid feeling that all along the old lady had been shamming and that now, with the nurse out of the way, she had hopped out of bed and was hiding behind the open door.

Rose nearly cried out, then the light from the window dimmed a little and she saw the old lady was under the sheets, lying still, and terribly flat, just the same as on the previous day.

She wanted to go away, but couldn't. She knew she'd never be able to stay there upstairs, on her own, getting tea for the nurse and the doctor, unless she assured herself that the old lady was still really alive.

On tip-toe she crossed to the bed and stared down. Surely there was no life there, she thought. Even the cheeks had a look of flatness, and the nose jutted up bonily as though fat and flesh of the past years had melted away, leaving skin tight over the bone. There was a sallowed look all over the features, like the pages of a book touched yellowly by age. Rose went on staring, at the greying hair, neat and orderly round the motionless face. There were still threads of brown there among the grey, still a hint of permanent waving that to Rose made the face seem more lifeless still.

She's dead, she thought in panic. Really and truly dead. They're pretending she's not, because then the house will all belong to that other Mrs Oatland and nurse won't have a job or cups of tea all day or . . .

Her thoughts broke into confusion, then reformed in some sort of order. She tried to laugh at herself, still staring down at that motionless face with the two cold blue eyes staring upwards at the ceiling. She told herself it was ridiculous to be silly and panic stricken. The old lady couldn't be dead. She was alive sure enough, though it didn't seem sensible to Rose that anyone can be called living who can't move or talk any more.

Abruptly, as she'd done the previous day, she bent over the bed and said, 'Mrs Oatland, if you can really hear and understand, try to blink – like my great-auntie did when she was sick. Blink once for "yes" and twice for "no". Will you do that? Please!' There was a sudden desperate urgency in her now to make that lifeless face reveal some sense of living. She pressed, 'Please! Please try! Once for "yes" and twice for "no". Do you understand? Mrs Oatland, if you understand me, please blink once for "yes". Will you?'

But there was nothing. Nothing at all, though she waited for what seemed a long time. Suddenly she couldn't bear it any longer. She swung round, so she wouldn't see the face any more.

CHAPTER 3

The child was afraid of her. That was all Sarah could think about at first – the horrible knowledge that she had become something that terrified a child. She was suddenly frantic to know exactly how she looked. She tried to cry out that she wanted a mirror, had to have it immediately, so she could peer into its surface and see exactly what sort of monster she had become over these last weeks.

It took her time to realise the child was speaking and more time to realise what was being said and then she was in a worse panic, trying to cry with her useless throat, 'Wait! Wait, child! Give me time to answer you. Wait! Please wait!'

She tried, desperately hard, to answer the child's plea, but she saw the eagerness slowly dying from the thin features and the child turning.

Oh no, don't! Sarah reproached her thin back. She knew she was going to answer the plea, too late again. Although it was useless now she let her right eye close in a slow wink that she was certain no one could have thought of as accidental. If only the child had seen it, she thought bitterly, if only she'd . . .

Then the child was turning. She said, her voice shrill with excitement, 'You answered me! Didn't you? Oh, I saw you, – right there in that mirror. See, when I turned I saw you – you winked at me. Once. Didn't you? Go on.' A thin brown hand shook gently at the sheet, crumpling it.

Bragg will be annoyed, was all Sarah could think. She'll be

angry about that crumpled bit under my chin. She heard the child saying, 'Go on, if you winked at me you, just wink again, once. I'll wait. You can't do it for a long time after I ask something, can you? Go on, answer me. Oh, wait, that's two questions.' The thin young face was serious and anxious. 'First, wink once for "yes" if you did really and truly wink before, – and then, after a bit, wink again if I'm right, that I have to wait and wait till you're ready to answer. Go on. Please!'

You don't have to add that last word, Sarah thought. Excitement touched her and in dismay she knew it was going to interfere, make it even harder to get through, but she clung to the child's promise to wait, and go on waiting, and after a little her right eye closed. Once. And then once again.

Rose stood straight again. She said wonderingly, 'So you're not dead, not nearly dead, and you must know about everything, mustn't you? You must know me. Don't you?'

Wink, went Sarah's right eye, after an interval, so long a time actually this time, because she was tiring fast, that she was afraid the child would give up in impatience, deciding that after all it was an illusion, just a coincidence that her eyelid was falling that way.

But Rose showed no signs of giving up. She stood there with stolid patience, thin hands clasped tightly together against her pink cotton dress, grave blue gaze on Sarah.

She said in that same grave, wondering voice, 'It must be only a little time, isn't it, since you could wink at all? Isn't that so?'

Wink, went Sarah's right eye. The grave, thin face was lit by a sudden smile. Rose nodded. 'I guessed it had to be like that, or they'd have found out. That nurse, and the doctor, though I guess he's not awfully good really at giving people time to do things,' she went on consideringly and sat down on the bed to go on chattingly, just as though, Sarah thought in delighted pleasure, she was a real visitor at last, not someone who'd come to view and whisper over the poor fish laid out on its slab. 'You know, I don't really think he's cross sort of underneath. Just, well, cross on top because . . . do you know,

I think maybe he's worried, and doesn't want you to know, or maybe, oh, I suppose you think I'm talking nonsense, don't you?'

The double wink came after a long moment. The child giggled. 'You know, you look awfully funny doing that – lying there all still, and everything, and just your eye going flutter, flutter, like . . .' The smile died, and her hands went over her mouth, the blue eyes rounding in dismay above them. Then, her hands back in the lap of her pink cotton dress again she said forlornly, 'I'm sorry. That sounded awful.'

Her gaze flicked up, to Sarah's face again. She stayed like that, gaze riveted on the still, elderly face, lips slightly parted. She's waiting for me to wink twice again, Sarah told herself. To say that no, she didn't sound awful. She tried, and knew in disgust and dismay that she was going to fail. The excitement of this longed-for breakthrough coming out of the blue, the effort expended on those other winks, had all been too much and she could only manage one wink.

One, she thought bitterly. One for 'yes'. She knew from the blankness in the young face opposite, in the way the child slid awkwardly from her seat on the bed, that her visitor had gone to be replaced by just another caller who simply didn't know what to do or say faced with Sarah's unmoving silence.

Often in the past few weeks Sarah had thought of the squandered gifts of words she had poured out heedlessly over the years, without thinking of them as the treasure they actually were, a link between herself and all other human contact, but she had never known the frustration that faced her as she looked now at the young downcast withdrawn features, or when a few hours before she had listened to the wall whispering to her of death.

Remembrance of that, of her need to talk to someone, to thrash things out and get some sensible explanation of what she had heard, drove out thoughts of the child's hurt. She knew she was again in what Bragg had called a 'lather of sweat', in spite of the drug the doctor had given her.

The child was no good to her, she fretted. She needed Bragg. That was it. Let Bragg come back and see her in a lather of sweat again and she'd once more start questioning the fact. 'Now what's wrong, my dear?' she would ask. 'Is it too hot for you? Too cold?' And she'd expect a reply, because, Sarah realised triumphantly, the child would tell them all now that Sarah's mind was still working, along with her right eye. Let Bragg know that and the woman would start questioning in earnest, and surely, in time, she'd come at last to, 'Is the window troubling you? The birds in the eaves? No? Then is it your bed being up against the wall here?'

For all her irritating ways, Bragg had sense. Sarah acknowledged that, triumphantly. There was a stubborn persistence in the woman that wouldn't allow her to give up till she'd seized on what was hurting her patient. And, surely, once the question of the wall was raised, Bragg would go on to ask why it troubled her.

Sarah went on thinking of that, trying to picture Bragg touching the wall, inspecting it, getting the truth about its hollowness, then realising that an overheard conversation must have caused the trouble; realising, too, it must be the Phipps who'd talked that day and upset Sarah. From there it would be another short stop to Bragg trying to find out what the conversation had been.

Oh, but she won't, Sarah fretted at that. She pictured Bragg going down the stairs, heavy-footed, and knocking at the sitting-room door and going in and saying, 'Look, my poor old dear upstairs is in a real state over something. I've worked out you can sometimes hear what's said down here, up there in her room. Weird, isn't it, but can you two remember what you were talking about today?'

They wouldn't tell, of course. Of course they wouldn't. They'd say . . . what? Sarah couldn't imagine, except that it wouldn't be the truth, and Bragg would probably be left with the impression that it was something about the division of the house, and that was all. But the pair downstairs would know that Sarah had heard.

But what did I hear? She pondered that and knew in dismay that the overheard talk was becoming confused, fragmentary, unreal, in her own mind. Now she couldn't remember the exact words at all, except for the bit about turning Palmer into a corpse. The rest was becoming a jumble.

What did I hear? She asked herself that again, tried to remember exactly and failed once more, but all the time fear was growing, because they wouldn't know she was forgetting most of it. They'd know, if Bragg questioned them, only that they'd been overheard.

She remembered that strange feeling when Murray Phipps had stood beside her bed, and she'd been afraid. She thought how that fear would be magnified now if he came soft-footed to stand beside her again, with the knowledge that she had overheard that talk.

She was feeling terribly ill. The child's face seemed to be floating, a pale blob, in shadows that moved and shifted.

Then she heard Bragg's voice. 'What are you doing in here? I never told you you could . . . oh!' Then her voice rose, calling the doctor's name. Sarah heard that, and the rising sharpness in Bragg's tone, 'Look at her! She's a lot worse than before when . . . Doctor, it's the child!' The sharpness gave place to triumph. 'It's the child who's troubling the old dear! Why, look at her for yourself. She was fine and quiet again when you went and just look at her now – covered in sweat again and looking terrible. I knew it was a mistake, but you can't tell that one anything. She saw another pair of hands to help out and save a few cents to come to her pocket eventually and so of course the child had to come, but look at my old dear yourself! It's her house and furniture and all that she's worrying over – the thought of what'll happen to them with a child loose among them.'

Sarah felt fingers on her pulse – fingers stronger and firmer than Bragg's – while the woman's voice triumphed,

'Now we know, and it's not to be wondered at, with the little imp creeping in here and pawing her things about. You were, weren't you?'

Sarah could see the child trying to shrink in on herself as though she were trying to escape notice, and punishment. She could have wept with the cruelty of what they were doing because now the doctor was standing upright again and his face, too, was stern and critical of Rose.

Bragg said, 'What did you touch? Did you break anything? Did . . .'

'I didn't . . .' the child's voice was shrill '. . . I didn't touch a thing. I thought she was dead. I had to come and . . .'

'. . . make sure she wouldn't jump on you while you were in the kitchen?'

The doctor's voice held no amusement, or even sympathy, only a kind of impatience, but Rose seemed to regain some of her courage, straightening, her chin up as she gave back, 'I couldn't see her in the bed. She lies so . . . so flat. I thought she was behind the door . . .'

Bragg gasped, a queer sound between a choke and a snort, as though she were struggling between indignation and sheer amusement.

The doctor said, 'What did you do? Poke her? Try to lift her? She seems to me to be terrified of something? Did you try lifting her? And let her fall?'

The spark of courage drained out of Rose. Sarah could see it happening, and Bragg made things worse. 'Well, she'll just have to go. Both of them. Mrs Abcons will just have to take her right away and find somewhere else.' Her voice was sharp.

Sarah's gaze caught the jerk of the small head, the frightened look in the blue eyes and slightly parted lips. She knew, in swift awareness, that probably there were few other people – and those not too savoury – who'd welcome a woman on her own, with a small child, and Rose was well aware of it.

It told in her face, her voice, her frightened denial. 'I never did a thing, and she was like that when I came in. She was! She really was! I thought she was dead and I came in and she wasn't. She was like that . . . and . . . and there was this bird.' Frantic now, Rose was intent only on getting herself out of trouble. 'There was a bird. Right there, on that window sill. It was that that frightened her. It was a big bird. Maybe she thought it'd attack her. Magpies do. It was a magpie sitting there. You know, they attack people sometimes. They do! If they think something's dead in a paddock they'll go and . . .'

'A bird?' Bragg's anger and triumph had vanished. 'I never thought of that. Oh, there are magpies right enough in that tree, but I never gave a thought of them frightening her. They're often down there on the lawn, though I've yet to see one up here by the window . . .'

Rose blurted out, 'Because you don't look dead. You . . . you move around, and they're scared.'

Bragg ignored that, and said briskly, 'Well, it's easily settled. We'll have screen wire over the windows, then she won't be frightened any more.' Maliciously she added, 'That'll cost Mrs Oatland junior a few dollars, and she'll squawk harder than any magpie over that.' Then, abruptly remembering the listening child, she added, 'You run along, Rose. Where's that tea you were going to make?'

Rose's voice quavered so desperately Sarah was sure that the doctor, out of her sight, was looking at the child in disbelief. 'It was a bird. Why don't you ask her if it wasn't a big bird that was on the window sill there and . . .'

'Ask her? Now, don't be silly, or . . . you know, if she can be scared of a bird she's reasoning all right.' Sarah was conscious of Bragg's face and body moving closer, of warm breath on her face, of Bragg's voice oozing at her, 'Can you hear me dear? And wink, or blink? You try blinking your eyes, once for "yes" and twice for "no", in answer to me. Now, was it a magpie that frightened you? Once for "yes", remember. Twice for "no".'

I have to be able to do it, Sarah thought, and realised in that same moment that the very desperation of trying was defeating her, exhausting her into complete immobility, while the seconds ticked on.

Abruptly, still out of Sarah's sight, the doctor demanded, 'Why suggest we ask Mrs Oatland, what's-your-name?'

'It's Rose.' The child sounded defiant again.

'Why suggest we ask her? Were you prodding at her? Questioning her? Trying to make her wink in answer?'

So you're not fooled with talk of magpies, Sarah thought exultantly, but immediately the child was denying frantically. 'I never did! I never did one single thing to upset her. I didn't! It was a bird . . . there on the window sill. It was going to come inside, I'm sure. On to the bed . . .'

'Along came a blackbird and pecked off her nose?' The doctor spoke absently. 'Well, she isn't answering anyway.'

Dear heaven, Sarah thought bitterly, I was listening to them. I wasn't trying then. She tried to make her throat move, to tell them to wait; make them know some way, any way, that she was capable of answering questions. Then listlessness, a cloying exhausting listlessness, closed over her mind and body at the knowledge that however much they questioned her they wouldn't light on the right questions to ask, so that she'd never have an explanation of that absurdly frightening conversation.

Bragg said, in that I-know-all-her-thoughts manner that so intensely irritated Sarah, 'The poor old dear just wants to sleep off her fright. She can't answer, even if she can hear. Rose, you run along home. I'll make tea myself.'

Sarah lay there, listening to steps going away – to the heavy plodding thuds that meant Bragg; to longer, softer steps that were the doctor's, and to a quick patter that would be the child. There was silence then and then the soft patter across the carpet again and Rose was whispering, 'I'm sorry. I was . . . scared.' There was shame in the whispered admission. 'They'd have sent us – me and my mother – right away, and there's only a horrid place we could go to. There was only it, or this. The other one was horrid. I was scared. At first, that is, and then later . . . why didn't you answer them?' The thin face came closer to Sarah's. 'Why didn't you answer? I didn't know what to do. I was going to tell, and then, you didn't answer. Was it because you thought I'd get into trouble? Because you see, I wouldn't have. I saw that afterwards. They'd have been so pleased at you being able to answer things – questions, and that – that they wouldn't have been angry at all. I saw that, afterwards, and I was going to tell. Then you didn't answer. I didn't know what to do. I'm so sorry about it. I thought . . . was it because you thought I'd get into trouble?'

Sarah's eye winked twice, after a long interval. The spate of huskily whispered words had confused her, but the child waited patiently and finally the two winks were given.

Rose gave a long sigh. 'Then it's like I thought. If it wasn't for fear of getting me into trouble, it was because you didn't want them to know you can wink? Have you been shamming all along that you couldn't? I don't understand that at all, but perhaps you don't want them pressing at you all the time, "Mrs Oatland, do you hear this and that or the other?" Or . . .' Sarah wished she could have laughed out loud at the considered '. . . I know – is it that other Mrs Oatland you don't want to talk to? For fear she'll talk and talk and talk and make you give in to things she wants done here?'

Why, how clever of you! Sarah was astonished, because she herself had never thought of that, but lying there, sheer panic swept over her, engulfing her in something close to downright fright, as she pictured Gwenyth, not standing rigidly by the bedside any more, but bending over it, pressing with cold words, while her cold gaze held Sarah's. 'Auntie, don't you think I should have power of attorney over your affairs? Auntie, don't you think it better you went into a home? This staying here with a nurse and doctor calling each day is eating up your capital. You'd be so comfortable in a nice rest home. Far less expensive, too. I could move in here and look after everything for you. Look, Auntie, your solicitor is here. All you have to do is give a "yes" and everything will be settled before you know it. You'll be safely tucked up in a nice rest home and I'll be here to take care of everything . . .'

Oh no, no, Sarah thought. It mustn't happen, and yet it would. Once let Gwenyth realise that constant pressure and nagging and wearing down could force her aunt into a permissive wink in front of witnesses, and it would be a one-way trip to an incurables' home for Sarah and a one-way trip for Gwenyth herself into the house, to queen it there.

She could think of nothing else. The Phipps pair were forgotten and Bragg and the doctor and even the child, till finally the soft whispering penetrated her panic, and she realised a question had been asked and was waiting answer. She heard the child repeat, 'Don't you want them to know? Wink once for "yes" and I'll tell them, and twice if I mustn't.'

The two winks were given before panic had had time to die; before she'd remembered that conversation that needed explaining, and there was no way of taking them back, of even amending the answer, of trying to explain that Bragg should know, but not Gwenyth Oatland.

The child was going away too, Sarah realised. She was already moving away from the bed, the whisper floating back, 'All right, then. I'll be silent as anything. Only you liked talking to me, didn't you? So I'll come again, if I can.'

The soft patter of steps began to cross the carpet again, then she heard the doctor's curt voice. 'Just what are you up to?'

As smoothly as oil flowing came Rose's swift answer, 'You forgot about the window. It's still open.'

'So it is, and you're on your way out. Not in. Come here. Outside.'

Sarah thought wearily, I should be worried about her. She's going to get into trouble again. On my account. In only a moment though, the child's problem was forgotten in remembrance of her own.

Rose said defiantly, 'I heard you coming and I was scared.

That's why I was coming out.' She added, 'You didn't give me time to close the window at all.'

'Because I think that magpie lives in your brain.'

Rose's thin face flushed. She knew she must look guilty, tempted to tell the truth, then remembered the old lady's winks that had asked for silence. Her gaze slid away from his and instantly his fingers closed over her thin wrist, towing her with him towards the stairs and down to the hall.

He said briskly, 'You're quite a liar, aren't you, what's-your-name?'

'It's Rose,' she snapped.

'Sure it's not Magpie?'

'There was a bird . . .'

'In your head. Tell the truth. What were you up to? Oh, for goodness sake,' he gave a little shake to the wrist he was holding, 'no one's about to eat you. Forget Bragg and her idiot talk of having you dismissed from the premises. Now, what were you up to? Listen to me, what's-your-name, because it's important. Mrs Oatland musn't be upset, yet she is, and I must know why. If there's something frightening, troubling, worrying her, we have to fix it or she'll have another stroke. Well?'

Rose was thinking. The talk of a stroke frightened her, confusing her, then looking clearly at the words she knew that everything would be all right. Of course Mrs Oatland had been frightened and worried – that her secret would be out in the open and young Mrs Oatland would come to the house, nagging and scolding – but now, Rose reflected comfortably, it was all right, because she'd been assured Rose wouldn't tell on her.

She said stubbornly, 'There was a magpie.'

Quite pleasantly the doctor said, 'You must be what's called a bird-brain.'

She nearly giggled, but his expression wasn't at all pleasant. It frightened her. He shot at her, 'Then tell me this? Were you trying to make her answer you? And did you succeed in it?' He gave another shake to her fragile wrist. 'Well? You told us to ask the old lady about a bird. You knew she could answer and would back you up. Is that it?'

Rose choked, 'But she didn't answer. You – the nurse. I mean – she asked, and Mrs Oatland never . . .'

'She didn't answer because she didn't want us – the nurse and I – to know she was hearing and could answer. Is that it? Rose, this is no time for childish secrets. If the old lady can really hear and give an answer of sorts, we have to know, and have to know why she's playing possum, too.'

It was all too confusing. Rose stood there, mouth slightly agape, and suddenly a soft, assured voice asked, 'Do you honestly think the old woman is playing I'm-sicker-than-I-really-am? Oh yes . . .' the assurance didn't dim even a trifle as the man stepped into the hall from the open doorway on Rose's left '. . . I was listening. You were, you know, speaking a trifle loudly. You're the doctor, of course – Holden, I think's the name?'

'John Holden.' The name came jerkily and was cut off by that assured voice saying, 'And you're wondering who the devil I happen to be. I'm Phipps, Murray Phipps. I imagine this is the Abcons child?' Without waiting for an answer, he went on, as though firmly assured he had the right to ask. 'Is the old girl shamming? Can she really hear and give a nod or something if she puts her mind to it?'

'Ask what's-her-name.'

'Well, what's-her-name?'

Rose hated them both, one for his rudeness, the other for his mockery. She said flatly, 'I'm going,' and slid between them, her hand already outstretched for the door knob. In another minute she was out in the open and running round the path towards the door to her own flat.

'Rose, wait!' She heard the doctor's voice and his running steps, but she didn't stop, merely throwing over her shoulder, 'Go away,' and then she had thrust the flat door open and was meeting Josie's startled gaze, which slid past her and changed first to fright and then to an anger so blazing that Rose cringed back against the wall of the tiny hall. Josie pushed past her and stood blocking the doorway. 'Get away from my daughter.'

The doctor halted, his arms outstretched, one hand on either side of the doorway. 'So you're her mother. Good. Tell me, what do you have to do with her to get the truth out of her? Paddle her backside? Bribe her with toffee? And what do you feed her on, come to that? She's thin as a rake handle. How long since you've had her overhauled? She's too nervous by a long way. Well?'

'Just who are you?' Josie's close-cropped brown head jerked back, her blue eyes narrowing as she looked up at him.

'He's a doctor,' Rose gasped from the shadows of the hall. 'I was in Mrs Oatland's room. There was a bird, only he says there wasn't.' Under Josie's swift-turning, coldly searching glance she used the one thing she knew would get her immediate sympathy and freedom. 'He . . . frightened me, Mummy.'

'Why?' Josie had whipped round again. 'What's this about?' She stood silent while the doctor answered her, then she said flatly, 'Rose doesn't lie. You're being absurd. You must know you are. That poor old creature would have no reason for cutting herself off from the sole human contact she might have. Would she?'

'She must, if she's shamming. The brat knows.'

'Brat?' Josie's dark brows arched. 'Nervous, a liar, and a brat. That's what you've called her so far. As well as underfed.' Suddenly her voice was shaking uncontrollably. She heard it and was appalled, but couldn't stop it or the shaking of her hands. She knew it was tiredness and the shock of Rose's frantic entrance, and then irritation with this man in front of her. She heard herself ranting, 'You men never do anything but criticise, criticise, criticise. Can't you ever do anything but . . .'

'Yes. Bring her to the surgery. Tomorrow. I'll overhaul

her.' As she stood there, open-mouthed with the shock of his retort, he added, 'Try tonight to get the truth out of her.'

Her lips came together with a snap. 'My Rose doesn't tell lies.'

She went on standing there, watching him walk away. She didn't speak, even when she had closed the door and turned to face Rose. She said, quietly, 'I was let off early, to get things straight here. Come and help.'

Rose's head jerked up. She said swiftly, 'Mummy, up there in Mrs Oatland's room . . .'

Josie's voice broke across the words, 'I told him you didn't tell lies. If you said there was a bird, that's the end of it.'

Rose knew there was no going back on it, that she was saddled now with the magpie just as – the thought nearly made her break into hysterical laughter – the old man of the poem had been saddled with the albatross for evermore. There was a sense of dismal aloneness in the knowledge, but under the scrutiny of Josie's shuttered expression she didn't dare to admit she'd lied; not now her mother had said in that proud, assured voice, 'My Rose doesn't tell lies.'

Rose remembered Josie saying that to the policeman, and the owner of the block of flats where they'd lived, to a whole pile of people, while that horrible caretaker had raved that she was a liar – about him at any rate. Even now Rose wasn't sure how it had all ended, except that they had hastily packed up and moved, and everyone in the flats had peered at their going from behind lace curtains and venetian blinds, and the caretaker himself had come out on to the step and yelled after them, 'I ought to sue you.' Rose remembered how her mother had turned, white-faced, expressionless, and said, 'My Rose doesn't tell lies.'

Rose knew that she couldn't bear to be caught out in a lie, for fear that Josie's loving expression would alter and doubt slide into her blue eyes, while she asked, just as the policeman had, 'Rose, are you sure you aren't lying about the caretaker? Maybe he even gave you a little fright, and you wanted to get sort of even by making trouble for him, hmmm?'

What did it matter anyway, she reflected in sudden comforting remembrance of two winks given her in a warm quiet
room. Mrs Oatland had told her not to tell the truth. That
was the thing to cling to and remember, she told herself, and
immediately past fright and future trouble were forgotten as
she danced down the hall after Josie.

The wall whispered with that assured voice, 'I'm on to
something odd, Val. Believe it or not, the doctor thinks your
old corpse is playing shams up there. Oh, you needn't look as
though someone's stuck a pin in you. It's no skin off my nose,
but it's interesting and has possibilities. If the doctor has cot-
toned on to the fact, the old biddy's told the kid to keep quiet.
Why, would you say?'

There was silence, then the tart answer, 'If I had a dear
niece like that I'd prefer to be laid out quiet like a corpse than
having her ear-bash me – "Auntie, you give your nod to this,
and a nod to that and to all else I want to do round here."
Right?'

'It has to be that, I'd say. Probably she feels she'll soon be
strong enough to stand up to ear-bashing, but for the moment
no one like the nurse and doctor are going to know, for fear
they feel it's their duty to pass the news on to dear Gwenyth.'

'So she tells that kid . . .' the woman's voice was impatient
now '. . . well, what's it to do with us? It'll keep the kid out of
our hair, that's all, running up to the old woman's room and
playing secrets with her. What's it matter?'

'It matters that your old corpse is an adult, my love, and if
her mind's okay she's not going to be happy with kid's prattle
for long. Wouldn't she welcome nice Mrs Phipps cooing at
her, "Dear Mrs Oatland, I know you can give a nod to questions, and I shan't tell until you tell me to, but how about I
read you the paper" . . . lord!' There was a sudden bang as
though, Sarah thought, the legs of a chair had been banged
down hard on the floor. 'Lord, how that expression of yours
bores me! Bovine, blank – all you need's a cud.'

Sarah expected a childish-sounding wrangle to develop between the two but, just as before, there was silence to his taunting, as though the woman was inured to insults and now they meant nothing to her, and after a few seconds he went on, 'She'll soon welcome you. Nursie will comment on it, be pleased to leave you in charge, and where do I stand then? I know, of course, the old lady can hear and be scared into fits if I go running upstairs yelling, "My father-in-law is taken bad." So I don't go, do I? I try to cope with things all by myself till it's too late. See the possibilities? A good excuse ready-made for me not to go rushing up for you.'

The whisper sounded harshly through the wall, 'What're you actually going to do to him? And don't stuff me with any more "You'll see, soon enough." I want to know. Now. Or don't you really know? Has all this just been talk?'

'I've never done or said one thing I'd do, without doing it, right down to the night I belted hell out of you after I'd promised that. Forgotten?'

He laughed. 'You've a mind like your face – bovine. Couldn't you see I had to know where we'd be, look the ground over, before I could see how it's going to be done? Could I say, he'll fall downstairs, when I didn't know if we'd have a staircase or not? Could I plan on some gadget going wrong when I didn't know what gadgets we'd have? Look round this place for yourself. Does it give you any ideas?'

'No.'

'Not even when you know there's a nice new gas stove put in in a hurry? Be sad, wouldn't it, if it wasn't connected properly, because Palmer's sense of smell has almost gone. But not quite. He might just manage to get a window open before collapsing. When I came in the gas wouldn't smell much, would it? And I might put it down to a simple faint at first, mightn't I?'

There was no answer, and after a little the man's voice went on in that assured confident whisper, 'There's a nice straight staircase out there. It would be so easy if Palmer went up with you one evening, carrying a few magazines, perhaps, and fell, on his way down again. Naturally he wouldn't want a fuss made. He might be able to get up, with my help, and tell me not to worry, so I wouldn't – or even get you, for fear of upsetting the old lady – and then, it was too late.'

I'm not hearing this, Sarah told herself with surprising vigour. This is absolute nonsense. No one could plan like that and talk about it and be so completely evil, but over that vigorous denial of her own hearing, the assured voice whispered on, 'There's a very nice little shower room down here, just the sort of thing to appeal to a tired old man. But shower floors are sometimes slippery, sometimes with dropped soap, and old men are shaky on their pins, too. If Palmer leaned in to turn on the hot water, and slipped and fell and knocked himself out, that hot water might run on and on, over him. Mightn't it? Hot water can scald, and kill and even drown.

'Perhaps you've noticed that light over the fireplace. Do you think it needs a new bulb? It might, you know, and Palmer's such an obliging chap, but he'd have to stand on a chair to fix it, wouldn't he? What if the chair toppled and he fell on to that sharp edge there of the grate. Skulls fracture quite easily. And how would I know it wasn't just a simple bump till too late?

'And do you see that framed picture over there? Rather charming, I think, but would you say that holding cord is fraying? Old men like comfortable chairs, and there's one in that corner, and pictures can fall, can't they? Of course, neither of us would realise the bang was serious. Palmer rather pooh-poohs a fuss, doesn't he? He might say, "Good God, boy, I've suffered worse bangs than that. Go get me a drink" and when I came back, he could be lying back, quite still. Couldn't he?

'There's that window in our new bedroom too. Did you notice the sash cord has gone? Perhaps Palmer might hear someone call urgently outside, and put up the window and lean out. Windows have fallen before this, unpleasantly.

'There's that piano down here too. I must remember to check it's well tuned before Palmer comes. We'll have some pleasant social evenings, that is, if the piano doesn't develop an ailment. Palmer might lift that lid – have you tried to? It's one of those old-fashioned pieces that weigh a ton – to see what had happened. What if his hands were slippery – the exertion of playing, you know – and the lid slipped and crashed on to his head? Skulls fracture, as I said before.

'We'll forget such items as electric fire, because it's summer, but summer brings bees, doesn't it? There are a lot of flowering shrubs outside our new kitchenette and no insect screens over the windows, which no doubt would bring a few critical comments from the coroner, as who can tell when a swarm of bees will enter a kitchen, or where they came from. Palmer's allergic to bee stings – oh yes, my love, I know a whole heap about my father-in-law. Palmer would run, of course, and an old man can slip on polished lino and fall, against the new stove perhaps, and knock himself out. The bees would panic too – they might sting him badly. Too badly. Mightn't they?'

The voice added gently, 'You're really very silent. I hope you're listening, my love, because houses are very deadly things – they can be terribly lethal in so many ways. Have you noticed that big mirror in our shower room? I wonder if it's really secure there on the wall, or if it mightn't fall and a big jagged piece cut Palmer's leg – badly. He wouldn't realise at first that an artery was cut, I expect – and how the old boy does hate a fuss being made. He'd try to patch himself with adhesive plaster – make sure we have some, won't you? How terrible it would be if I walked in later – too late – and found him unconscious. Very unconscious.'

The voice stopped and there was only silence. There was silence in Sarah, too, which had nothing to do with her paralysed voice. There was a silence of thought that blotted out any comment, any fear, any horror, at what she was hearing. She simply lay there, thinking of nothing at all, and the silence went on and on, till thought came back and she was certain the two downstairs had left the sitting room altogether.

Then the woman's voice whispered up the wall, 'Never speak to me like that again.'

'You wanted to know. Now you do. Stop sitting there and go to the phone. See if Palmer's home. If so, tell him we've found a place and want him to come for a visit soon. Give a broad hint that I've my eye on some property and am more than keen on it. That'll bring him running to stick his oar in before I get a chance to close on any deal.'

'How soon do you want him here?'

'As quickly as possible. The sooner it's over the better. In any case if I use the stove, that framed picture, the bedroom window, it must be quickly, before it's obvious we've been around long enough to know the things were defective. There isn't going to be one shred of blame, one fraction of an inch of doubt turned my way.'

Always the first person, Sarah reflected. She wondered if he cared a jot if suspicion and doubt and blame rested on his wife, decided he would have to, because if the woman was blamed she would surely blurt out his part in it; and from there fell to wondering why two who so obviously disliked one another should be partners in such an evil thing, deciding that necessity must over-ride dislike – that perhaps the woman would have legacy rights to Parker's money, but not the – she couldn't think of any word except 'stomach' – but not the stomach for disposing of him, while the man did, and his benefit would come from her.

Then, as though answering the questions clamouring in Sarah's thoughts the voices began again, the man first, saying lightly, 'Besides, I fancy escaping the hot weather and going to Europe. Doesn't the idea of a white Christmas appeal to you, my love?'

'Yes, providing you're not there with me,' was the swift bitter answer.

'I'm afraid I will have to be – for a little while. It wouldn't look respectable if immediately on the old boy's death we took off in separate directions . . .'

'And besides, you want to be sure of getting your portion don't you? Remembering that little clause in the will – what was it again? "Providing the said Valma and Murray Phipps are still joined in matrimony and living together." I can never remember the legal blarney, but that's it, isn't it? And I could, couldn't I, tell the lawyers that we'd parted days, weeks, before Palmer died.'

The man chuckled. The sound, to Sarah, held genuine amusement. He said lightly, 'You might, dear, but for the fact that Palmer will die in our home, seeing us dwelling in married bliss, which is another reason for a quick job. I have no intention of letting him see through the bliss, and how long do you think you can play the contented little wife?'

'Just as long as you're likely to be able to play the devoted husband. Listen to me, Murray . . .' suddenly all whispiness, all softness was going from the woman's voice. It was as assured as his own '. . . I'm not going to Europe or anywhere else with you. Where I go will be my own business. The lawyers can put my departure down to grief – a need to be alone – or whatever they like, and as soon as it's feasible I'll start divorce proceedings. Let them think what they like. We won't be the only couple who've stayed together just so we can gain under a will and . . .'

'But perhaps the only couple, my love, who gained their legacy through a sad, abrupt accident. Oh no, we're staying together. I told you, no finger of suspicion is going to point. For heaven's sake, Val, use your brains!' Exasperation replaced the assurance. 'Accidents are always investigated. Do you want the police noting that we were at loggerheads? It'd be only a step from that to them wondering if we couldn't go on living together, but wanted that money, so staged an accident. . . well?'

All the woman said was, 'Wouldn't it be funny if he died – naturally – on the way here? Planes are lethal and taxis and . . . dozens of things.'

'Cold feet, my love?' was the question and then there was only silence.

———

CHAPTER 4

It was the next morning that the whispy voice sounded in Sarah's bedroom; not through the wall, but there beside the bed, almost lost under Bragg's treacly gushing that cut across the soft, 'anything I can ever do', with a bright, 'Well, I won't say there aren't times I could do with an extra pair of hands, Mrs Phipps. The old dear isn't so heavy, but she's a dead weight; can't help herself an inch you know, and it's really a job for two people. I did suggest to Mrs Oatland – the niece, I mean – that another nurse to come in for an hour each day would be a good thing, but of course I might have . . .' she stopped, then after a moment added flatly '. . . of course all this is very expensive as it is, though I must say . . .' in spite of an obvious effort, grievance rode high in the admission '. . .I thought her – Mrs Oatland's – idea that I get the household help to give me a hand was just plain silly. Mrs Furlong's over sixty, for a start, and so slow she barely gets the place clean before she goes. Of course . . .' the flatness was back '. . . she's cheap.' Abruptly she asked, 'Do you work, Mrs Phipps?'

'No. We'll be looking at houses. My father is coming too – tomorrow . . .'

The rest of it was lost to Sarah. All she could think of was the Roderick Palmer she had known as a stage star all those years ago coming to her home as a guest and . . . what? She tried to think what the new stove downstairs would be like;

found herself bitterly regretting that broken sash cord in the window of the dining room, which was now to be a bedroom; hated herself for putting up the big mirror in the shower room because the light was dim in there and a small mirror didn't seem to catch the light.

Dim, she thought, and dwelt on the word, sickened by it, because dimness was a weapon. In that small dim space Roderick Palmer wouldn't notice that the mirror was almost free of the wall – till it fell, smashed to dangerous slivers . . .

But you can't, she thought in confusion, make a piece of broken glass cut an artery. Roderick Palmer would jump backwards, out of range . . . but of course he wouldn't, she thought, feeling really ill now. Murray Phipps would have all that nicely planned. It would seem the old man had jumped all right, and tripped, and crashed, striking his head on the basin or floor, so he was knocked out. It would have to be that way. There wouldn't, she thought in mocking cynicism, be need of sticking plaster. It would just seem Roderick Palmer had knocked himself out, and fallen on a jagged sliver of mirror and an artery was cut, so that he simply bled to death, unconscious, knowing nothing to the end . . .

In front of her unmoving eyes was a horrible picture of Palmer going into that little dim room, to stand facing the mirror, seeing in it his son-in-law come in behind him, turning to face him, a half question on his lips that was never uttered, because he was struck down. Then the stage would be set and it would be a horrible accident and, just as they'd planned it, no finger of suspicion or blame would rest on them. The blame would be hers, Sarah Oatland's, for not seeing that her mirror was securely fastened. Or no – suddenly, ridiculously, she could find amusement in her imaginings, realising it would be Gwenyth who'd get the blame because she had let the place. The responsibility would rest squarely on her. Sarah could imagine Gwenyth, red-faced, furious, being censured in court by some cocky little coroner.

Only it wasn't funny. Not a scrap funny. The amusement

was as swiftly gone. She tried to shut her mind to further imaginings, and heard the whispy voice saying, '. . . some time to help a little. I could sit with her, for instance, while you could go out for a breath of air. I suppose you go out shopping sometimes, too, and there's . . .'

'I try. Oh yes, I have my rights, as I pointed out to Mrs Oatland. There's an old friend of the old dear's comes and sits once a week. Mrs Oatland cried off. Did it once and she was a bundle of nerves when I came back. Actually shaking.'

It was news to Sarah. She didn't remember Gwenyth ever having sat beside the bed. She listened with real interest to Bragg explaining, 'Just after the stroke that was. She said the old lady's eyes suddenly opened and her jaw fell, and she said to herself, My God, she's gone! and she just sat there, too scared to find out! Mind you, that does happen when she's asleep. Would it scare you?'

The whispy voice denied it, 'No. Not at all. I'm used to old people.'

'I suppose, come to that, your father is quite old.' The suggestion came reluctantly, as though Bragg feared to have past illusions shattered. 'I was trying to work out last night how old he'd be. Is he able to care for himself still?'

'Roderick?' The whispiness had given place to astonishment. 'Why, he's the most capable person . . .' She stopped, the words bitten off so sharply, the silence afterwards so prolonged, that Sarah could guess the reason. The woman was regretting the admission; fearing almost certainly that it would be remembered; that the nurse might afterwards say in some gossiping sessions, 'They wouldn't have inherited for years and years, except for that accident. He was young for his age, in good health . . .'

Afterwards, the pause so long that Bragg must have noted it and puzzled over it, Sarah was sure, Valma Phipps admitted, 'He's sixty-three. He still travels a little. Oh, not the stage. His voice went, you know – that was before he married my mother. Afterwards he started investing – small businesses, that sort of thing. He still has those interests.'

'So it's just a holiday for him? You won't be tied down caring for him?' Bragg said.

'No. I told you, I can spare some time. Today, for instance. Before he comes. If you'd care to go out today I'll come up.'

So soon, Sarah thought and was seized with panic. She reflected on that whispy voice pressing at her, 'Mrs Oatland you can hear me, can't you? Do please answer me . . .' and knew that she wouldn't reply. She daren't now. Too much had been said down in that sitting room. Far too much. If ever the Phipps pair found out now about that whispering wall, there'd be . . . but imagination became bogged down in panic and panic in weariness, so that she ceased to think, or even hear, what was being said.

'Mrs Oatland!' The urgent whisper reached her only faintly. The child had to keep repeating her name, asking urgently, 'Mrs Oatland, can't you hear me?'

Wink, went Sarah's right eye at last and a breathless little giggle rewarded her.

'I knew you were really awake. Your nurse is having lunch in the kitchen, 'cause I set the table in there to help Mrs Furlong. Nurse said I should have given her a tray in her own room, and Mrs Furlong said, "Well, if you're too proud to eat in here among the pots and pans, Nurse, you could pick up the table and take it to your room." Nurse said back, "Really, Mrs Furlong, there's no need to be offensive."'

Sarah wished she could have laughed, the mimicry of Bragg – treacly voice holding outrage – was so good. She listened fully awake and interested now, as Rose prattled on. 'And Mrs Furlong said, "I'm not being offensive, Nurse, I'm being frank, which is a different thing, you telling me so when we discussed my floor-cleaning the other day."' Regretfully she added, 'Then Nurse told me to run away, so I did, and I came in because she'll be ages over lunch. Mrs Furlong says she chews every mouthful ten times, which is good exercise for the jaws, but Nurse doesn't need it anyway because she talks so much she gets a lot otherwise.'

The soft voice held urgency again, 'Mrs Oatland, I just wanted to ask if there's anything I can get you? Is there anything you want?'

Sarah thought, confused again, How do I answer that? If I tell her 'yes', she won't ask the right questions. How does she know I need a policeman, or someone who can deal with that dreadful pair downstairs?

After a long moment – too long, she realised – the child said anxiously, 'Mrs Oatland, can't you hear me?' And then she gave a little chuckle, 'Oh, of course, there must be lots of things you'd like, and you're thinking, aren't you, which ones I could maybe get you, and which ones'd be any use? You take your time. I'll wait.'

So what do I say, Sarah wondered anxiously. 'No'? I might as well. Yet to say 'yes', and let the child question her would keep her there for a while, and bring her back later.

Wink, went her right eye, and Rose said eagerly, 'I'll ask you questions. If it's something you don't want, don't answer at all. Just answer if it's something you'd like, and I'll ask . . .' her thin face grew doubtful '. . . oh, I can't ask Nurse to get it, can I?' Her expression brightened, 'But I can get it myself, so don't worry. Now, what would you like?' The narrow dark brows furrowed in thought. 'A book? Oh, no don't answer that. That was silly, wasn't it? You couldn't hold a book at all. I could read to you perhaps, but I don't think I'd be allowed to. I'll just have to sneak in when I can, like now.'

Why aren't you at school, Sarah wondered, and as though she had picked up the thought and was answering it, Rose went on, 'I didn't go to school this morning. I have to go after lunch. Mummy said when we came back that I might as well offer to help up here till after lunch. You see, this morning, I went to the doctor. Oh, you needn't be alarmed. I haven't anything like spots. I haven't anything, in fact, only your doctor was quite cross and my mother says he has a lot to learn, including a bedside manner, because he said last night I was underfed, and a liar. But never mind about that bit. That doesn't matter at all. He said last night to bring me to the surgery, and my mother said, "Well, we'll go. You may be skinny, but that's nature and not underfeeding" and she said to the doctor this morning, "Rose is quite healthy, and well fed. I was skinnier than she, at eleven years old." And the doctor said, "Good lord, how did you avoid falling down the plug hole when you had a bath?" and Mummy said, in her heavens-above-what-next voice, that's how I think of it to myself you see, "You've quite a sense of humour, haven't you?" and he said, "Anything wrong with that?"'

She paused to regain lost breath and prattled on, 'And Mummy said, "My husband had one. And nothing else." And she just never talks about my father, because . . .' there was hesitation now in the soft voice '. . . because he left us. He just never came home one night.'

For a brief moment there was silence, then the child went on, 'And the doctor asked, "What should he have had?" and my mother said, "A bit of gumption for a start, and a sense of responsibility and the will to do some hard work, and stick at it, and make a decent living for his family." She just never talks like that, only she did this morning, just as though she couldn't stop. There were a whole pile of things she said my father should have had, and when she stopped the doctor said, "Tried to make him into the sort of man he was never meant to be, did you?" and my mother said, "So you're blaming me – how like a man to stick up for another," and he said back, "I'm not blaming you. I'm pointing out he was probably never built to be all those things you wanted. I haven't met him, or heard his side of it, have I?"

'My mother never said anything, which was odd really, because it's awfully hard to make her stop talking when she's cross, and the doctor told me to take off my dress and next thing he said, "Good lord, do you work yourself to a standstill and then spend the money on lace petticoats for a child?" and my mother looked crosser than ever and said, "It's my money and I've said nothing about working myself to a standstill," and he said, "No. You don't need to. You look it. How old are you?" And when she said twenty-eight – that's a fib though really,' Rose confided, 'because she's thirty, the doctor said, "You look forty. By the time you're forty you'll look sixty. All work and no fun makes a plain Jane. Remember it and, if you want to buy lace slips, buy them for yourself," and . . .' there was a soft giggle '. . . she said, "How do you know I don't?" and he said, "I know. A woman who keeps her mouth so tight as you hold yours has forgotten how to be young and frivolous and coddle herself with lace and fripperies and expensive powders and soaps."

'My mother looked madder than ever and she said, "You make me sound like the television ads – ah me, my fiancé said my twin sister looked years younger than me, all because she uses X brand soap." And then, do you know . . .' the young voice held wonder '. . . she laughed. Really laughed, I mean, and she doesn't do that often, and he guessed. He said, "You want to do that more often and you'd look twenty," and then . . .'

Rose stopped. She said then, dismayed, 'Oh, I'm sorry. I didn't mean to talk and talk like that. I've tired you, haven't I, and I didn't mean to.' Sarah's eyelid closed twice quite effortlessly this time, because she had loved the prattling, the feeling that here was a real visitor at last, not speaking in hushed tones of subjects suitable for the near-departed, but making Sarah part of living and life again; and it had taken her mind away from other, horrible things.

Remembering, ease and pleasure began to slide away again. She wished the child would start talking again of things remote from the house and the Phipps pair, but she didn't. She said instead, 'Now, what would you like me to bring? Oh, do you know I've just thought of something. It'll have to be things I could think of all by myself you see, or they'll wonder why I bring them, 'cause I can't say you asked me to get them – not unless you want them to know?'

The voice held question, and that brought panic back. Then she gave a double blink.

Rose nodded. 'All right then. What would you like? Flowers? There are some lovely roses in the garden outside our door. Mrs Oatland told my mother that piece of garden was for us to keep nice now. My mother said real low, "A penny saved is a penny gained", but I told her there were lots of flowers already and I'd buy others with my pocket money if she liked, and she said that wasn't what she meant, but she didn't explain. Would it cost a lot to buy some little plants, do you think?'

She smiled at the two winks, but Sarah felt the futility of them, when she wanted to say a lot; to tell the child not to buy one single plant, and not to weed or water either. How typical of Gwenyth, she thought wearily. The garden had never been any trouble. Most of it was shrubs that needed little care, and there'd always been boys willing to come for a few dollars when she needed help to cut the grass. The rest she'd done herself. Gwenyth could have coped on her own but, no, she'd seen a chance of free labour and used it.

Rose asked again, 'Shall I bring you roses then?' and Sarah gave assent. She wished she could have said, 'You're the rose I want most, my dear' and knew again the frustration of not being able to make any real contact with anyone.

Rose said, 'Good. Now what else could you have?' She fell silent, her brow furrowing and after a long pause she said, 'I can't think of anything. Yet there must be something.'

Sarah wanted to say, 'Oh there is. For instance, I wish someone would remove that horrible painting. Bragg put it there and Gwenyth noted it at once and told her it belonged downstairs, but Bragg wouldn't budge. She liked a nice bit of seascape, so she explained, and now it faces my bed when I'm not here by the window, and I loathe the wretched thing. The curtains, too, irritate me terribly. They don't belong to this room at all. I wish I knew what had happened to the long yellow ones. When the sun shone through them the room turned golden. Now it goes a sickly green. I suppose Bragg thinks it's restful.

'I'd like a bird, too,' she would have gone on to explain 'one that chirps and sings and brings a bit of life into the room. Even a cat, a nice plump, cosy cat perched on the foot of my bed would be a comfort . . .' Then she pictured Bragg's face at the sight of a cat on the smooth counterpane and wanted to laugh.

Oh, it was wretched not being able to make her wants known, she thought then. There were a million things she would have loved to have. Still, roses would do for a start. Her sense of smell was still there and roses . . . Her thoughts broke. Sense of smell, she reflected and was thinking again of Phipps, with his talk of the gas stove and Roderick Palmer's sense of smell being gone.

I want a policeman, she thought frantically, but Rose was asking, 'Would you like to see someone?' Eagerly now she questioned on, 'Is there some old friend, someone who doesn't come often, I could tell to come? I mean, someone I could tell about you hearing things and winking and that and who'd keep it a secret, but come and visit . . .'

Is there, Sarah wondered, and names went flickering through her mind, to be discarded in despair. She'd made no new friends since David's death, and their old ones had been mostly his. How odd to realise, only now, that she had lived so much through David's zest for life. With him gone she had settled down into dullness. That was what it amounted to, and from the names that came and went she wouldn't get much help, she was certain.

Oh, they would come, and some would keep the secret. Or would they? She pondered that, realising they probably wouldn't. They wouldn't perhaps mean to let it out, those good, and elderly, and oh so dull contemporaries of hers, but it would be such a delicious bit of gossip to tell to another friend over tea that it would slide out willy-nilly. She could just imagine a tea party with one greying head bent towards another while the whisper buzzed, 'Can you imagine, that niece of hers is such a grasping creature the poor old thing can't even admit she can hear and be questioned for fear she'll have the life badgered out of her.'

It would be all over the town in no time, she thought wearily. Worse, one of them would almost certainly feel it her duty to run to the doctor – in an effort to protect her from Gwenyth. Then Bragg would know. From there it would be but a step to Bragg's confiding in Valma Phipps, that eager helper of a sick old lady.

She realised she had hesitated so long that the child was questioning again, 'Would you like to talk to my mother?' She clapped her hands to her mouth. 'Oh, no, I can't tell her, because she told the doctor I couldn't possibly be telling lies. Well, there's Mrs Furlong?' At Sarah's quick double wink the child giggled. 'I didn't think you would. She's gloomy, isn't she? While I was helping her she told me all about her husband and brother and her mother who're all dead. I think all her relations must be dead, except for her nephew. He went wrong, and she doesn't like to think about him.' Pensively she added, 'She talks about him an awful lot though.

'Oh, I'm babbling again. I'm sorry. Who else is there? There's Mr and Mrs Phipps.' At Sarah's urgent double wink, Rose said, 'I don't know them, but their father is coming and my mother says that once he was known all over the world, and my grandmother used to have a terrific crush on him. His name's Roderick Palmer. Would you like to meet him when he comes?'

Sarah's assent was swiftly given, more swiftly than ever she had been able to lower her eyelid before, but when it was given she thought helplessly that the answer would get her nowhere. Even if Roderick Palmer was coaxed up the stairs to this warm quiet room – and how would the child tempt him up ever? – there'd be still no communication between them, no chance of warning him.

Suddenly she was so tired she just wanted to sink away into the oblivion of sleep and instantly – how closely the child must have been watching her, she thought vaguely – the soft voice said, 'Oh, you're tired. I'll go away now. But I'll come back. When I can. With roses. And I'll remember about Mr Palmer. I'll find some way of bringing him up so you can see what he's like.'

The tone was so gently soothing, so firmly promising that vague amusement reached through Sarah's weariness and she wondered if the child thought that she, Sarah Oatland, like that unknown grandmother, had once had a terrific crush on the old singer.

When Sarah woke again the room was filled with the sickly green light that she hated. She knew the green curtains were drawn over the windows, though she couldn't see them. All that day her bed had been in the middle of the room, the bed-head against the far wall. Bragg had spoken to Mrs Furlong that early morning about a man coming to fix screens, 'Though he won't come in here,' she had added decidedly. 'He'll be working from outside. I insisted on that.'

He was working now. It was that that had woken her, Sarah realised, the clattering from outside. She was thinking about it, wondering what sort of screens they would be and if they would spoil the appearance of the house, when the woman spoke.

'Don't worry about the noise, Mrs Oatland. There's a man fixing screens outside the windows to stop the birds worrying you. He'll be gone shortly.' Then she asked, 'Do you recognise my voice? I'm Valma Phipps from downstairs. I'm sitting here with you while Nurse does a little shopping.'

There was a moment's pause before the whisp of voice added, 'I know you can hear, Mrs Oatland, and nod – or perhaps you give a blink? – to questions. Oh, don't be at all alarmed. If you want it kept secret for a little while that's your business. I don't regard you as half dead.'

Which neatly puts her into a different category from Gwenyth, Sarah thought cynically.

'I think of you as very much alive. You have a right to your privacy, a right to make what decisions you can. You've decided you don't want your family, or Nurse, to know about this. That's your business.'

And none of yours, Sarah thought, but the voice pressed on, 'I shan't bother you at all. I just want to help you, and you must be terribly bored with things as they are. Now, I've been making a few enquiries – from Nurse, and from Mrs Furlong. She's worked for you and for a few hours each week for a long time, hasn't she? She tells me you love books, but doesn't seem to know your favourites. There's a terrible jumble of every kind in one of the bedrooms up here – brought up, Mrs Furlong told me, before downstairs was rented.'

It was ridiculous to feel anger, Sarah told herself, at the idea of the woman prowling through the rooms. Mrs Furlong had sense of a sort. She wouldn't have allowed a stranger free access, but just the same she lay there hating the thought of this woman's hands touching David's beloved books, riffling the pages, perhaps reading, in smug amusement, the little comments he had often made in the margins of some point or paragraph.

Valma Phipps was asking, 'What would you like? I'll find the books you love best later on today, and tonight I'll come up and relieve Nurse for a little and read to you. What shall it be? Dickens. I often feel, do you, that he was really a very cruel type of person. Would you like his books, though? Or a modern novel? A romance perhaps?'

After a moment she said, and now impatience underlay the smoothness of the words, 'Why don't you answer me, Mrs Oatland? Is it because I haven't told you what to do? I think it's probably a blink you can give, isn't it? So give me one blink for "yes" and two for "no". Now, let's start again. Would you like Dickens?' After a long pause she pressed, 'A modern novel? A travel book? A romantic story, Mrs Oatland?' Now there was sharpness too, so that the voice seemed altogether different from the whispiness of her first attempts. 'Mrs

Oatland, answer me! You can. I know quite well you can, and it's so foolish of you to refuse to admit it when I want to help you.'

Sarah found malicious satisfaction in her denial of that pressing voice. She had to give the younger woman credit for persistence, if nothing else, as over and over during the next couple of hours she tried to gain an acknowledgment from Sarah. Sarah found her presence tiring, as well as irritating as the time dragged on. She was frightened to drift towards sleep for fear the persistent voice would gain an acknowledgement jerked from her half-unconscious mind, so that it was sheer relief to hear heavy-footed steps across the carpet and Bragg's voice, 'Shopping is getting worse year by year. Everyone seemed out today. Must be the fine spell. I'm a bit late, aren't I, Mrs Phipps, but better late than never, and I saw the screens were up and the workmen gone. How did the old dear take it?'

'Never a peep out of her,' was irony for Sarah's ears alone, but Bragg chuckled richly.

'Didn't expect one, did you? I meant, did she seem upset?' Warm breath touched Sarah's cheek and Bragg's face loomed across her vision. 'You're fine though, aren't you, my dear, and it was for your own good. Now the birdies can't annoy you. . .'

Unkindly Sarah reflected what malicious satisfaction there would be in having a record cut of Bragg at her most inane, to be later played back to her with blunt candour, and then she was sorry because the spicy smell of carnations reached her and the other woman was saying, 'I didn't forget you while I was out, my dear. Brought some carnations for you. I thought, Well, she might be able to smell as good as myself, so there they are.' The flowers came closer, the smell fragrant with memories of walks through the garden; of David planting carnations year after year . . .

Across her memories cut Valma's quiet remark, 'You talk to her as though she understands you?'

'Who's to say she doesn't?' Bragg was the professional again, her voice smug with knowledge. 'We don't really know how much these cases take in. Sometimes it's just a vacuum, I think. Sometimes they hear and know everything that's going on, even though they've no way of showing it. But you've been stuck up here long enough. I'll pop these in water and take over. Maybe you'd help shift the bed – it moves easily – we had special castors put on – over by the window. That's the spot she likes best, poor dear.'

The wall began whispering, as Sarah had been sure it would, as soon as Valma was downstairs again. Sarah lay, the hated green curtains moving gently in the breeze through the new wire screens, almost holding her breath for fear the sound of it would bring Bragg back. She knew what would happen now if Bragg heard those whispers. Full of importance, of a chance to gossip to a new-made friend, she would gallumph, heavy-footed, downstairs and rap on the door and say cheerily, 'Guess what? I've discovered my old dear can hear right enough. Now I know why she likes that wall by the window so much. You'd never believe it, but up there you can hear your voices coming up behind the wall. Now . . .' Sarah could easily see Bragg's arch look and wagging fingers, 'Now you two be careful or all your secrets will be known to the poor old thing.'

Or would she do that, Sarah suddenly wondered. Would Bragg do that, or keep quiet? Knowing that Sarah couldn't tell on her, and later on she could even justify herself with the excuse that to tell would deprive Sarah of her one small enjoyment in life, Bragg might sit there by the bed, sharing avidly in the lives of the Phipps. What then, Sarah asked herself, if the wall whispered again of murder?

Excitement touched her, to die away. She was positive that never again would Murray Phipps speak in the way he had done the previous evening. The woman had told him not to, and obviously, from his secrecy with her before, he liked keeping his plans to himself. Tomorrow, she remembered sharply,

Roderick Palmer would arrive, too. There'd be small chance then of the wall whispering anything but polite conversation between the three of them.

So there was small chance of Bragg hearing anything revealing. Sarah was sure it would take a lot to convince Bragg that someone in the house was actually plotting the death of another. All that would be gained by her knowing was the chance that the Phipps pair would learn that the horrible, evil talk of the previous evening had been heard.

The green curtains rustled gently. Valma's voice through the wall was hardly more than another rustle, 'I can't make her out. I offered to read to her – anything she chose, but no. I couldn't get a scrap of acknowlegement. Honestly, Murray, I think you and the doctor are being totally absurd. She's just . . . not there, if you follow me. Not that it seems to me to matter one way or the other. I've made friends with dear Cornelia – did you know that's her name? She's so-o-o-o-o grateful. Funny thing is, I think she really and honestly cares about the old woman. She brought her home carnations and talked to her as she might babble to a pet puppy. If you're interested, she's at daggers-drawn with Mrs O. junior. Murray!' Her voice rose, 'Are you listening to me?'

'Yes, my love. I was thinking.'

'What about?'

'Your old corpse. She puzzles me. Maybe she doesn't like your face, or . . . Val . . .' his voice sharpened, '. . . were you a trifle too friendly with the nurse? Would the old biddy get the idea you were becoming bosom sisters? That might have kept her from letting on to you that . . .'

'Oh, what does it matter? Whether she can hear or not doesn't . . .'

'I've told you. If we know she can hear and be frightened I'd be unlikely to go dashing upstairs yelling for you and exclaiming that Palmer was lying around half dead.'

'It doesn't seem to matter much, except . . . what are you

going to do exactly to . . . no, don't answer that . . .' She amended swiftly '. . . I don't want to know!'

Sarah could picture her standing there, hands pressed to her ears, shutting out any chance he might have had of speaking as he'd done the previous day.

She expected to hear his assured voice taunting, but when he spoke again it was only to say, 'Watch the brat, Val. She'll be home from school soon. Watch her. If she really talks to the old woman she'll wait her chance to sneak up and get gossiping. Follow her up. You can surely think of some excuse. Offer more help if you like, or take up some fruit. Anything, but get the nurse out of the way for a bit and let the kid have free rein, then make some excuse to pussy-foot after her. Try and catch her and the old woman having a question-and-answer session. Now listen to me. It's a simple job for you, and it's important. When the time comes, I don't intend having any mistakes. I can't trust you, you're too unpredictable and go to pieces. You'll be nervous to start with. I don't want you saying the wrong thing and her hearing it and noting it and getting it through to the police afterwards. I want to know how much we can say in front of her and how we can use her. Oh yes, we can use her. You have only to blurt out about her being able to hear, etc., etc., and the police will be up there and you can lead the questions to her so that she lets on exactly what we want them to know.

'In fact,' he finished triumphantly, 'we'll have the perfect witness – one who can back us up, yet not say a thing more than we want her to. Now you do what I said – keep watch for the brat coming home and then trot upstairs after her.'

What would Bragg have made of that conversation if she'd heard it, Sarah wondered, and decided that the other woman would have been merely confused and bewildered by it. There was nothing frightening in it, only the suggestion that Sarah was shamming part of her illness. Bragg would be annoyed about that. In her annoyance she might even thrust any questions about the rest of the talk right out of her mind.

She lay there wondering what she was going to do that afternoon when Rose came back. If she didn't answer the child, Rose was going to be hurt and bewildered, perhaps even frightened that Sarah had suffered some new stroke so that she couldn't respond any more. In that case she might rush to Bragg to pour out her worry, but before that Valma Phipps would be there, pressing, 'What are you doing, Rose, talking to the old lady as though she can answer?'

Sarah went on fretting endlessly, 'What am I to do?'

She had come to no decision by the time sleep claimed her, and when she woke again she knew the room was filled with roses. The scent overlay that of the carnations, and for a confused minute she thought she was in the garden, in one of the old deck chairs, and David had come to wake her, one hand on her shoulder. She lay there expecting to hear his voice saying, 'Wake up, sleepy-head, there's a cuppa waiting.'

Then she knew the hand was too light in touch for David. It was a child's hand. Her eyes opened and she saw Rose's thin features. The child's lips were slightly parted in anticipation, the small irregular teeth biting into the pale lower lip as though she were holding her breath. Then she said, her blue eyes reflecting the eagerness in her whisper, 'Can you smell them, Mrs Oatland? I picked all the ones that smelt the very best.'

Sarah assented eagerly.

'I'm going to bring the vase over so you can see.' There was the rustle of steps over the carpet, then the fragrance grew stronger, and they were there in front of Sarah's eyes – a blaze of scarlet and pink and a solitary golden one. Suddenly she felt tears close. How odd she thought, and unkind, too, of the golden bush to flower only after she couldn't visit the garden to see it. It hadn't flowered the previous summer, though she had cossetted it carefully, but perhaps, she thought confusedly, that had been the matter. Perhaps flowers and people had a lot in common – too much cossetting was as bad as too much neglect.

Maybe, she reflected in wry amusement, the rose bush had resented, as much as Sarah now did, the constant poking and pulling at it, the constant watering and feeding, the constant anxious inspection.

'Aren't they pretty?' Rose asked, and Sarah winked in answer.

The blooms receded, out of her sight. After a moment the light steps came back and the child said at her side, 'Nurse said I'm a good, thoughtful girl.' She gave a faint giggle. 'I came up, quiet as a mouse. I thought maybe she wouldn't even let me in, and she was sharp at first and asked what I was doing, and I said, "I picked some of the roses from the garden for Mrs Oatland, 'cause she can't go down and see them any more," and she was pleased. She said I was a good, thoughtful girl, no, child. That was it, a good, thoughtful child. Then Mrs Phipps came up. I didn't hear her coming – she walks terribly softly – and I gave a frightful jump and nearly dropped all the roses and she said, "Did you think of the flowers all by yourself, Rose? Or did someone ask you to bring them?"

'I said I thought of it myself, and Nurse said, "Well, dear, you obviously like the poor old soul and now you know she can't hurt you, don't you?" and when I said yes, Nurse said I could sit in here for a little, while she put the roses in a vase and perhaps had a small cup of tea.' The soft giggle sounded again. 'She said that this morning and Mrs Furlong said that Nurse must own a lot of shares in Indian tea plantations and I said, "Oh, is she rich?" and Mrs Furlong laughed like anything. She said she meant Nurse drinks so much tea anyone would think she was helping the tea market along. Anyway, she's gone to have a cup with Mrs Phipps, so we can talk. If you like?' she added hastily.

Sarah's eyelid closed once and then, after a moment, reluctantly, hating herself because she saw the eagerness and pleasure die out of the small face, she gave another wink.

Don't go away, Sarah pleaded silently. All the words she couldn't speak seemed stuck in a hard, bitter lump in her throat as she looked at the downcast young face, but she knew she didn't dare have Valma Phipps walk – so softly, as the child said – into that warm quiet room and hear Rose chattering as though she expected an answer.

After a moment the downcast expression lifted a little. 'I suppose you're tired. Well never mind. I'll come back tomorrow. That is, if you like?'

Sarah's right eye closed once.

'Oh good. I'll go away when Nurse comes, but I'll remember. . .'

'What are you doing Rose?'

Sarah could only think that she hadn't heard a single sound till the whispy voice spoke – only it wasn't particularly whispy now – it had the tone of authority, of someone demanding an answer, a truthful answer, given promptly.

Rose gave a little gasp, 'Oh, oh Mrs Phipps, you frightened me again!'

'Why? Were you doing something you shouldn't have?'

'Oh, of course I wasn't. I just . . .'

'Talked. Why? She can't hear you. Can she?'

'No. But I was just telling . . . telling . . . I mean, Nurse talks to her, you see. She said no one knows how much Mrs Oatland really does know, and she talks to her and I was just saying . . .' there was a pause, such an obvious pause, Sarah thought ruefully, while the child tried to remember exactly what she had said. Then finally Rose said triumphantly, 'I held the roses up to her face so she could smell them, and I was telling her I was going away when Nurse comes back, but I'd remember to bring her some other flowers soon.'

'Really?'

The tartly doubting word might have silenced someone far older than Rose, but the child stiffened. Sarah could feel her against the side of the bed, and then she said, with a casual artlessness that made Sarah want to applaud, 'That's right. Oh,

Mrs Phipps, my mother told me that your father is coming tomorrow and that he was a great actor once, or no, a singer I mean, and do you know, my grandmother had a terrific crush on him!'

'Oh, really.' This time there was only a complete lack of interest in the words. She added flatly, 'A lot of women had crushes on him.'

'So Mummy says. Like people with pop stars now. Only I was thinking, my grandmother would be about the same age as Mrs Oatland, that is, if she'd gone on living, only she didn't. But maybe Mrs Oatland knew your father, too, and maybe she'd recognise him and be pleased and happy if he came up here and she saw him.'

There was a sudden jerk of laughter, then the woman said, 'What an odd kid you are. Fancy thinking of that of all things. Oh, well . . .' she hesitated, then added at last '. . . Maybe he'd do it. I don't know.' Then abruptly, sharply, she demanded – so swiftly that Sarah was sure the child would fall into the trap – 'When did she tell you she'd like to see him?'

Had there been something in the woman's expression, Sarah wondered afterwards, that had warned Rose, put her on her guard? Because without obvious hesitation she said, apparently puzzled, 'What do you mean, Mrs Phipps? Do you mean Nurse asked me to ask you . . .'

'Oh . . . leave it!' The woman was moving away, Sarah realised. She had never been in sight, and now, going, her footsteps were plain on the carpet. She added, 'Nurse won't be long.'

In the silence, with the steps gone from hearing, Rose said softly, 'Why does she creep like that? She . . . spies.'

Sarah's eyelid blinked agreement.

'You don't like her?' At the two winks that answered, Rose nodded gravely. 'I don't, either. Or Mr Phipps. He smiles.' It was such an odd statement that Sarah wanted to ask for an explanation, but Rose was saying, 'Maybe Mr Palmer won't be very nice, either. Did you think of that? Oh, you did. Good, then you won't be disappointed, will you, if you don't like him at all. But I was rather clever, wasn't I, the way I asked?' she questioned proudly. And then she added, 'But you said you didn't want to talk. I'll sit quietly, I promise.' And to Sarah's regret and disappointment there wasn't another word from her at all.

The wall whispered later that day, 'She didn't think of that by herself. She may be cute as a new cent piece, but someone's told her to bring Palmer up there and who else would it be but the old woman?'

Valma's voice doubted this, 'I can't fathom how she'd do it, unless she can really and honestly speak, and it'd be crazy to stay quiet if she could do that. You might be able to browbeat a tired, sick woman who can only blink in answer to questions, but if she has her voice I bet she'd give dear Gwenyth a dose of it.'

'It's obvious,' the man's voice scorned. 'The kid has been cute enough to ask if she wants to see anyone and has run through all the names she can dream up – probably prattled about Palmer coming, come to that. So she got a wink or a nod to bring him up to be looked over.'

'So what do we do?'

'Depends on Palmer. We can't force him to go up, but there's no harm in him going. You never know. Look, we can hint we think she can nod or wink, or something, but won't, for fear of being browbeaten, but Palmer might get her confidence. He's just the sort to be interested and flattered, and once he gets a nod from her we're back at what I said before – if I know she can be scared out of her wits by someone rushing up and talking of possible deaths in the house, I'm not going to rush up there for you, till too late.'

'What are you going to do? Yes, I know I said I didn't want to know, but I have to. I'm scared of touching anything in the damn place, if you want to know.' The voice rose in something close to panic. 'Everywhere I look now there seems a possible trap, and I can't stand it.'

'Mirror, mirror on the wall, what is the deadliest trap of all,' the answer taunted.

'Mirror . . .' she was obviously teetering between doubt and confidence '. . . you're going to use the mirror?'

'Did I say so?'

Yes, you did, Sarah thought. Or hinted at it, but it needn't be true. Quite possibly isn't, because you can't trust her. You've told her so. You're frightened she'll back out at the last minute; might upset all your plans; might go to see what you've done, how you've tampered with your trap, and spoil it.

The dawnlight, but not an end to sleep, because Sarah hadn't been able to sleep at all. Bragg knew it. She came in at first light, carefully darkened hair hidden under rollers and a net, and her uncorseted figure revealing, through the print dressing-gown, unsuspected bulges and shapelessness. She bent over Sarah's bed and exclaimed, 'You haven't slept. Now I wonder why? Bed too hot, maybe? Or not hot enough. That's the trouble, my dear, you can't say, and I can't know – not unless I was to get in there with you . . .' she laughed at herself '. . . and even then I wouldn't know how you felt, would I?

'Oh well, my dear . . .' her plump hands smoothed at already smooth sheets '. . . we all have our troubles. There's Mrs Abcons down there, for one. Taken bad in the night with a pain. She came and knocked me up. Timid as anything, but straight to the point. "I need help, Nurse," she says. "I've got to be able to get to work in the morning. I can't afford time off. We're too busy." When I pointed out, after telling her it looked to me she'd been eating food that was a bit off, that they could always get someone else at that bridal place, she said, straight to the shoulder again, "That's what I'm afraid of. Someone else might prove better at it and then I'll be out and I won't get the same pay elsewhere." So I dosed her, but if you ask me she won't go anywhere today. I asked if I'd fetch her the doctor . . .' the plump hands were still at work round Sarah '. . . but no, it seems they've had a set-to, and she wasn't giving him the chance of crowing over her and telling her she didn't know decent food from bad, she was such a poor mother and wife. According to her the doctor told her first that the child looked underfed, and then that she'd treated her husband quite wrongly. Believe me, her voice was as sour as her sick stomach when she told me, "Men are all the same. I told him how Roy, my husband, walked out. He walked out on his job first. He'd walked out on a whole string of jobs before that, and Rose and I had to eat, as well as him, but he never thought of that, just walked in the door and said jauntily, 'Never let me take a job again where there's an Irish foreman. You can't argue or work with a man like that.'" Mrs Abcons told him flatly that he couldn't work with anyone and that was his trouble and he said, all of a sudden, "You're quite right, and I can't go on living with you either" and went. Just like that.'

Bragg sighed. 'She's not divorced, mind you. He died a few years later, though she never set eyes on him again. She was that angry the whole story just poured out of her. The doctor told her that perhaps her husband had told her the flat truth and that if she'd had the sense to enquire why he'd really left all those jobs, she might have found out he was really ill or too physically weak or just wasn't trained for the jobs, and had probably been sacked and was too proud to admit it. "No man'd relish admitting he was too sickly or weak, or untrained to keep down a job. Men have their pride, you know," he told her. "So've women," she said back to him, "and I had too much to go running after him and beg for explanations and him coming back."

'She told me she burst into tears then. She was furious about it, and the doctor just said, "And you've regretted the pride ever since, haven't you? Oh well, you'll know better next time." As though there'd be a next time, she scorned to me. She told him that, too, and he promptly told her the child needed a father and she needed a husband to shake the hardness and bitterness out of her. She had a retort for that, too, told him to his face he needed a wife, to teach him a little civilised behaviour.'

Bragg straightened, and laughed, the rich gay laugh that was at such variance with her oozing voice. 'I'd have loved to have seen them at it. Oh well, dear, you just lie there quietly till I have my shower and straighten up and then I'll be back to fix you for the day.'

Sarah was left to reflect in amusement on how much she was learning about the world outside her room, without moving a finger or toe, or speaking a word. In the space of a couple of days she'd learned an incredible amount about everyone in the house . . . amusement died on the heels of the thought.

Half of her wakefulness during the night had been due to her straining ears, trying to hear some whisper, some sound in the quiet room, that would be the wall whispering again of death, though she had known quite well that with her bed in its night-time position against the far wall she had no chance of hearing anything at all.

But now the wall seemed to have a life of its own. She could almost sense the bricks lining the cavity wall soaking up the evil from the words echoing upwards. She knew that she would never again be happy in that warm, quiet room. For always now, memories of her life and happiness with David there would be overshadowed by memories of whispering voices, talking of death.

She promised herself that the first thing she would do when once more she could speak would be to ask to be taken from the room. There were a million things she needed and wanted to say, but everything was secondary to that one request now.

She lay there, half dozing, wondering what would be the second thing her newly restored voice would say, and suddenly she was terribly tired and terribly cold, remembering that before she asked to be moved from that room, she must tell of the wall and the secrets it had spoken.

By then it will be too late, she reflected, thoughts broken and confused by that tiredness and coldness. The mirror would be broken, or the picture fallen, or the stairway forever ghosted by the crumpled still figure of an old man at its foot.

I have to get through to someone, she told herself, even while admitting the hopeless impossibility of that. She had a moment's wild, hysterical laughter as she pictured one of her callers making bright conversation, once they knew they could reach her, and coming at last to that impossible, crazy question, 'Have you heard of any good attempted murders lately, Mrs Oatland?'

But the wild humour gave place to tears, slow helpless tears that rolled down her face and soaked into the smooth sheet, because she couldn't move to wipe them away. Such a little thing, she wept anew. She couldn't even do that – not even wipe away one tear, let alone prevent an old man from dying.

She thought, and the coldness grew, I couldn't even stop them killing me, if they find out I know. I'd lie here and watch them coming and feel them and die, without a movement, a call for help.

The child came back at mid-morning. She came in on tiptoe, but Sarah heard her, because all morning her ears had been straining at sounds, waiting for the wall to speak again, once Bragg had rolled her bed towards the window and settled her patient for the day.

Seeing Sarah's open gaze, Rose said, 'Oh good, you're awake. I'm to sit with you while nurse goes down to my mother.' She settled herself by the bed and added gravely, 'My mother's sick. Nurse says it's the meat paste sandwiches at work yesterday, but my mother said something queer. She said – I wish you could talk and maybe explain it, Mrs Oatland, but, well – "I think I'm just sick at heart. To be blamed for everything that way, and I did try to be understanding and patient, but how could I go on being that with a child to feed and keep?"

'Mrs Oatland . . .' now the small face was furrowed with anxiety '. . . do you think it means my mother is in trouble at work? She worries terribly about that happening. She's always frantic for fear she'll be late, or an order'll be lost, or a customer will be angry, or someone will complain, because if anything goes wrong they might put her off.'

The grim emphasis might have been funny but for the anxious little face, the worry in the soft voice. Sarah's two answering winks were given without real thought, only the idea to reassure, and she was rewarded by a beaming smile, and a lifting of the anxious frown.

'It's a pity you can't tell me what you do think it means, but so long as she won't be put off, that's what matters most. Of course being sick matters too, but Nurse said anyone can get sick, and she'll ring the shop herself, because everyone listens to trained nurses exactly the same way they listen to doctors and never think to argue, which is only right, Nurse Bragg says, because many a nurse with years and years of nursing behind her knows a whole sight more than many a young doctor.

'My mother said, "Well tell me what you think. Am I to blame or not?" and I thought I was going to learn what it was all about, only they realised I was there and I was told to come away and sit with you, and that's how I came to meet him.'

The breathless voice ceased, then began again, 'He's not a bit like I expected, though honestly I don't know how I really did expect him to look, and he wears glasses – ones with big black rims. They make him look awfully solemn. Oh, I'm getting all mixed up, aren't I?' she said. 'I didn't tell you what happened. I came out of our door and there was Mr Phipps's car at the front. It's a nice car – grey with red seats inside. He was carrying luggage inside and there was this other man just stepping out of the car and I went up to him and said, "You must be Mr Palmer."

'He doesn't really look old,' she assured her listener, 'though his hair's white. He has a little grey moustache too, and solemn eyes, like I said, and a round, pinky sort of face. He doesn't look at all like someone important,' she confided earnestly.

'Mrs Oatland, would you recognise him? I mean, does he sound a bit the same as he used to be when you knew him?'

Sarah debated the point. She was vaguely disappointed. Surely Roderick Palmer's features had been lean? And his hair, of course, had been dark. She couldn't remember a moustache either, and certainly not spectacles. The disappointment grew and then she laughed at herself, reflecting on how twenty years had dealt with her.

After a little, Rose said, 'You're not answering, so I expect that means you don't really know. Is that right?' With the affirmative wink from Sarah she went on, 'Well, anyway I said to him, "You must be Mr Palmer," and he smiled – he has a nice smile. Not like Mr Phipps's smile.'

Sarah wished she could have asked for an explanation of that point, but Rose was rattling on, 'He smiled and said, "That's right, lass, and who are you?" So I told him and then Mr Phipps came back. I think he was cross at first, though he smiled just the same. He's always smiling.' There was discontent in the soft voice. 'He told me to run along and that I should be at school, so I started to explain about my mother, only he wasn't really listening. Mr Palmer was, though. He asked me all sorts of questions and seemed really interested, so . . .' she drew a long breath. 'At last I said, "Mr Palmer, there's someone who'd like to meet you – upstairs. She knew you when you used to sing," which was the wrong thing to say, because Mr Phipps asked, quick as a flash, "How do you know she did?" but I was just as quick, because I said back, "My mother said she's pretty sure of it, because all old ladies Mrs Oatland's age were quite crazy over Mr Palmer, like my grandmother was," and Mr Palmer put back his head and laughed. He has a nice laugh, too. Mr Phipps didn't laugh, though, he just went on smiling and then he said, "I'll tell you all about it later on, Rod. Come on inside – Val's waiting," and he took

Mr Palmer's arm and almost dragged him in and just left me standing there.

'So I don't know if Mr Palmer will come or not,' she finished ruefully.

Does it matter, Sarah wondered bleakly. What if he did come? She still couldn't reach out to any contact with him, to warn him. Even if she had the use of her tongue, how would the story sound anyway? He might think she was crazy.

Then the child asked, 'Is he to know, if he comes, that you can wink?'

What am I to do? Again that unanswerable question. If he knew there was the chance he would tell the Phipps pair . . . Then she thought, But they're certain already I can hear, and fear and panic came back, because now her position was worse than ever. She'd been a fool, she realised bleakly. Now if the Phipps pair found out about that wall, there'd be no chance of them deciding that after all Sarah hadn't listened at the right or wrong moment. Her stubborn resistance to admitting she could hear and respond would give her away completely now.

Slowly her right eye closed as she fought down that rising wave of panic. Her heart was fluttering and she felt that at any minute she would be sick. Now she wanted the child to go, for Bragg to come; and she knew again the agony of frustration in not being able to ask for the simplest things. She realised the child was speaking again, but the words were just a jumble of sound in her ears, and made no sense; then it stopped and she knew in relief that Bragg was coming, heavy-footed, across the carpet. Talking too. Slowly the sound began to form words she could understand and she knew that Roderick Palmer had come. Panic gave way slowly to a vast surprise that he should have come so quickly, then she realised in wry amusement that he was probably curious to see what the poor old fish, who had once been his fan, was like laid out on her slab.

Bragg was saying, 'Here we are,' as though Sarah couldn't possibly have been aware before that her bed was shadowed now by the presence of people. 'Rose, your mother's asleep, my dear, and will be fine soon. You can make her a nice fruit squash later on when she wakes.' Her tone changed to curiosity. 'How did you come to think of asking Mr Palmer to come up here?' Then, without waiting for an answer, she added, 'It was good of you, Mr Palmer, but as you can see the poor old thing isn't capable of acknowledging you're here. I don't know for certain she can even see you properly, but maybe . . . well, you know, I talk to her just as if she can hear, because for all we know she can. Perhaps you wouldn't mind sitting for a bit and just talking – about the old days perhaps? I'll run and make a small cup of tea for us all if you would.'

'Certainly.' The voice, to Sarah's straining ears, was acutely disappointing. This wasn't the man she remembered at all. Gone were the rich cadences, the full-throated masculine voice. The word was *reedy*, and when he went on the words came monotonously toned. 'Will you stay with me, Rose?'

Sarah was lying there, dwelling on her disappointment, telling herself how stupid it was to feel that way, and listening to Bragg's steps going away. She wasn't aware of a silence that grew and grew, till the child's voice came shrilly, 'She can really hear, only it's a secret. You mustn't tell. She doesn't want to be . . . to have people she doesn't like, pestering her. Only really she can hear, and if she isn't too tired she'll answer, with a wink.'

The monotonously toned voice was still that, but sharper as Roderick Palmer questioned, 'Is that so, Mrs Oatland?'

Wink, went Sarah's right eye, in assent.

Now the voice was tinged with faint amusement. 'Well, congratulations on having the spirit left in you to make a decision for yourself and keep it.'

What a refreshing breath of commonsense you are, Sarah thought in gratitude and knew a rising sense of elation at the thought of getting into some sort of contact with someone adult, someone who might speak to her of adult things, treat her as an adult and let her forget for a time that she was as helpless as any tiny child. More helpless, she amended then. A child could scream if danger threatened.

She waited eagerly for her visitor to say something else, and after a moment he said, 'Rose, how about joining Nurse and leaving me to chat? You can be a help and keep her out of the way as long as possible. How about it?'

A soft giggle, a breathless, 'Of course I will,' and a scamper of steps over the carpet and then the uncadenced voice said, 'You don't fancy being old-deared and talked to like an infant, eh?'

So he'd taken Bragg's measure already, Sarah thought in amusement and winked her assent.

'Right then. How do you like having your home cut up this way? Murray's told me the situation. Like it? Or not?' At the two winks he nodded, his mouth grim. 'Matter of dollars and cents though, I expect,' he pointed out. 'You needn't worry about your furniture. Val's a decent little housekeeper. Her mother trained her well. Tell me, do you like Val?'

Confused, Sarah hesitated. She wished she knew how he felt towards the woman downstairs. It was impossible to answer for fear of angering him, upsetting him, even driving him away, but abruptly he said, 'Don't be afraid of hurting my feelings. Answer honestly. What's the good of us chatting if you aren't. I'll never get to know you if you hedge. Just remember that Val's my dead wife's daughter – not mine. I never met her till she was grown up.'

To Sarah's double wink he merely nodded, asking, 'What about Murray?' and then he nodded. 'We agree there. I often feel like asking him what he has to grin about all the time. Gets on my nerves. He's been a good enough husband to Val, though I wish they'd have some kids. Probably waiting till they settled, of course. Looks like they'll be doing that soon. Tell me, do you think you'll get better?'

The pink, plump face – Rose had been right about that, Sarah thought – creased in a quick smile at her answer. 'Good. If your brain's working and your sight and your hearing, you can't be all that bad. Tell me, does anything frighten you?'

It was a surprising question; one, she thought gratefully, that few people would have thought of asking, because she was apparently living in a cocoon of security where fear – apart for from her health – could have no place. She was washed and dried and fed and comforted and warmed and sheltered, without a scrap of effort on her part.

At her assent he asked, 'What? That niece of yours will try and take over the place and bustle you off to the old crocks' home?

'You are? Forget it. I'll have a word to your legal men if you like and have the woman put in her place. Well? Right, I'll see to it. She can kick at me if she likes. Kick Val and Murray out, too. I'll soon find them something else. Now, what else? Afraid of that nurse of yours? You're not. Didn't think you would be. Goodhearted type, under that silly manner. You like the child, so there's no fear about her and her mother, so what's left? Afraid of your doctor? No? Good. What about death, then, are you afraid of that?'

The double wink was given without thought, only desperation, the need to reach him and warn him. Unspoken words were a hard knot again in her throat, choking her, and of course he misunderstood, asking instantly, 'Like to see your clergyman?'

That was laughable. She had always disliked Mr Simpson with his fluttering gestures and vague manner. Now he would be nothing but an irritation. He would talk to her of the beauties of heaven, perhaps even of the joy of seeing David again, but the thought that it was someone else's death that was worrying her would never occur to him, and murder would be so outlandish to him he probably, she thought unkindly, hardly knew how to spell the word.

Her winks were vigorous and the smile came back to the plump pink face. 'Bit of a drip, eh?' he said. Then the smile went. He said thoughtfully at last, after a long hesitation, 'I don't see what I can do about it. We're all afraid of death, I expect, in one way or the other – scared of a good blistering after the event . . .' a fleeting smile touched his mouth again '. . . or frightened of the way we'll go. Now me, do you know what I'm afraid of most about it all? Being stretched out there in the mortuary without a stitch on me while they lay me out. Hurts my dignity. Silly, isn't it? But I can't stand the idea of them talking about my varicose veins, and my bit of a paunch, and my lack of teeth. They say no man's a hero to his valet; to his mortician I reckon he's just a plain mess.'

The hard knot was gone in bubbling amusement. She longed to say, Me, too, but I never knew anyone else shared that absurd dislike.

'Well, what else are you frightened about?' He went on questioning, then stopped, his gaze travelling round the room as though seeking something to give him a pointer. At last, rather lamely, he said, 'Anything frightening you in this room?'

What do I answer? She fretted at that. If she said 'yes', he'd go over each item, one by one. He might finally come to the fireplace wall. And if she winked assent to that question, what would he do? Investigate, of course, till he discovered its secret.

She tried to reason clearly what would happen then, but she was tired. In spite of enjoying his company, tiredness was creeping back and her thoughts were becoming confused. All she could think of was that he would eventually think of a conversation frightening her; and would start to question everyone in the house.

Which he mustn't do at all.

That was the one clear thought. He mustn't start questioning what had been said down in that room below. He would never be given the truth, but the Phipps pair would know she had heard that terrible talk.

Suddenly it seemed there were actually whispers in the room now with her, first Valma's, 'But why worry? The old corpse is nearly that – she can never tell,' and then the man's assured, confident, 'If she can hear and see and use her mind she's not too bad. One morning, this week, next month, next year, she may be able to speak. However long it is she'll have remembered and she'll speak, or if she can move her hands instead, she'll write it out, all we've ever said, ever plotted, ever done. And we'll be done, too.'

'We can't afford to let her live.'

It came down to that, Sarah knew and there wasn't strength left in her to answer anything, because panic was back.

————

CHAPTER 6

The wall was speaking and even through the brick the difference in tone was so marked Sarah might have laughed, if she had been able. Yet there was something horrible in those social voices, those platitudes that mocked at the words that had echoed up before.

'Another sandwich, Father?' That was Valma. 'I remembered, you see, that you couldn't stand mustard.'

'You've a good memory, Val – got it from your mother.'

'Along with other things.' That was Murray. The assurance was still there in his voice, but now there was no mockery, no irritation, no rudeness to the woman. 'She's already scrubbed your little bedroom out from ceiling down, I should think. I only hope you won't wake to the ghost of Cinderella. You see, Rod, your room was originally a kitchen, so I'm told, and then an office of sorts, and now your bedroom. Probably the servant sat there among the cinders while the Oatlands gave balls.'

'Probably never gave 'em,' was Palmer's retort.

'Well not actually balls, but dinners. Quite grand affairs, if you can believe the present one. She's hardly eligible for a prince though – over sixty and a bit odd, according to Val. Val, you see, has been offering a hand upstairs and has been getting all the gossip in return.'

Resentment held Sarah. A fierce resentment at the idea of the woman discussing her and the past and David with anyone. 'She spies,' Rose had said of the woman, Sarah remembered.

Roderick Palmer said quietly, 'I always thought that was another thing in which you took after your mother, Val – in avoiding a sick bed. I remember when one of her best friends was ill, she'd never so much as visit. Said it made her feel ill herself. You always seemed the same.'

Now Sarah was certain of something. He didn't like his daughter by marriage. Or perhaps 'like' was the wrong term, because there surely had to be some vague liking for the woman or he wouldn't have left her everything he had.

Or could that be, she wondered, because there was no one else. Both his wives had died, his son had died. There was probably only Valma Phipps left to him in the world.

There was pathos and bitterness in the thought of an ageing man, once a world favourite, seeking some assurance that the one person left to him had qualities he could admire, and respect and love. Because that, she realised sadly, was what Roderick Palmer was seeking. It showed in his soft query, 'Have you changed, Val?'

Valma Phipps was aware of it, Sarah realised, as instantly she challenged, 'You've been disappointed in me, haven't you, Father? I know I refused to come back to nurse Mother. I'm afraid you'll have to blame Mother herself. She was afraid, sickened by illness of any sort, and you know it. I grew up with that. She was so sickened herself I grew frightened of it. It's funny, though, since she died, and I've been married, I seem to have lost it. Along with a lot of other things. She influenced me a lot, I guess. Of course, she was pretty strong-minded. You know it. Still . . .' she poked shrewdly at him, '. . . you must have admired her. You married her, after all, and stayed with her and . . .'

'I've no use for divorce!' The words came with crack-like force, reminding Sarah of what had been said before in that room, the mention of the will and its phrasing. It was Roderick Palmer's hatred of divorce that had led to this. If it hadn't been for that, Valma might have divorced her husband a long time ago, Sarah thought bitterly, and still remained in the old man's favour. There would never have come the desperate day when Valma had decided she wanted a divorce, and her inheritance, and could wait for neither, so that she'd put the problem to Murray and from that . . .

Or had he been the one who had pointed out facts to her – bullying her – carrying her along with him?

Not that it mattered, she thought, and suddenly as the smooth voice below said, 'Try a meat paste sandwich, Father?' she was seized with panic so violent she could feel the force of a scream trying to leave her mouth.

She remembered Josie Abcons and a meat paste sandwich that had been bad. She thought of Murray's mocking, 'Mirror, mirror, on the wall, what is the deadliest plot of all?' and then she could hear Valma's bitter cry, 'I'm afraid to touch anything in this damn place if you want to know! Everywhere I look now there seems a possible trap . . .'

Relief from panic came with Palmer's thoughtful comment. He said, 'I think I'll have another ham instead. Now Murray, let's get down to facts. What is it that appeals to you so much about this place you have in mind?'

To her ears, as tiredness came sweeping back, the words became a jumble of sound. She didn't try to fight the tiredness this time. Nothing important was going to be said, she was certain, nothing important to herself, at least. She lay there, thinking of nothing, drifting towards sleep and then abruptly, shockingly, she was awake again, because the child's voice was exclaiming in breathless wonder, 'Why, the wall is talking!'

Sarah's eyes opened, but she couldn't see the child's face, only one thin arm and a small hand. She realised that Rose must have her head bent towards the wall, listening, and now in the silence she could hear the self-assured voice say, '. . . your opinion. Val's quite interested, anyway.'

Whatever was answered was lost under the child's own

whisper, as the thin features came into Sarah's sight. They were flushed, the blue eyes wide and excited, 'Why, Mrs Oatland, you knew the wall talked, didn't you? Oh, that's why you like this corner so much! But why hasn't anyone said that? Oh, I can guess.' She nodded wisely and laughed softly. 'I know how it is. There was never anyone before living down there, so Nurse never found out, 'cause the only time anyone was down there was when Nurse took doctors and visitors down there to talk and you listened!' Her tone was faintly chiding.

Any amusement Sarah might have felt at it was lost in stark panic. When Rose asked, 'Have you ever heard anything exciting?' It was instinctive to wink 'no', because even if she had given assent it would have gained her nothing. There was absolutely no way of getting through to Rose how exciting, and how terrible, the talks had been; and Rose must never rush through the house, she warned herself frantically, telling the story of the wall, whispering mischievously, 'She heard something exciting, too, once. I wonder what it was.'

She willed Rose to ask if she wanted the wall's secret kept, but the child prattled on, 'Why, Nurse said to my mother when we came that they didn't know if you could hear, so the doctors never talked about your health in front of you, but talked downstairs, over a small cup of tea.' She giggled suddenly, 'And you knew, just the same. It's rather clever of you; naughty, too,' she said with an adult air. 'My mother always tells me listeners never hear any good of themselves. I hope you did.'

Sarah gave one wink, but she was willing the child still to ask that vital question about keeping the wall's secret.

Instead Rose said, 'I'm glad, and maybe you know you're going to get better?' When there was no answer she nodded wisely again, 'Oh, I see, then it would be perhaps.' At Sarah's assent she smiled, 'I hope it's a big perhaps,' then her eagerness was gone. 'Oh,' she cried in real distress, 'you won't be able to listen in to the doctors any more!'

No, I won't, Sarah remembered, but there were so many other things to trouble and worry her now that she dismissed the brief upset and anger almost as soon as it touched her. She forgot it completely when Rose said, 'And have you thought that now Nurse will probably find out you've listened? 'Cause the people down there will talk and talk all the time and Nurse is sure to hear.' She stopped, then added in delight, 'Oh no, she won't. I've just remembered! Mrs Phipps said to Nurse, "My husband and father will be out on business for the next few days, Nurse. They're looking over various properties. I shan't be going often. They'll be leaving first thing and I've the cooking and cleaning to do, so I've begged off. I'll be free most afternoons to give you a break if you'd care for it," and Nurse said,' the mimicry was so good Sarah was startled, "You're a dear kind person, Mrs Phipps." So you see?'

All Sarah was seeing was the flat – that so lethal place, as Murray Phipps had called it – empty during the day, while she decided that whatever was planned was planned for the night. She became aware of the child repeating eagerly, 'They'll be out, and Mrs Phipps won't talk to herself, will she, and at night you're over the other side the room, aren't you, so the street light won't fall on the bed. So I don't think Nurse will find out – yet, anyway.

'I won't tell, because then they'd know you can hear and you'd get tired listening, wouldn't you? And then you might forget and answer, mightn't you, and then they'd expect answers all the day long.'

Yes, I might, reflected Sarah, as she winked once. There was sweet relief in the knowledge that she had a few days of grace before Bragg found out about that wall and went running through the house to tell everyone; a relief that died so quickly she had hardly time to taste its sweetness before it was gone in the onrush of knowledge that a few days grace was useless after all. By then Roderick Palmer would be dead and her position would be worse than ever. She would remain as a silent witness who would have to be silenced for good.

'So that's settled,' Rose said comfortably. She went on, 'Really, why I came up was because the doctor came. Nurse sent for him after all, and when he came she went down with him to see my mother and I was sent up to sit here. He remembered my name today, but he called my mother Mrs Alcorn and she was cross. She asked him didn't he get anything right ever, and he said, "I'm right about one thing: your health needs attention. A healthy young woman wouldn't be laid out flat from one miserable sandwich. I rang your workplace. The other women were slightly sick. Note I said slightly. Which means the sandwich spread was only slightly tainted. Conclusion reached: you were in poor shape to start with."

'Then he said, "It's no good telling you to have a holiday, but a change is as good as a holiday sometimes. You can come fishing with me on Sunday, and if you haven't fished before it'll be a complete change for you, so don't argue about it."'

Regretfully she confided, 'That was when I was told to run along, so I don't know yet whether we're going or not, because Mummy was wearing her in-one-minute-I'll-explode face. Mrs Oatland, did you like talking to Mr Palmer?' At Sarah's single wink, Rose said, 'He likes you. He says you're a spunky old girl.'

Brief amusement touched Sarah, only to die at the reflection that far from being spunky she was scared stiff.

Rose said, 'When I leave you I can spend fifteen minutes with Mr Palmer. Mummy says I can accept his invite, only no longer than that, because fifteen minutes of me is enough to change his opinion of me, she reckons.' There was a soft giggle. 'She says it's really a mercy I can't pester you. Mr Palmer is going to show me a little box with seventeen secret compartments. He bought it in Zanzibar. Have you ever been in Zanzibar, Mrs Oatland?'

The soft voice pattered on, but now Sarah wasn't paying attention. She was tired again, and could only reflect on the fact that the spunky old girl, as Roderick Palmer had dubbed her, was going to fail him.

She hardly noticed it when the child was joined by Bragg. She heard only vaguely the child asking what Bragg was going to do now, wanting to know if perhaps she was going to feed Mrs Oatland, or wash her, or tidy the bed.

Bragg laughed at that. 'Fancy yourself as a nurse do you, my dear? No, I'm not going to disturb her. You can see for yourself she's dropping off, poor dear. We'll leave her be. I'll whip up a fruit jelly for her tea while she sleeps. Now you run along, like a good girl.'

The rest was just a jumble of sound. Sarah was glad of it. She was lost in despair now, dwelling morbidly on the thought that her home – her beloved home – was filled with death. No other thought seemed to matter. Even when the wall began whispering, when her room was quiet again, she paid no heed at first, till she realised it was the child's voice speaking.

Attention caught, she heard '. . . a secret, you see, because they'd know she could really hear everything and it wouldn't look nice, would it, for an old lady to be listening.' The tones were suddenly prim. 'So you must be careful, or Nurse will find out and everything will be spoilt. So you see I told you, 'cause I thought you could make sure no one talked in here when Nurse might be up there and could hear the wall talking that funny way. It doesn't matter at night at all, because the bed's moved and you have to be right against that wall before you hear it talking.'

There was the sound of soft, reedy laughter, then Roderick Palmer said gently, 'Now there's a woman for you to admire, Rose. Everyone thinks she's nothing but a helpless log, but she has all manner of little secrets. I wouldn't mind betting she knows as much as you or I do about happenings in the place. Well, we'll make sure the wall doesn't talk at inconvenient moments. I'll fix it some way. Now come and see my box and see if you can find out its secrets.'

Sarah was thinking gratefully that now she had another reprieve, another time of grace before she was found out but, as fleetingly as it had come and gone before, relief came and went, because nothing was solved. One day, very soon, Roderick Palmer simply wouldn't be there any more, and the wall would talk and talk and betray her.

Valma's voice was soft. So gentle, so whispy, it hardly seemed to disturb the warm still air of the bedroom. 'You might as well take a breather,' she said. 'I know how you've been rushing up and down all day. How's Mrs Abcons? I'm a complete fool where illness like that happens or I'd have offered to help down there. As it is I might as well be useful up here. Murray's taken Father out.'

Which means you're going to take another opportunity to make me acknowledge your probing questions, Sarah thought in irritation, but when Bragg had finally gone, there was only, for several long minutes, the click of knitting needles, before finally Valma's soft voice said quietly, evenly, as though she were speaking of quite commonplace, everyday things, 'We know, Mrs Oatland. I heard the child with Father, you see.' As gently the voice continued over the click of the knitting needles. 'No wonder you didn't want me to know you could hear. Of course, it's quite obvious to Murray and me why you've kept grimly quiet. You heard everything Murray said that evening, and before. It's a wonder that you didn't drop dead from shock.' Then the needles stopped. The click-click began again. Quite crudely and brutally, she said, 'It's a pity you didn't. Now you've become a problem, for disposal.'

———

Just like a piece of refuse, Sarah thought. There was no resentment in the thought. No panic either, which was peculiar, she reflected vaguely. It was as though she wasn't really vitally concerned at all, as though she had become a spectator on the sidelines of drama.

The soft voice repeated, 'Now you've become a problem for disposal,' but by then Sarah's mind and eyes and hearing had become alert. In satisfaction that verged on ironic amusement, she knew that that determinedly quiet voice held stark fright. There was a tiny tremor in the voice, a jerky motion to the moving hands, a little twitch in one cheek muscle.

The woman couldn't stop talking either. Her fright and nervousness had to be talked out to someone who couldn't answer back, couldn't point out flaws. The words flowed faster and faster as she went on, the needles clicking busily. 'You see, you're dangerous now. So long as you live, so long as there's the faintest chance you'll come to life again and speak or be able to write, or tell what you know, you're dangerous. You might die and never, never, tell, only there might come a morning instead, and it could be years from now, when you'll wake up and tell everything and then where will we be? Even if we went right away, from this house and this town and even over the seas, we'd be tracked down eventually, because there are investments I can't dispose of – I just draw the income, so the police would find me, wouldn't they?

'Murray says this is the sort of thing – extreme danger, extreme shock – that might do the trick and bring you back to life too and then where will we be? We can pretend it's a joke, a story we were thinking up, lots of things, if Father's still alive, but if he's dead . . .'

There was only the click-click of the needles, then she began again, dismissing those last words as though there was no question that Roderick Palmer had to die, and Sarah with him. 'If you're tough enough not to have been shocked to death by what you found out, you're tough enough to recover, to betray us, to ruin everything.' She added flatly, 'And you're not going to.

'I know what you're thinking,' the words babbled on, 'you're thinking now I could lift your head and slide out one of these pillows and press it, firmly, over your face, aren't you? And it would all be over. But it won't be like that. It can't be. Murray says two deaths in the same house together is impossible. Unless it's all so natural looking. Don't you see what a problem you've become?'

As though the whole situation's my fault, Sarah thought in amazement, and in mockery and astonishment at herself, her eye winked once.

The needles stopped. The woman moved, came hesitantly to the bed, and the pale face came closer to Sarah's. 'You winked. You were telling me "yes", weren't you?' The voice rose. 'Why, you're, you're inhuman! To lie there and wink that you agree, that . . .'

Should I have winked twice, Sarah mocked herself and told her I wasn't a problem, hinted that I'd quietly die to save her some trouble?

The pale face came even closer. Valma Phipps said violently, 'Do you know what Murray said? He said, "Get some way of making the bed stay there against the wall tonight. When she hears what I have to say, when Palmer's out of the way, the old witch might die of fright yet, and save us some trouble."'

In one smooth movement the face was gone and the chair was occupied again. The needles began clicking busily and then the voice, soft, gentle, said, above the sound of Bragg's coming, 'She's quite all right, and dropping off again. I'll stay for an hour, if you'll set your alarm.' Then, hardly waiting for the other woman's assent and thanks, she said gently, 'Why don't you leave the bed where it is tonight, Cornelia?'

The Christian name was spoken a trifle smugly, as though, Sarah thought, the silent listener was being told, 'Look what great friends I am with your nurse. I can do anything with you. You'll find no help there.'

Valma went on, 'Don't you think she might like to see the stars occasionally? They wouldn't keep her awake if she wanted to sleep, and it would be a change if she can see things clearly. Now the windows are screened she'll be quite safe. You said yourself she likes that corner.'

'It's just a feeling I have, and you know, you could be right. We'll leave the old dear there tonight and see how she likes it. Oh, I can always tell if she's pleased or otherwise about something. If she likes it there, there'll be no harm in leaving her there for good, and save a bit of effort besides. It's no joke, even with those castors fixed on the bed, to be always pushing it around on my own.'

When the footsteps had gone away again, leaving only the sound of the needles clicking busily, Valma's soft voice said, 'I didn't want to do that. I told Murray I wouldn't, but . . . it was your own fault!' The voice rose in anger. 'Lying there winking at me, as though you didn't care a jot about it all and you must, or . . .' The needles stopped, and again the pale face came close to Sarah's. 'Or do you care? You haven't much to live for, have you, after all? Lying there, not able to move, not knowing if you'll ever move at all again. Maybe you don't care about dying at all.' The voice was a whisper 'Do you?'

Sarah's eye winked twice and went on winking, because suddenly there were scalding tears welling up and overflowing down her cheeks.

Roderick Palmer came back with the evening, to seat himself by the bed and say, in the reedy voice that now didn't disappoint her at all, 'Your nurse is going to coddle you a nice egg, whatever that means. She seems a bit astonished I'm up again. Suppose she is, come to that. I told her I was interested and thought I'd come to chatter, even if you couldn't hear it. Pointed out I might be taken your way myself before the end and I'd like to feel someone would take a bit of trouble. "Too true," she says, in a kind of gloomy satisfaction sort of way. "Have you any physical troubles, Mr Palmer?" Lord, I thought, she is going to have the pants off me any tick, to look at my varicose veins. Anyway, she's coddling that egg, so you needn't worry about her walking in.

'You know, secrets are all very fine, and it's your decision after all, but you'll have to let on to your doctor soon. Could be there's new treatment they might try if they know you're getting a bit of life back.'

Sarah winked urgently, once, but he took it as assent to his suggestion, not, as she'd hoped, that he should tell the doctor at once, and after all, she reacted, what did it matter? The doctor didn't spend much time with her. He wouldn't be likely to quizz her with questions that mattered, that let her tell what was going on in the house.

Roderick Palmer went on, 'Mind if I smoke?' and at her double wink, pulled out his pipe and bean, slowly filling it. She watched with interest and something close to sadness, remembering how long ago it had been since a man had sat in that room filling a pipe, in just that slow, finicky way.

'Young Rose told me about the wall,' he told her, and half turned, looking at it with interest, then swung back to face her. 'Val and Murray said anything to interest you down there?' At her one wink he chuckled. 'I'll be eager to hear what it was when you can tell me about it.'

Abruptly he asked, 'Anything about me?' At her single blink he pressed her, 'Something good?' When there was no answer he nodded. 'Bad, eh? Interesting that. Would it be about my money?' At her quick assent he said again, 'Interesting that. I've left the lot to Val. No one else to leave it to. Not a scrap of family left besides her. Oh, there are a few charities I've named. Haven't much use for charity as a general rule though. I reckon it makes for spineless character. A helping hand's okay when you're down, but too much . . . that's as bad as nothing.

'Back to Val though. I thought she should be the one to have it, with Murray. I've put in conditions though; tied some of it up so she can't spend the lot on foolishness in a few years and then regret it. Actually I was thinking more of Murray there. I want their marriage to stick fast, and Murray's a bit of a fool about money. He could run through the lot and then she'd be at his throat – rightly enough of course – but it wouldn't help their marriage any.

'Tell me, would you mind if I had that piano tuned up and used it a bit?'

Her double wink was frantic, almost fumbled. She saw the surprise, and doubt, in his face, then he said slowly, 'You do? I wouldn't hurt it, you know, and I'd get a first-class man to touch it. It's a good piece, but neglected.'

He was watching her for some sign that she'd changed her mind. When there was nothing, a slight frown creased between his brows, but he said only, 'Right, then. It'll be left strictly alone. I'll see to that.'

So that's one plan that's failed, she thought smugly, knowing the heady satisfaction of having manipulated events, but satisfaction was gone on the heels of the knowledge that he wasn't going to ask her permission to touch his bedroom window, or sit in the chair under the large framed picture, or go into the shower room and stand by that lethal mirror.

He asked then, 'Is there anything else down there you don't want touched? The decision can be yours. I'll see it's respected,' At her reluctant negative – because how could she get through to him that the whole place was, as Murray

Phipps had said, a deadly thing – he nodded, satisfied, and said, 'Tell me, have Val and Murray ever discussed the future, when I'm gone? Not gone home, I mean, but dead and gone?'

There was a faint smile on his lips. It stayed there with her assent and his asking, 'Do they think they'll be happy with the money?' and his instant response, 'That's a foolish question, of course. Who wouldn't expect to be happy with more money? Perhaps what I meant was, are they happy now?'

The smile died at her assured negative. 'I thought so,' he admitted glumly. 'Oh, everything is fine on the surface, but there are signs . . . but you said they thought the money would make them happy. Are they short of money then?'

'Perhaps then,' he said reflectively, 'I could make some arrangement now, for the present, not let them wait.'

Hope soared in Sarah, only to die at the reflection that however much they were given they would, almost certainly, want more and more and, whatever they were given, there would remain the problem of herself – the silent witness who any day might be silent no longer – who'd seek out Palmer and tell him what the wall had whispered to her.

'You know, Sarah . . .' the name slipped out as though he was long ago used to its use, bringing warmth to the coldness closing in on her '. . . I'm glad she isn't my own. Val, I mean. I can look at things without bias. I mean by that, if she were my own, I'd be bound to take her side, be influenced by it, ago- nise, I expect, over her troubles, from her slant of them. With Val it's different. I'm clear-eyed. A lot of her troubles are her own making. Why doesn't she stand up to Murray a bit, for instance?' There was irritation now in the reedy voice. 'Doesn't she have a mind of her own?' Astonishment at her quick wink jerked a brief laugh from him. 'Oh, so you think she has? I wonder how she's shown it – so it's not all, "Yes, Murray, no, Murray," down there, is it?

'You know, Sarah . . .' his tone now was indulgently affec- tionate '. . . you're an old stickybeak. You get quite a kick out of it, don't you, lying there and knowing more of what's going on here than anyone else in the place? Well, tell me this, is there anything like another woman?' At her negative he pressed, 'Or man?'

The smile came back. 'It's not too bad then, and here's your coddled egg coming.'

The thought of her egg arriving with heavy-thudded steps down the hall was so ludicrous she was lost in enjoyment of it, and almost missed his whispered farewell. 'Goodnight, Sarah. Sleep well.'

Twice her right eyelid closed, but he'd already gone. Anger and fear touched her and were gone in the acceptance of facts, because she knew that even if he had seen he could not have done anything, except whisper, 'You don't expect to sleep well. Why not?' And how could she have answered that?

She had no way of telling how late it was when the wall began whispering of death again. She knew that she had dozed a little and woken to surprise it, and that the stars had been paled by the moon and brightened again as it had crossed the strip of night sky she could see. It seemed a long time since Bragg, curlered and night-creamed, had peered at her and gone away again, to her three hours sleep before the alarm woke her to come, grey-faced and yawning, for another inspection of her silent charge.

She was sure that Murray Phipps knew all about those three-hourly visits through the night; that it was midway between them that the wall mocked, 'She's a witch, that old woman up there. Who else bar a witch, in her position, could get through to Palmer about the piano? Oh yes, my love, she did. Didn't you, old witch in the corner?' the wall mocked up to Sarah.

'No, it's so obvious it's painful. He was keen as mustard on having it tuned up and then, all of a sudden, this evening, he says quite sharply it's not to be touched. She's dangerous, Val.' Now the voice had lost its mockery, was sharply angry. 'Have you considered the idea that dear Palmer might ask if we quarrel and fight and she gets through to him that all isn't as sweet as it seems on the surface? She'll do it, if she can. What if he decides he ought to change his will? Perhaps put in a few other safeguards for the sanctity of marriage, for instance? Tie us up for years together before we touch a penny? He could do it. He could easily stipulate we have to be married ten years and produce three bouncing brats before we collect. Thought of that? In fact, have you thought he could tie it up and damn well leave the lot to what the lawyers call legal issue? In other words, the bouncing brats?'

There was a jerk of laughter. 'Your face reveals all, as the adverts say. Have you thought, then, how an old woman could die?'

'Don't!' The voice begged. 'Come away back to . . .'

'No. That wall between the two other rooms is paper thin. I've noticed it. Palmer can hear us, and perhaps if the old witch is frightened enough she'll die of shock anyway.'

'She cried,' Valma said quietly. 'She cried. She doesn't want to die.'

'For . . .' the anger was broken off short. 'Neither do I. Oh, I know they don't hang you these days, but there's prison. Ever thought about it? It'd be worse than being stuck up there in a bed without movement or speech. Oh yes, it would be. She's protected and cosseted and cared for. In there, in prison there's none of that. You're as much tied down as the old witch is, and you're not cosseted with it.'

After a minute he said, the whisper quite flat and unemotional, 'Stop staring like that. Do you think this is fun? Pleasure? My seeking? I'm telling you flatly we can't afford to let her live. Even if you backed right out now and wouldn't touch Palmer for anything under the sun, you'll never know another minute's peace from now on. Any minute she could come to life again and then she'll squawk. You needn't kid yourself Palmer won't listen. He might be incredulous – at first, but he'll keep on listening and he'll know she isn't spinning a tale like that for a joke. He knows the wall talks. He'll remember her determined silence, except to himself and that kid. He'll be at his lawyers so fast he'll burn the pavements, and then he'll send for the police.

'You don't know him very well, do you, Val? Oh, I don't think we could be charged with anything if he wasn't touched, or there wasn't so much as an attempt at touching him, but I know enough of him to know that once he's proved someone untrustworthy he takes steps to see that person isn't untrustworthy somewhere else.

'Oh yes, my love, that's quite true. He'll go to the police and say, "This woman planned my death. Watch her." Think of it, Val. You marry again and your husband dies. Next thing you know the police want to know how and why and are probing, asking how much you gained. Oh, you could be innocent and proved so, but how will you enjoy the interval? With fingers pointing at you? Perhaps you get a job instead. Perhaps a legacy when the employer dies. The same thing will happen. Perhaps, if Palmer heard there was a legacy waiting, he might step in first and say to your employer, "Watch this woman. She planned my death, for a legacy."

'He could, and might, give a hint to any employer, "Watch this woman. She would do anything for money, even kill." You see, Val, that old woman, helpless as she is, is completely dangerous. So, how many ways can an old helpless woman die?

'She can't . . .' Sarah, so fascinated that now fear was forgotten, could imagine the man ticking off each item on an upraised finger '. . . be attacked and killed accidentally by a burglar, surprised in a raid on her valuables, because she can't move or cry out or otherwise be a danger to him.

'No more can she die with electric shock, because she touches nothing. There's not even an electric blanket, because it's summer. Neither can she fall, or burn herself critically, or collapse in her bath and drown, or eat something poisonous by mistake.

'She can't cut herself, nor die in a car crash. A tree can't fall on her, nor can she slip on a polished floor and fracture her skull. She can't die of sunstroke or pneumonia from getting soaked in the rain, and neither can she go swimming and drown in the sea, or in the rivers and lakes from an overturned, sinking boat. She can't trip in the street and go under a bus; nor be attacked by a bag snatcher. She can't go near a golf course where she could be hit, fatally, by a golf ball played too vigorously by mistake. She can't be knocked to the ground among crowds and accidentally trampelled on, nor killed by debris falling from a building site.

'There can't be a hunting accident, and however depressed and unhappy her present state could make her, she can't change it by suicide, or what looks to be such. She can't accidentally lock herself in the coal cellar and starve, or trip over the cat and break her neck; turn on the gas stove and forget to light it so there's an explosion or she's gassed.

'She can't, my love, even stand on a chair to fix a light bulb and break her skull that way. In fact, that helpless old lady is better protected against death than you or me. Did you realise that before? It's a fascinating and chastening thought when you dwell on it, to realise that the healthiest young person in the world has a hundred times more chance of dying before nightfall tonight than a helpless, paralysed old woman.'

There was silence. How crazy, Sarah was reflecting in fascination, yet how true it was. To most people who came and peered at her and discussed her in hushed voice, she was already dead, yet she might well outlive them all.

Except for the two downstairs, she remembered then.

Valma's voice broke the silence, jerkily, 'She could . . . have an overdose . . . medicines . . . you know. She must have dozens I expect. You . . .'

'Can you see the Bragg sitting meekly by while the coroner and court condemned her for carelessness? Because that'd be the only way that could be wangled. It'd have to appear that Bragg had made a bloomer and she'd scream to high heaven before she let that idea become concrete fact. She'd be out to find a scapegoat, and, remember, there's going to be another death. Can't you picture her connecting the two, fossicking and ferreting till she unearthed something to grip . . .'

'He needn't die here. Why need he? If you can get rid of that old woman we can go right away. We can wait, can . . .'

'I doubt it. I've a nasty suspicion your old corpse has got through to him already that everything down here isn't moon-light and roses. Oh, use your brains!' Now the assurance gave way to impatience. 'If you knew a wall was echoing every con-versation down here and you had your share of normal curios-ity about how our marriage was making out, what'd be the first questions you'd ask the old woman? And I don't like the way Palmer was looking from one to other of us tonight, as though he were weighing every action and word on a new set of scales. I just don't like it. I think she's talked, haven't you, old witch up there in the corner?' His voice mocked up to Sarah.

'Oh no, we can't afford to wait. It has to be quickly, and both of them, and two deaths are one too many – unless they die together. It has to be that way, that's all.'

How?

The question bothered at Sarah all the rest of the night. Bragg came in for her usual inspection, yawning and dawn-grey of face, and fussed over her, and Sarah barely noticed either the light or Bragg or the fussing. She simply went on pondering that question, how could a vigorous man, who could walk and talk and do a thousand things, die the same death as an old helpless woman in a cocoon of safety?

Murray's words had given her a new vision of herself – as something imperishable except from natural causes and the processes of old age. She was looking at herself down the cor-ridor of uncounted years, with Bragg ever at her side, furrows deepening in her long face; while her callers dropped away one by one because they hadn't been cherished in her safety. The thought of it was appalling, and yet perversely, was to be preferred to immediate death.

She even puzzled over that, amazed at herself, telling herself impatiently that one day among those years she might well wish desperately that everything was over and finished with, yet she knew the stark fact remained – she wanted to live and she intended to fight to live with whatever means she could find.

So find the means, she told herself and found only frustration instead. Plot, she willed herself. Plan, she willed herself. Plan, devise, scheme. Get on with it, Sarah! Her brain was as fertile, as brightly clear, as Murray Phipps's, she was sure.

She knew that the wall was no help now. Never again, except in darkness, when she was alone, would it talk. There was irony in the thought of Roderick Palmer carefully seeing that the Phippses didn't betray her secret unwittingly, while the two of them were doing exactly the same thing.

Even if Bragg heard now, she'd forgotten that terror of Sarah's before. That had been long ago dismissed with the story of the magpie and the fixing of screens. Now even Bragg wouldn't ask if the Phippses had said anything upsetting that Sarah could have heard. Bitterly she reflected that if she had, Roderick Palmer might have seized on it and come up to her and questioned, patiently, carefully and somewhere, some way, he might have lighted on a question that gave him some faint idea.

But it was no use thinking of 'ifs' and 'buts', she told herself impatiently. The thing was to face the fact she had to find some way to fight, for herself and for Palmer too, and immediately she was back to that one question. How could the pair of them, so dissimilar, the one vigorous and active, the other inert and helpless, die together?

———

CHAPTER 8

Rose came back in the morning with another golden rose, which she laid on the coverlet where Sarah's gaze could reach it. She said, 'I brought that as an excuse for coming, and I can't stay long, because my mother is still sick. I have to stay home from school again and help look after her because she says she won't be be ... beholden ...' she stammered over the word '... to anyone, not even to Nurse and certainly not to the doctor. You see, he told her he'd come again and she said "no", and he said "yes", and they kept arguing and then she went red and said – she was terribly cross – "The truth is I can't afford you, so there," and he said, "Good lord, is that what the trouble is? I wish people wouldn't be so full of false pride," and he sounded crosser than she did. Then he told her he wouldn't charge her anything and she got madder than ever, and he snapped, really snapped, at her, "I can't stand people who won't accept an offer of help. It's nothing but a form of inverted snobbery," which I didn't understand at all,' Rose confessed.

'My mother didn't either. She asked what the devil he meant. That's what he said,' she told Sarah. 'He said it was just saying, with your nose in the air, that you didn't want shoes and wouldn't have them for a gift and that you hated the damn things and didn't wear them because you saw no sense in buying them when all the time your feet were blue with cold. It was all pretence and quite silly and he wanted to know why she didn't develop a little sense.

'That was when she told him we weren't going fishing with him on Sunday,' she added forlornly.

There was a faint sigh, then Rose added, 'But I know who's going somewhere tomorrow night. Nurse Bragg is. Mr Phipps is taking her to the theatre. Did you know that?' At Sarah's negative response, Rose said, 'It's true, and she blushed like anything. Truly. She said, "Oh, Mr Phipps, but even if the tickets were given you for nothing, you should be taking Mrs Phipps," and he said, "It was Val suggested I ask you. She's not really keen on stage shows. She'll sit with the old lady till we come back."'

Sarah turned the words over carefully. That there was some special purpose in that invitation she was certain, but the more she dwelt on it the more bewildered she felt. There seemed no sense in it. If death came to the house it would be through the man, Sarah was certain. Valma Phipps, for all her eagerness to hold Roderick Palmer's money, would never have the stomach to kill with her own hands.

Slowly her mind groped with the set-up, as she pictured Bragg and the man leaving the house. Left would be Josie Abcons and the child, out of the way, and Valma, upstairs in this warm quiet room with Sarah herself, while Roderick . . . where would he be? She was back at that question. How could a vigorous man and a helpless woman die the same death, together?

'Are you listening, Mrs Oatland?' The small voice probed and, when she gave assent, reluctantly now, because she wanted to concentrate on that problem and that odd invitation to Bragg, Rose went on eagerly, 'Perhaps Mr Palmer will come and sit with you instead and then you can talk. Before he goes to sleep, that is. Nurse asked about him, you see. She said, "But won't Mrs Phipps want to sit with your father-in-law?" and he laughed and said, "Oh, no. Rod's a bit of a dull stick in the evenings. He likes to get to bed early, though he doesn't sleep well. He takes these sleeping tablets all the time. I wish he wouldn't."'

Sarah found that difficult to believe. Roderick Palmer seemed the last type to resort to the pill bottle. He was very like David, she thought musingly, and that was really an odd reflection too, she decided, when the two men were physically so dissimilar, but she couldn't imagine David ever resorting to a bottle of pills to make him sleep. He would have gone walking till he was tired, or called up some crony and stayed up talking to him, with the hours flicking by unnoticed.

Death, she remembered, lay in sleeping pills and she pondered that, remembering Murray Phipps's scornful dismissal that she, Sarah, could be overdosed. So death couldn't wait for her in a bottle of pills, she decided, almost amused at the detachment she was showing to the problem. In any case she herself wasn't given them, so wipe out sleeping pills, she told herself briskly.

She couldn't, though. To every action of Murray Phipps there was a carefully thought-out reason, she was sure. There was a reason for that invitation to Bragg; another reason for that mention of sleeping pills.

You'd better find out what it is, Sarah, and fast, she admonished herself and then frustration swept back at the remembrance she couldn't ask the simplest question, even of Rose.

The child asked, 'Don't you think so?' and when Sarah remained unmoving, she accused, 'You weren't listening at all,' and then, 'Oh well, it doesn't matter. It wasn't important.'

But it might have been, Sarah thought frantically, and her eye winked once.

Rose laughed. She said, 'Oh, it wasn't. Not really. I was just asking if you didn't like pipes. I do, but I don't think Mr Phipps does. He thinks they're unhygienic. He said Mr Palmer smokes too much, and he's sure it's bad for him, especially at night last thing and didn't she think a combination of smelly old pipe tobacco and sleeping pills was the limit?'

The limit of what, Sarah wondered vaguely. For once, she decided finally, the man must have been speaking idle chatter.

Not about the sleeping pills. There was something important about that, she was sure, but Roderick's pipe smoking could have nothing to do with death, not unless the tobacco was poisoned with some mysterious substance, and that was patently absurd.

The thought was laughable – for a moment – then amusement slid away as she dwelt on the word 'smelly old pipe'. Roderick's sense of smell, she remembered abruptly, was defective, and slowly fear grew, as she connected that with the sleeping tablets, the smell of tobacco, a flat occupied by one old man alone.

Slowly a picture formed and dissolved and came together again. She remembered the new gas stove that might, just possibly, be found to be badly connected; and an old man, drowsy with sleeping tablets, smoking his last pipe of the day, never smelling the gas that crept slowly out of the kitchen and through all the rooms of the flat. She saw the pipe fall gently from his hand and his head sink back, and upstairs . . .

But I'd still be alive, she thought in wonderment. Valma Phipps will be here. She'd smell the gas, long before it even hurt me, let alone killed me, so it's all absurd, or am I supposed to promptly die of shock?

Her head was beginning to ache. She wished now that the child would cease prattling. The soft little voice was a drone of irritation while she dwelt on the problem. Abruptly she thought, Yes, Valma will smell it, and she'd do what anyone would do smelling gas from downstairs. She'll run down the stairs and find Roderick unconscious and she'll . . . what?

Thought bogged down, then finally she knew. Valma would drag the man outside. That was how it would have to be. She'd drag him out and work over him, but of course it would be too late. Too late for Sarah too, because Valma wouldn't have thought, of course, of searching for a gas leak. She'd forget about that. About Sarah too, and slowly the house would fill with gas, and a frail old woman . . . well, no one would expect her to survive that, would they?

No one would even bother wondering if perhaps she had been given a special dose of gas – she was sure, she reflected cynically, that Murray Phipps's inventive mind would find a way of fixing that – just to make sure she did die.

When Bragg and Phipps finally came back the gas would have been turned off, of course. No one would know exactly how much had filled the upstairs rooms, and no one would care, either. It would be just a sad double tragedy, and everyone would sympathise with Valma in her distress, at having forgotten the helpless old woman upstairs. No one would blame her at all, and in a few months everything, with Roderick Palmer and Sarah herself, would be simply forgotten dust.

———

CHAPTER 9

She wondered how Bragg could possibly have known, because her patient's face could surely show no expression at all now, and there was in her such a concentration on trying to outwit the pair downstairs that fear seemed to have left her.

Yet Bragg had known, at the first sight of her apparently, that Sarah had spent a bad night. When she came in, crisp in her white uniform again, the darkened hair out of its pink plastic curlers once more and her figure chastened into curves instead of bulges, she said, 'Well, that didn't work, did it, my dear? A pity. I thought it was quite a good suggestion or I'd never have left you there, but you do seem to enjoy being there by the window. I'd love to know what it is that you don't like about the nights there. Would it be shadows, I wonder?'

Now, thought Sarah, and her right eye closed twice on the reflection that it was important to get through to as many people as possible in the hope that one might, just possibly, hit on a question that might lead to help.

She expected an immediate reaction, an exclamation, a wild cry, even a rush from the room to rouse the house and her disappointment was acute when her signal was ignored, when Bragg's voice oozed on in a low monotone as she prepared Sarah for a sponge bath. 'It couldn't be birds in the night, could it, because they're asleep, except for night birds of course, and I've never seen them round here–too many cats in the neighbourhood. It wouldn't be cats now, would it? Their wailings sound like murder being done out in the darkness sometimes . . .'

Sarah's eye winked once. She willed Bragg to notice it, and to harp on the subject of murder – that so important word – but the voice rolled on. 'Of course there was a bit of a breeze last night. I wonder did the curtains play tricks as they swayed about? Or the trees outside?' Again Sarah's winking eye was ignored. 'Or was it just the strangeness? I know one can get settled into a routine. If it's disturbed it can cause real distress sometimes. Did you think, perhaps, that I'd forgotten the bed should be rolled back to the other side of the room for the night? Did you keep awake, expecting me to remember and come back to do it?'

Carefully, expertly, she got Sarah into a clean nightgown, and then she said quietly, 'So you can hear, and answer too, my dear.' The surprise was so great Sarah couldn't answer that at all, but Bragg went on, 'Oh yes, I never talked to you just for nothing, Mrs Oatland.'

Sarah felt a stab of pride, a feeling of rebirth, and even amusement at the first use of her name. It was as though Bragg was admitting, Now you're a person again. You're Mrs Oatland once more. No longer the fish on the slab, or the poor old dear.

Bragg went on, triumphantly, 'I know that sometimes a sick person can try too hard. That just defeats itself. I've often thought maybe when you tried answering the doctors when they tried reaching you, you were so tense and nervous you failed simply because of that, so I've kept talking to you and waiting for some response when you were relaxed and not so desperately anxious. Now tell me – do you feel anything else is coming back to you – a bit of feeling in your legs? No? Arms?'

Impatiently Sarah answered, as patiently Bragg probed and questioned – but always professionally. Hope slid out of Sarah and was replaced with a quiet question, 'Are you afraid of suddenly dying, Mrs Oatland? Here in the night? Alone?'

At Sarah's agreement, the younger woman nodded slowly,

straightening from smoothing fresh sheets over her patient. She said, 'I thought so. It's now you're getting better that sort of thought will come and frighten you. I could see at once you'd had a bad night, but from now I'll see you're not alone at night.'

A malicious, delighted glee filled Sarah. She hardly heard the added assurance, 'If your niece baulks at the extra expense of help at night to sit with you, I'll shift my bed in here,' because she was thinking of the pair below having their plans disrupted, by Bragg always being . . .

The glee and the triumph were both instantly gone in the remembrance that tomorrow night Bragg wouldn't be there, a guardian against death in the night. She'd be out with Murray Phipps and in the chair by the bed would be Valma, the knitting needles clicking, and downstairs an old man falling asleep.

Bragg's hands smoothed the counterpane, and gave a reassuring pat to the neat cocoon that was Sarah. 'There, Mrs Oatland, you're set for the day, or is there something else you want?'

What a simple thing to raise one's self-esteem, Sarah reflected wryly, but how delicious the question was. To be reminded that now you were once more a person, with desires and wishes, but there was the problem still of getting your wants across, even when Bragg had nodded to her answer.

'What would it be now?' Bragg's long face twisted, her mouth thoughtfully chewing over the problem, along with her mind. She said at last, almost apologetically, 'There's not much that would be of use to you. Perhaps you'd care for another pillow? No, I thought not. A visitor then?' The furrows of effort were gone from her face at the answer. 'Mrs Phipps now? No? The doctor will be along later in any case, you know. I shan't ring him especially. Would you care for Mr Palmer now?'

Her gay laugh rang out. 'Oh, you would.' There were such depths of meaning in voice and face that Sarah was annoyed;

would have given anything to snap, 'Don't be an idiot creature! Do you think I'm going to swoon at his feet like some teenager with her current idol?'

She fretted all the time of waiting about what Bragg might be saying to Roderick Palmer, and worried at the grin that widened his mouth as he came into her warm quiet room, to stand by the bed looking down at her.

'So the great secret's out, Sarah,' he said, and drew up a chair, settling beside her and bringing out his pipe. The sight of it made her forget everything but danger and fear, but he was going on. 'That means you're feeling a whole lot stronger and full of life, doesn't it?'

Yes, she agreed vigorously, and longed to add impatiently, 'Roderick, I want to *remain* full of life. Help me.'

All the old frustration of not being able to reach him, to ask for help for them both, filled her as he said lightly, 'Feel capable now of dealing with that niece of yours, do you?'

Gwenyth, she thought, and reflected in amusement that Gwenyth and her pettiness and silliness had long ago become nothing but a pinprick.

There was silence then, filled for her with impatience, before he said, 'I wish I felt capable of dealing with Val – in the right way. Now look here, Sarah, last night they got out of bed in the small hours. I heard 'em. They nicked off together to the sitting room and I knew this was going to be a private talk they didn't want me to hear . . .'

Sarah was barely listening. She was thinking, He wasn't asleep. He couldn't have taken sleeping pills or he would have been asleep and not heard them move.

His voice flowed back into her consciousness '. . . wall like paper. They know that, and this was private, and I frankly admit I pussyfooted out of bed too and tried to listen, but I couldn't hear. Now look here, Sarah, tell me honestly, did you hear them talking in the night?' At her quick assent he questioned her and hope rose eagerly again. 'Was it . . . well, a good talk? Or was it something I'd have been . . . you think . . . upset about?' He stopped. He sounded defeated when he nodded and said, 'So it was. I wish you could tell me the whole thing, Sarah. I'm desperately worried. There's something wrong down there. I may be a bit of a fool sometimes, but I'm not so much of a fool not to notice when a woman's jumping out of her skin at every trifle, and that's what Val's doing.

'Now look, Sarah . . .' He stopped, gazing at her anxiously. 'Am I upsetting you with all this?' At her quick denial, he said, 'Stop answering if I am. I want to know this. Are they breaking up?'

Yes, winked her right eye triumphantly.

'Is that definite? Not just a guess?' He drew a long breath. 'So that's that. And they're covering it up so I won't know? Right? All right, that's settled, but I can't make sense out of it. I mean by that, what's the use of covering up if it's definite, Sarah?' His voice was bewildered now. 'If they're going to bust up, I'll have to know sooner or later. You see that, don't you? So why the bother to cover up? They know I won't like it, and you see, I'm clinging to that. You say it's definite. You did, didn't you? That's right. That means they've said so, and you've heard them, but Sarah – they haven't broken up yet, and I'm hoping they won't.' Triumphantly he added, 'Don't you get it? Why bother to cover up if it's so definite? Oh they're talking, but talk and action can be two different things. I think maybe they're talking loud and hard and definite and nasty to each other to see how it sounds, yet all the time they know I'm going to hit the roof and they're wondering if they couldn't yet make a go of it if they really tried.

'Don't you think I'm right?'

She wanted to tell him he was a fool, a poor deluded fool who was trying to convince himself of possibilities. She wanted to say a dozen things, but all she could do was give a double wink. She saw his expression cloud. He drew vigorously on the pipe, chewed on the stem of it a moment, then said, 'You don't. I wonder why?'

He shook his head. 'And you can't answer that, so I'm

stumped, or . . . Sarah . . .' There was silence for a long moment before he asked, almost diffidently, 'Sarah, be honest. Are they thinking, perhaps, that I might die soon?'

Yes, winked her eye, and she waited, breath held, for him to press on. Tears of disappointment, of rage, of terror and sheer grief, stung at her eyes as he said, instead of questioning on, 'I had a check-up a few weeks ago. I'm in good shape, and we're long-lasters, my family. Several of us've marched into the nineties with our backs straight still.

'I'm going to have to put it to them straight, that's all, and have it all out. I didn't want to, and that was just being cowardly. They can't go on this way. Neither can I. So I'm going to tell them straight I could live to be ninety, barring falling under a bus perhaps, and that I can see for myself they're play-acting in front of me, and what are they doing behind me?

'Then, I'm going to tell them they can have a bit of money now and start all over,' he told her eagerly. 'You told me they were worried over cash. Well they needn't be, but I won't just hand it over, Sarah. I'm going to see they invest it – in a business venture they can work together. If they work together they might see qualities in each other they've overlooked up to now.

'It's a chance, isn't it?' He was almost pleading.

When there was no answer he gave a rueful shake of his head. 'Well there's one thing, Sarah, you're honest, bless you. I suppose you think I'm an old fool.' At her sharp assent he chuckled. 'And being ridiculous?' The chuckle turned to open laughter that filled the room.

They came in procession that morning. It was a tribute to her new status, she realised, and she might have been amused and interested, if there hadn't been so much desperation in her to try and find help.

The doctor was first. He thumped her chest and peered into her eyes and called her Mrs Oakshot twice and Mrs Elm once, with Bragg patiently correcting him each time, and then he shot at her, almost impatiently, 'Nurse tells me you're afraid of dying here alone in the night?' and at her assent he sounded more impatient still. 'Nonsense. I'm more likely to die than you. When I leave here I'm going to meet half a dozen maniacs in cars just driving a single mile. I could be skittled by the lot. I simply don't think about it.'

Then he shot at her, 'You've too much time for thinking. That's your trouble. Keep her occupied, Nurse, and don't raise your eyes to heaven. Heaven only helps those that help themselves, so do a little of it. Use your brains. Mrs Elm used to play chess. Get the board out. If you finger each piece she can tell you what move to make each time. Can't you?'

So I can, she thought in astonishment and pleasure as his sharp voice went on. 'She could play simple card games too if you hold the cards in front of her so she can give a wink to tell you which to deal. Read to her, too. Something lusty and a little bit shocking so she won't fall asleep at your droning. And rally her old friends round to talk to her of what's going on outside this room.'

He bent over Sarah. 'Stop thinking about dying,' he ordered. 'Think how much you can do already and use your time for thinking out more things to do. You could even study French grammar. Get one of those record things and listen to it and by the time you start talking you'll be ready to plan a trip to Paris. Dying? You simply haven't time for it!'

I haven't, Sarah agreed. She wanted, terribly, to do all those things – play chess again and cards, and keep up with new books – the thought of Bragg's voice shrinkingly skirting the lusty bits brought real amusement, and most of all she wanted to plan that trip to Paris.

Why not, she asked herself when he'd gone. She'd never again be happy in the house. She hated it now, so it could be sold. Gwenyth would have a fit, but what did that matter, she planned recklessly. It could go and the furniture too. She wouldn't be able to bear it either, thinking that the Phipps pair had sat at this table, and in that chair and slept in that particular bed. She'd sell the lot and spend the money recklessly on a trip round the world.

If she got better, that was, she reflected and a little of the exhilaration died, to die completely as she remembered that the Phipps pair were there, in her house, using her furniture – and using her, too.

The child came next, to confide in her, 'The doctor went down again to see my mother and he told her you're getting better because you can answer questions now and your mind's ticking over like new clockwork. That's what he said, and I said "Oh, I know. I've known for simply days," and he said, "I know you did. You're a real little liar, aren't you?" and he reminded my mother he'd said all along that I'd been talking to you and wouldn't admit it and he asked her, "Now who was right of the two of us? You swore she never told lies, remember?" and she said, "Well I was wrong," and she was furious,' she finished mournfully. 'She told me afterwards that she'd never, never believe me again and I'd made her look a fool, because any woman ought to know her own child better than that, and for heaven's sake, what sort of a mother did he think she was now?'

My fault, realised Sarah and promised herself to put it right. If I have time, she instantly amended. She lay listening eagerly, hopeful the child would speak again of that mysterious invitation to Bragg, but Rose was too lost in her own troubles. All she would speak of was Josie Abcons's anger and her face was still mournful when she went and was replaced by the clergyman.

Sarah had never liked him. She remembered that David had once called him a Twitterer. He twittered at Sarah now in a pleased coo as he patted her lifeless hand. 'Such a wonderful thing, such a wonderful change, such a hopeful sign.' He breathed peppermints and tobacco over Sarah as he twittered on, 'You're on the mend, Mrs Oatland, on the mend.'

But I'm not, she wanted to protest. I'm going to be broken for good and all and never mended again if you, or someone else, won't ask the right questions, and she tried to put anger into her eyes and knew she'd succeeded, because his own lean brown face jerked back and he sat there blinking at her in silence.

Then he asked, the twitter muted, 'Is something troubling you?'

That's better, she silently admonished him and gave vigorous assent, waiting hopefully.

'The thought of the future?' He nodded gravely. The twitter mourned, raven-like. 'Of dying, Mrs Oatland?' He shook his head over her assent to that, reproving, 'We should never fear it, Mrs Oatland.'

She knew anger was glazing her eyes again and that he could see it. The rapid blink of his own eyes returned and he said, 'Perhaps you think I am speaking foolishly?' Mutinously she winked assent.

He looked down at his long fingered hands, carefully inspecting the nails for a long, silent moment. 'Why?' he asked, and then sat staring at her.

As helpless as I am, thought Sarah bitterly. We're two adults and he has plenty of intelligence, and I know I have, and I need help and it's his place to give it, but we simply can't reach one another.

He tried though. She felt respect and even faint liking for his careful questioning, his trying to pin down what was wrong. He began with, 'Am I being foolish because you have a special fear about it?' and hope rose when he said, 'Is it fear of the manner?' He probed carefully. 'Do you think it might be painful?' and while she was sure gas wouldn't be so she gave assent, which made him question her, 'Unpleasant? Very much so?' He gave his hands another long inspection and her hopes soared when he said, 'Do you imagine sometimes it might come through . . . through the actions of other people?' He went on rapidly without giving her time to answer, so that her single wink became lost among the jumble of words, confusing him. 'I mean by someone's fumbling with medicines or letting you get too cold or the sheets cover your face or . . . well, matters like that?'

He sat in silence after that. She could have wept with the frustration of it, but tears wouldn't help. They'd hinder, she knew, and fought them down, because her eyes were her sole communication, and they couldn't fill with tears now; they couldn't wink and blink and become useless to her, too, because of useless tears.

Then he said slowly, 'I think all this is out of my province. The doctor felt it was a matter of . . . the soul, the after-life perhaps, but . . . it seems to be his province after all. Doesn't it?'

She didn't answer that, because there was really no way of answering it and after a little he said, 'You feel it's a matter for us both?' Then his clouded gaze cleared. The twitter came back with his triumphant, 'You feel we should get together and discuss it? That if I tell him now what you've told me . . . certainly, but of course certainly.'

She couldn't decide what hope lay in the promise, but everything now was something to clutch at and try to use. I've done what I could, she told herself tiredly. He knows now I think death could come through someone else. Surely – hope rose again – surely if they talk it all over they'll come to see.

Then she was shivering, realising that two might mean that there should be two people here. Two. All the time. Murray and Valma together.

Esmay Laurence came next. Sarah's first thought, as her one-time crony was ushered in, was how old the other looked, and the next a startled realisation that it must be how she had looked to others for years because Esmay and she had shared a desk at school.

It's all these faces, she told herself confusedly, and never seeing my own. Bragg isn't so old really and her skin is good. Beside Esmay she looks young.

Even Esmay's voice sounded old, Sarah thought. She promised herself that that was something else she'd see to in the future. When she could talk again she'd make sure she didn't speak with an old woman's drone.

She wouldn't either be always pointing up the passing years the way Esmay was doing, she thought unkindly, inching herself into the chair, and pulling faces and saying, 'Oh my, I'm not getting any younger, am I?'

Settled, her old friend peered down at Sarah. 'They tell me your wits are working, Sarah, as good as mine. Insulted by that, I suppose, aren't you? You always fancied yourself as being brainy and me as a bit of an addle-pate. Well, you'll need all your wits. That niece of David's is downstairs telling your nurse that now dear Auntie is mentally capable she can do a bit of business with her lawyers. She'll be at you now to give them a wink to her taking over you and the house. Going to let her?' At Sarah's denial she laughed. 'She might be a match for you, just the same,' she said. 'Know what you ought to do, Sarah, give them a wink to sell the whole place up and use the money to get yourself a couple of nurses and some luxury. Well?'

Her round brown gaze widened in shock at the assent. Shrewdly she asked, 'Is it because of what Gwenyth's done to the place?' She nodded at the answer. 'Thought so. Mention selling to you before, and you'd have thrown a fit, but now it's not like yours any more, eh? You'd rather it went all together than be cut up piecemeal?

'Do you like those tenants of yours?' she demanded. 'No? Hate 'em?' she suggested and shook her head at the answer, though she admitted, 'Can't say I like the fellow myself. Grins all the time as though he's trying to sell himself like a grocer with a pound of rather nasty cheese. Sarah . . .' her hand flicked out to touch gently at Sarah's cheek '. . . how about getting rid of them? Giving a wink to make them go?'

Now why on earth didn't I think of it, Sarah wondered, then dismissed her anger at her own stupidity with the reminder that never before had anyone asked her that simple question that would bring safety, because if the Phippses were gone from the house they'd have no excuse to enter this warm quiet room.

Or would they? She thought about that anxiously, then decided that surely, if she made her hate of them known to Esmay and everyone else, there'd be no possibility of Valma, in her gentle whispy voice, offering to take dear Nurse Bragg's place any afternoon she liked to ring to Valma for help.

Slowly her right eye closed and Esmay gave a jerk of malicious laughter. 'Poking Gwenyth's eye out, aren't you? But it's your house. Wait'll she comes up with that nurse of yours, and I'll tell her flat you loathe the sight of your tenants and want them out – double sharp. Right?'

Right, Sarah's wink agreed.

There was softness in Gwenyth's voice, smoothness in her face and anger in her bright, dark eyes, as she stood by the bed and said, 'I'm afraid that's quite impossible. Naturally, Auntie, you don't like the house being divided. Perhaps, now you're capable of deciding things again, we can arrange something else, but for the moment they'll have to stay. Mr Phipps paid two months rent in . . .'

'Pay it him back and tear up whatever lease you gave him,' Esmay suggested impatiently.

'Do you think he'd want to do that?' Gwenyth snapped.

I don't, thought Sarah, and knew defeat.

———

CHAPTER 10

Roderick Palmer came back before lunchtime, and this time Valma was with him, tightlipped, gaze downcast except for a brief dulled glance at Sarah. He carefully placed a chair for the woman, then sat down himself and said, 'I've told Val what you've let out to me, Sarah.'

And cut our lifetimes even shorter, Sarah reflected bitterly. Now they'll be desperate, they'll hurry things up, for fear you'll run to your lawyers and change your will, and either cut them out or tie them down with so many restrictions they'll find it impossible to live up to them.

You've robbed us of hours, her gaze reproached him, but he went on heavily, 'I've never thought much of hiding things, and I'll give Val credit for not trying to bluff her way out and saying you were mistaken or having fancies or something.'

Pale eyes met Sarah's, in mockery, and Sarah reflected wearily that Murray Phipps would have long ago dismissed that defence as being so feeble it was worthless. If Sarah, her voice restored, spoke out and continued to speak, and her mind was shown to be as vigorous as her voice, it would be of no use at all to speak of a sick woman's fancies.

Roderick went on comfortably, 'I said to Val that now I must have you worried, talking my head off the way I did, and you unable to tell me to shut up, and that it wasn't your problem, so we'd come up and tell you how we've worked things out. Or aren't you interested?'

There was a faint wistfulness in his voice. She was acutely reminded of David, thrashing some problem out to her, adding that last query, asking her for reassurance that he could go on using her as a sounding board. And she was interested in Valma Phipps, she thought in wry amusement, as she winked her 'yes' to him.

His face lit up. He leaned forward and said earnestly, 'It's going to be the way I suggested, Sarah. I'm seeing my lawyers tomorrow and starting them preparing the ground for me handing over a sum to Murray and Val.'

Tomorrow, Sarah mused and met again the mocking pale glance from the woman that said, as clearly as though the words had been spoken, Let him plan. Nothing will ever be signed.

He went on, 'It will go on buying a suitable business. I've suggested a hotel, Sarah. Val's a marvellous manager when she sets her mind to it. Her mother trained her well. And Murray's been assistant manager at an hotel. A small place would be fine. Later on there could be a bigger one if they feel they can manage that.'

A wisp of voice said gently, 'It's so marvellous. I can't believe it's really going to happen. It's going to be a new beginning . . .'

And we'll all live happily ever after, Sarah reflected in real amusement, and then in impatience wondered why Roderick Palmer couldn't see through the woman and her sweet-voiced platitudes and pretended gratitude. Anger took over then, as she realised that Roderick's actions were going to be another shield to the pair as well. Now when he died there'd be no murmurs that his daughter and her husband had gained a fortune, that couldn't be countered with the true statement that he had been about to make a settlement on them.

Valma repeated, 'A new beginning . . .'

'Tomorrow,' Roderick Palmer promised.

Tomorrow night, Sarah added silently to them both. Tomorrow night, that's the new beginning.

There was a solemn conclave in Sarah's room that evening. She lay there reflecting that to an outsider, peering into her lighted bedroom, it must have looked hilarious, two men and three women seated solemnly round her bed, waiting for instructions from her motionless figure, but to Sarah it meant a chance of reprieve and there was the hunger of desperation in her eyes as the doctor said, 'We've talked about you. You're afraid, are you, that Sister's going to hand you over to someone who'll make a mistake in caring for you, when you can't say a word in protest?' At her quick assent he assured her, 'That's a common fear, in your condition.'

Bragg's voice, brisker than usual, sounded straight on the heels of Gwenyth's retort, 'Solved, if she was in a good home with trained staff available night and . . .'

'Solved with another pair of hands at night here,' Bragg countered, and the two women sat glaring at one another.

The clergyman twittered, 'There are several church homes . . .'

'. . . run by good souls, inhabited by good souls, who think only of their wretched souls.' Esmay Laurence shook her grey head at him. 'Sarah's got a bit of life in her, and I've never known her to take a close look at her soul in her life. Do you want to go to a home, Sarah?' She looked round the circle in triumph. 'There. She doesn't.'

'Money . . .' began Gwenyth.

'. . . is the root of all evil,' Esmay countered brightly. 'Stop being evil-minded and dwelling on it, that's my advice to you, my lady. There's plenty of money in this place. The furniture can go for a start. Sarah doesn't want it. Do you?' She nodded triumphantly again. 'There, you see. For a start, there's that dresser in the dining room – should be in the dining room, but now the house is all upside down goodness knows where it is, but I've always coveted it. I'll give you a dealer's price for it, Sarah. If you say "yes" I'll get a dealer round tomorrow and . . .'

Gwenyth's face was scarlet. 'You know very well I wanted that dresser and that I've . . .' she stopped.

Esmay laughed maliciously. 'Then you buy it. Well?'

Perhaps I ought to be shocked, Sarah thought. Instead she was amused, even exhilarated by the haggling over her possessions. It was quite absurd to remember now that only a week ago she would have been acutely distressed at the thought of anyone at all buying the dresser. Now it was simply part of a house that she could never live in again.

The doctor said, as though he hadn't heard the squabbling, 'We can get you another nurse. It will be expensive. It will take time, too. Will you settle for someone reliable to sit with you while Nurse is out?'

When there was no reply, Bragg offered coaxingly, 'There's Mrs Phipps now, Mrs Oatland. She's a very . . .' Her mouth opened and stayed open in surprise at Sarah's negative.

Esmay laughed. 'She hates the woman.' She leaned forward. 'Don't you, Sarah?' she asked gleefully, then leaned back in satisfaction. 'There, I told you she did.'

They were all staring at her, Sarah thought. Let them dwell on that, she told herself. Let them dwell on it and seek a reason . . .

Hope slid away again. 'A sick woman can hate anyone, especially someone she resents having in the house,' Gwenyth said.

There was a general leaning-back in chairs, a sudden losing of interest, then Esmay said, 'I'll sit with you, Sarah. It'll be a change to talk all I like without being interrupted. Your nurse can give me a ring when I'm needed. Will that satisfy you?' At her assent, Sarah knew that the whole matter of her hatred of Valma Phipps was forgotten, yet she felt contentment in the knowledge that tomorrow night it would be Esmay who would come up the stairs and sit with her in Bragg's absence.

Or would it?

She ignored the watching circle, closing her ears and eyes to them as she mulled it over, searching round and round it in anxious enquiry and then drawing a hard breath of relief because she couldn't find a way that Esmay – as determined and stubborn a person who ever lived – could be prevented from coming.

There wasn't, she thought with satisfaction, even the chance that Bragg would call on the Phipps woman instead, not now that Sarah had made her attitude plain.

She thought, So their plans are finished, but she knew it wasn't true. There'd be another plan and another and another till they'd got rid of her.

She didn't understand the child at all. Her first thought on waking was sheer irritation at being disturbed, her second fright at the cold small hand touching her cheek. Only then did she start making sense of the words stuttering close to her ear, and they were so ridiculous she was annoyed all over again at having been woken to hear them.

Rose was saying 'He's a magician. He sees into the future. He looks in the mirror and he sees the future.'

Her face came close to Sarah's. 'I used the lift, you see,' she confided, and at Sarah's double wink, the small face withdrew again. The child asked, 'What does that mean?' and sat frowning, then her face cleared. 'Oh, I know. You mean you don't see at all.

'I was telling you . . .' her soft voice reproached Sarah '. . . that I was making Nurse's tea, and I saw the lift that goes down, and . . .' She hesitated, then admitted, 'I got inside and it went down – oh, only a little way, and then it stuck. I thought I'd never, never get it up again and before I did he came into the room down there. That was the dining room, wasn't it, only now it's a bedroom, and he came in and she did, too, and I could hear them quite plainly . . .'

Another spy hole, Sarah was reflecting, amused now, and then amusement gave way to astonishment. 'He was looking into the mirror and seeing the future . . .'

One small finger pushed the blue-framed spectacles up Rose's thin nose, holding them pressed there a minute, then slipping away as the child went on, 'He was asking the mirror to tell him what was going to happen and then . . . and then he said he could see it. In the mirror.'

Sarah was concentrating on that one word 'mirror', remembering that arrogant, assured voice taunting, Mirror, mirror, on the wall, what is the deadliest plot of all.

Rose asked abruptly, 'Can he tell the future?' When there was no reply she sighed. 'You don't know, of course, but he was asking it what was in the future and then he said, really loud – I heard him quite plainly – "I can see the future, Val. I can see it plainly. I can see tomorrow night!"'

There was another hesitation, then Rose went on, 'And she called out, "Don't. I can't stand the way you go on with that mirror. You're always standing there and gazing and asking and . . ." She stopped then because he broke in and said himself, "I can see tomorrow night."'

Silence stretched out. Sarah could have screamed with fury at it. Her gaze sought the child's and couldn't quite reach it, and there was another scream in her at the fury of not being able to turn her head as she willed. She waited, real and surprising pain rising in her throat from that unuttered screaming, but the child went on sitting in silence.

Then abruptly the small pale face came fully into Sarah's view. The blue eyes behind the spectacles were wide and dark and frightened, and the words, when the child spoke, were breathless and so soft Sarah almost lost them, 'Something terrible is going to happen tomorrow night. He said so.'

What? Sarah waited impatiently for that query to be answered, but all Rose said was, 'And he meant it. Really. Because she said, and her voice was real scared, "I won't listen. I won't! How can you go on staring into the glass that way, as though . . . as though it's all there in front of you and . . . put that glass down!" She was terribly, terribly upset.'

The soft voice breathed, 'Mrs Oatland, I don't want to believe he can really see the future,' as though she was begging for reassurance. Then, as if impatient now with Sarah's lack of response, her voice rose. She demanded, 'Do you think something . . . the thing he says . . . will happen . . . tomorrow night?'

The single wink was given before Sarah had time to collect herself; to remember that Rose was a child, who needed reassurance. Only when she saw the shock and dismay in the small thin face did she realise what she had done. She tried to retrieve it by another wink, but there'd been too long a pause, and the young voice was almost anguished. 'You know he can see the future? You know it'll . . . oh, that's dreadful!' Rose cried.

Soft footsteps pattered across the carpet and were gone, but already the anguish, the dismay and fright were lost to Sarah. She was thinking only that she hadn't learned the one important fact – what was going to happen tomorrow night.

It was Roderick Palmer who first thought of the game. He came in that night, his face a little rosier than usual, to settle himself beside the bed and say, 'You can choose the subject tonight, Sarah. What shall we talk about?'

That held bewilderment, and he gave a sly little chuckle. 'That fooled you, didn't it, but why not? I had an idea. You think of something you want to talk about in particular.'

Murder, she thought instantly, but he was going on, 'Then I'll rattle through the alphabet. When you get to the letter that heads your subject give me a nod. Then I'll try and find the exact word.' He tapped his pocket complacently. 'I've brought up a little dictionary so I can run through its words. If you've the patience we'll get to the right word in the end.'

Bless you, congratulated Sarah and the prick of tears scorched her eyes, because there seemed a prospect of help at last. She listened raptly as his monotonous voice went through the alphabet, stopping at her quick wink at the letter 'M'.

His eyes twinkled then. He asked, 'Is the word "me"? Do you want to talk about yourself? No? Then myself? Oh well, we'll try again. How about marriage?' At Sarah's sharp, impatient, double blink, his brows went up. 'Not interested? I wonder – Sarah.' He hesitated, then went on, 'Don't answer if it annoys you, but, was your marriage happy?'

He nodded. 'So it was. I'll tell you something. I've been married twice, but I don't feel like it. My first wife lived with me for a month, gave me a son, and then treated me as a neighbour she'd prefer to keep on the other side the fence. I don't believe in divorce, and she didn't want one, so we stuck it out. Next time round I chose a different type of woman altogether. Oh, we were happy enough in a way, but there was something missing. A whole lot. We never really got close to one another at all. We couldn't talk. Not really talk, I mean. We'd just sit around making polite social noises at each other, without any arguing and sparring and exchanging ideas at all. It's a funny thing, Sarah, but for all your silence I can talk a darn sight easier to you than I could to her. But there . . .' he leaned across and touched her shoulder, consolingly '. . . I was forgetting. We were playing the word game, weren't we? Trying to find a subject you'd care to chatter about.

'Well, there're molecules,' he chuckled, 'but don't ask me to talk on that. Wouldn't mind betting you didn't know what they were, anyway. Then there's mussels and market places. Like to talk about the latest fashions?'

Oh no, no, Sarah thought. Angry now, she would have given anything to strike out at his stupidity, to hurry him along, to make him say the one word she wanted to hear, but he went stolidly on through memories, and men and maladies and money, to medicine.

'I'm bad at guessing, aren't I?' he said, crestfallen, and fumbled in his pocket to bring out the small dictionary. 'Now let's see, where are the "M"s. Here they are. What about mammals, Sarah? No, I didn't think that was it. Or merry-go-rounds or monkeys, eh?' His fingers flicked through the pages. 'There's mirrors . . .' His hands became still. He asked sharply, 'Sarah, have they held a mirror up to you lately? Let you see yourself? I bet you've wondered sometimes . . .'

For a moment that other urgent word was forgotten, swept away in an instant by the one great desire to see herself again, to know what she had become. She gave an urgent blink of her right eyelid, and delightedly he slapped down the little book on the bed and crossed to her dressing-table. He hurried back and held the mirror in front of her.

It was a shock.

Not because she was aged and cruelly altered, but because there was a blank smoothness, an unreality to the face she knew so well. There was no life in it at all. Even the lines that had been there before her illness seemed smoothed out. She looked ageless and lifeless, like a doll, she thought in dissatisfaction.

He let her look for a long time – too long a time, really. Then he went back to his chair. He said with satisfaction, 'There, you see, Sarah, you can choose what we'll do in future. It's just a matter of patience. Now you've seen yourself in the mirror. Were you pleased?' There was sudden anxiety in his face and eyes.

No, she admitted, and he looked crestfallen. 'Have I done the wrong thing in holding up the mirror for you, then?'

She denied that, and some of his dismay slid away, but he held up the mirror to view his own face, smiled a little and said, 'I don't fancy my own face sometimes. Tell me, Sarah, do you think then that you've altered much?'

She didn't know what to answer. Most women, she reflected in wry amusement, would have been glad to have seen wrinkles erased and past strains and stresses and laughter smoothed out and forgotten, but not she. She wanted them back, all of them, and life to take away that doll-like mask.

He was still holding the mirror to reflect his own face when Rose's voice came from the shadows of the room, asking breathlessly, 'Can *you* see the future, too?'

'Eh?' He turned, peering at her, 'Why, it's young Rose. And what are you doing up here, eh?'

On the defensive she said, 'I brought a picture. It was in the paper. A picture of the town gardens. My mother thought Mrs

Oatland might like to see it, now she can see things and . . .'
Then she demanded again, '*Can* you see the future in mirrors?'

The man started to laugh. 'Now what on earth put that
idea into your small head?' he asked. 'Not me. I can't, Rose,
though of course people say sometimes that they can.'

'But Mr Phipps does.'

Sarah's heart gave one great flutter of fear. The room
seemed to darken and sway, and she wanted to cry out in terror, to try and protect the child, to urge silence on them both
over those betraying words. All she could think of was them
being repeated to Murray Phipps and his sure knowledge that
the child had overheard something, as she, Sarah, had done.

But Roderick Palmer was exclaiming in astonishment,
'Murray see the future? That's the last thing . . .' He burst out
laughing. 'Oh, I see, he was having a game with you, was he?
and . . .' he half turned '. . . you know, Sarah, I never knew
Murray spared much time for children. It just shows . . .'

'He didn't,' Rose began, then was silent.

'Oh . . . ho?' He looked at her in amusement, 'Listening to
what doesn't concern you, were you? Oh well, we'll forget it.'

But Rose wasn't to be silenced. Her voice piped shrilly,
desperately, dismayingly, through the room. 'He said . . .
tomorrow night . . . someone was going to die.'

So that was it, Sarah thought grimly and wondered whose
face it had been Murray Phipps had been seeing in the mirror
glass as he'd said that.

Then Roderick Palmer was saying, his voice amused, 'Of
course they will. Every night of the year someone dies, Rose.
Didn't you know that? That was just a silly sort of joke, my
dear. Looking in the mirror, was he, and saying he could see
someone dying tomorrow night? That's just a silly kind of
joke. Don't you agree, Sarah?'

Her double wink came swiftly. He looked astonished, then
nodded gravely. 'Oh yes, I see. You think it was stupid, eh?
Because it's frightened Rose. Well, I agree, you know, though
Murray wouldn't have known she was listening. Did he,

Rose?' When the child shook her head he nodded. 'There, you see, Sarah. He didn't know but I agree, it was a stupid sort of joke. Rose, you show that picture to Mrs Oatland, before we do anything else. We're playing the word game,' he explained.

When the child didn't move, Roderick Palmer said almost chidingly, 'Come and show the cutting, Rose. Then we'll play the word game. Do you know what that is?' When she shook her head, still not moving, he explained, asking, 'Can you think of a word that begins with "M" that might be the one?'

Rose reflected, one leg twisted behind the other, the top of her tongue pressed between her small irregular teeth. Then she said, almost hoarsely, 'Mysteries.'

'That it, Sarah?' Roderick enquired.

Sarah hesitated. It wasn't the right word, but she was sure they would never come to 'murder', that impossible, ridiculous word to speak in this warm, quiet, enclosed world of hers. 'Mysteries' would have to do, she decided. For a start, anyway, and her eyelid blinked once.

'Well, what a girl you are, Rose!' Roderick Palmer exclaimed. 'Show your cutting and then we'll talk about mysteries. Come on over here, Rose. Bring a chair. You're better at this than I am, evidently. What sort of mysteries do you think Mrs Oatland wants to talk about?'

Rose's gaze sought Sarah's and held it. For a moment there was a wordless communication between them – brought about by fear and anxiety, Sarah knew, though those emotions had different roots.

Then the child said, 'In this house . . .' and at the man's puzzled look she added, her voice shriller '. . . mysteries in this house. I . . . funny things that happen and . . .'

'You mean there've been mysteries in this house? Is that right, Sarah?'

After a moment she agreed.

'What mysteries?' He turned almost eagerly to the child then. 'Is there some special history connected with this place, Rose?'

The blue eyes, behind the glasses, were dark and secretive and unhappy. She said at last, 'I don't know. I meant, funny things . . . now. Not history, like you said.' The words started coming, faster and faster. 'Things like that mirror and Mr Phipps, and Mrs Phipps being nice to Nurse and then laughing and him saying I'm useful if there's an accident, because how does he know, and I'm sure I wouldn't be at all, and then my mother saying he's the very finest person she's ever met when she hates him frightfully, so she said and then . . .'

Sarah knew, despairingly, what was going to happen. Roderick had no way of knowing how to pick the grain from the chaff of the babbled words. He wasn't to know there was rich grain at all, and just as she'd expected he seized on the last words, 'Murray? Your mother hates Murray, yet thinks he's the finest . . .'

'Oh, no!' The denial came explosively. 'At least, I don't know what she thinks about Mr Phipps. I mean the doctor. She said she hates him 'cause he's dreadfully rude, and he called her a fool and a whole lot of other things and now she just gazes into space and says he's the very finest person she's ever met, and there's someone for me to admire and respect.'

Roderick was openly laughing before the words had stopped. He said lightly, 'There's no mystery there, Rose. It's a woman's privilege to change her mind about everything from tablecloths to friends. Do *you* like the doctor?'

'Oh yes,' the answer came enthusiastically. 'He gets cross, but it's all on top really and underneath he's nice. He's just pretending, I think, like my mother I expect when she says she hates him. I wish people wouldn't pretend.'

'And does Mrs Phipps pretend?' Roderick Palmer asked quietly. 'You said that she's nice, Rose, and then she laughs. What did you mean by that particular mystery?'

The child's cheeks had reddened. Her gaze was lowered, evasive. 'I didn't mean anything. I was only saying . . . or rather . . .'

'You meant, didn't you, that Mrs Phipps is nice to Nurse

Bragg to her face and laughs at her behind her back? Isn't that right?'

'Yes.'

'A lot of people do things like that,' he told her quietly. 'It means . . . perhaps you don't like a person very much, but you make an effort and be polite and kind to them.'

In the silence Sarah was thinking again of the mirror, hoping that they'd return to the subject and that Rose would tell exactly what she'd heard Phipps say, but Roderick seemed sure now that he had dealt with the important part of Rose's mysteries, that nothing was left. He said briskly, 'Sarah, is there some special history connected with this house that you want to talk about?'

'History', she reflected. That wasn't the right word at all. History was a year ago, two years ago, a hundred years ago. Her mystery lay in the present and the few days previously.

She didn't realise, till he spoke again, that she had taken so long thinking what to answer. 'You're not answering, so you're not sure what to say. There's a mystery, but it's not history. Is that right?' He nodded at her agreement, then asked, 'What do you think it would be, Rose?' Without waiting for her answer, he said, 'We've disposed of the mirror, so it isn't that. I was wrong, of course, about you wanting to look in a mirror, wasn't I, Sarah? Rose had told you about Murray's foolishness with the mirror and talk of the future, of course. That was the mirror you wanted to talk about, wasn't it?'

She agreed, and felt cross with him when he smiled and said complacently, 'Well, we've disposed of that. Rose, what mystery do you think is left?' Now he was looking at the child and not at Sarah at all, so that she couldn't, even with an urgent double wink, tell him that he was wrong.

Rose was silent. He looked back at Sarah, and her rage grew, because she had no way of telling him what was wrong now – the whole thread that had been gently unwinding had now snapped and broken and she was back where she had started, she thought bitterly.

Bragg brought the final confusion. She came in tiredly and was immediately co-opted by Roderick into joining in his word game. But her tiredness dissipated with her gay, youthful laugh and her sly remark, 'The only mystery I know round here is who'll get the dining-room dresser. They're both at it. They've both been back – Mrs Laurence and Mrs Oatland – to have a look at it. They met up on the stairs going up.' She laughed again. 'Who's going to have it, Mrs Oatland?'

Roderick was chuckling, too. 'So there's a mystery, Sarah. Who's to have it?' He touched her shoulder again. 'Your niece? No, I thought not. So it's to go to Mrs Laurence then?'

Bragg heaved herself to her feet, 'Then in that case I'd best go and tell them. They're down there in the spare bedroom about to carve one another up.'

Sarah closed her eyes. Her chance, her hopes, were gone again. She didn't want to see either Esmay or Gwenyth. When they came in, Esmay with quick, hopping steps that spoke of triumph, and Gwenyth, strident-voiced and vocal, Sarah refused to open her eyes or give any acknowledgment that she could hear the voices pressing at her.

It was Esmay who brought the session to a halt, 'We're driving her crazy. Goodnight, Sarah. I'll be off, but I'm coming to lunch tomorrow and by then you'll have decided definitely about the dresser, I hope, and give me your word about it. Between friends a wink's as good as a signed contract.'

The night was brilliant with stars that paled the sky to a washed-out grey. Rose had put her glasses in their case and to her the sky was blurred, a glitter of sequins. She loved it that way and her face was sulky when Josie Abcons entered the bedroom they both shared and said, 'Rose, you should have been asleep ages ago! I told you . . .'

'I couldn't sleep.'

The flat tones held no expression. Josie said, 'Why not?' automatically, but she wasn't really listening. Her mind was on other things. Only when the flat youthful voice ceased did her thoughts grope backwards, seize on the words, worry at them and discard them finally as quite absurd.

'What nonsense! Lie down, for pity's sake. This time you can lie there and go to sleep. I shan't warn you again. This is the second time I've tucked you in, and I have to sleep, too. I have to get back to the salon tomorrow. It's Saturday and I just have to be there.' Now her voice was anxious, the lines of harrassment, so well known to Rose, back between her dark brows.

'It isn't nonsense,' Rose said slowly. 'Mrs Oatland thinks it's true, that people can.'

'What?' Josie pulled off her robe, preparing to get back into her own bed, but hesitated. She sat down on the side of the child's bed. 'Do you mean to tell me the old lady actually believes you can see the future in mirrors? Oh well, that's not so odd really. A lot of these old people believe in crystal gazing and Tarot cards and that sort of thing – seances, too, for that matter – that's getting in touch with the dead, if you don't know.' At Rose's disgusted yelp, Josie smiled. 'It's not more ridiculous than seeing the future in mirrors.

'Rose!' Now her voice was edgy. 'You didn't tell the poor old soul what Mr Phipps is supposed to have seen, did you? You said it was something bad? You didn't . . .' At the embarrassed wriggling under the bedclothes, she pounced, pulling down the sheets to reveal the child's face fully. She said grimly, 'Now tell me the lot! Everything, from start to finish. Go on, hurry up!'

Rose knew the tone of old. There was going to be no escape, and she didn't want to escape anyway, she knew quite well. She wanted to tell someone the whole story and be reassured. She began breathlessly, 'I got into that little food lift thing in the kitchen and it stuck.'

'You had no business to do anything of the sort.' Josie began automatically to scold, then brushed it aside. 'Oh well, leave that. You hid in the lift and started it and it stuck. Right. What then?'

'I could hear. Through the bottom of it. I could hear them downstairs. I heard Mr Phipps come into that room that's a bedroom now and Mrs Phipps was there, too and she told him to stop staring in the mirror and he laughed and said, "Mirror, mirror on the wall, tell the future, tell me all" and she told him to stop it, that he gave her the creeps, and he said, "But I can see the future, Val. I can see it plainly in the glass. I can see tomorrow night." He sounded as though it was really true, as if he could and she knew he did, too, because she called out, "Don't. I can't stand the way you go on with mirrors, always standing there and looking into them and asking them to tell you things," and he said back, "But it's real, I can see tomorrow night in the glass."'

Rose drew a long breath. 'She told him to stop it, that it was too much for anyone to stand the way he went on, and they started squabbling like anything and he was real rude to her and called her a silly cow . . .'

'Rose . . .'

The child shook her head stubbornly at the warning tone. 'Well, he did. And then he told her this awful thing was going to happen tomorrow night and she said she hated bad jokes, and he said it wasn't a joke at all.'

'Well?'

'He said that tomorrow night he was sure that Mr Palmer was going to die. He did, Mummy. Truly. And she was awfully scared, and started to cry and tell him he was dreadful.'

Josie stood up. She said distantly, 'I think we'd best see Dr Holden again tomorrow, Rose. You're becoming a terrible little liar. Maybe it's being left on your own so much of the time. I'm beginning to wonder how many things you've told me are true and how many not. Oh well, leave it, but honestly, Rose, this story is . . . oh well, perhaps you did hear something and you've done a bit of embroidery on it, hmm? Isn't that it?' Her voice and slumped body both spoke of utter weariness. 'Oh leave it, pet. All right, I'm not angry, so don't cry, but this is all nonsense. Whatever you heard, or didn't hear, it's all nonsense. Maybe you heard something and it frightened you, but it would all have been a sort of silly teasing. You said they were squabbling. Well, when grown-ups squabble they do silly things, annoying one another by silly speeches. Oh well, you wouldn't understand, I suppose, and it does sound ridiculous, but . . .' there was bitterness in her voice now '. . . but when grown-ups quarrel they can be so ridiculous it's unbelievable, pet. Now curl up and go to sleep. Oh, Rose, please! I have to try and sleep myself. I have to work tomorrow.'

After a moment she added, more gently, 'Listen, pet, don't be silly. Don't you see it's all nonsense? If Mr Phipps thought his father-in-law was going to die tomorrow night he'd be terribly, terribly upset and he'd be making plans to stay home and be on hand. But he isn't, pet. He's taking Nurse Bragg to the theatre. Haven't you thought of that? And he's bought her a box of chocolates. He did that this afternoon. So how could he possibly think old Mr Palmer was going to die? See? Now, haven't you been silly?'

Gently she disengaged the small arms that had been thrown round her neck in a violent hug, tucked the sheets round the small thin body again and thankfully moved to her own bed.

Her voice was a caress in the darkness as she switched off the light. 'It was all nonsense. You do see now, don't you?' The answering voice was happy again, light and sleepy now, 'Oh yes, it was all nonsense. I do see. I was silly, wasn't I?'

———

The house had been full of noise all through the morning, so much that Sarah was realising how everyone must have tip-toed during her illness, hushing one another at the slightest sound. It had been like a morgue, she had reflected wryly, but now she was coming to life, so they thought, and life was beginning again all round her.

Bragg had been more bustling than usual and had talked unceasingly, to Sarah's rising irritation, of the coming evening and the theatre visit. 'You'll have to be good while I'm gone,' she had joked to her silent patient. 'I wouldn't say that Mrs Laurence had too much patience, even if she has a kind heart.'

It was the thought of Esmay that bolstered Sarah's spirits, even after the dismaying visit of the child, flushed and bright-eyed that morning, who came dancing in with another rose and the whispered confidence, 'I was silly. So silly my mother thinks I need medicine or something. Oh, I was silly. Really. I thought it was true, and it wasn't, of course, because you see he's going to the theatre tonight. You do see, don't you?' she asked anxiously. When Sarah's two blinks registered, her small face was downcast again, but only for a minute. She laughed and said, 'Oh, I do babble and get mixed up, don't I? But you see, yesterday I heard what Mr Phipps said about see-ing the future in the mirror and of course that's nonsense. Oh, I don't mean it's nonsense for everyone,' she added hastily. 'You think people can see the future in crystals and things, don't you? You said so yesterday. But not Mr Phipps. He was just having a silly joke in saying he could see in the mirror and see Mr Palmer dying tonight. It was nonsense, because if it was true Mr Phipps would stay home tonight and be terribly sad, wouldn't he, only instead he's taking Nurse to the theatre. So you can see just how silly I was.'

At Sarah's urgent double wink she only laughed. 'Oh yes I was. You needn't be polite. I was very silly.' Then she added softly, close to Sarah's ear. 'But I think it was a horrid joke, don't you?'

The quick steps pattered away across the carpet and Sarah had only one thing left to cling to – the fact that Esmay would be there that morning, not Valma Phipps at all. She clung too, to the hope that Roderick Palmer would come up again and play the word game, but though the house was full of noise and doors opening and shutting and Mrs Furlong running the vacuum cleaner, her only companion all morning was Bragg.

She was alone, though, when the crash came.

She had been half dozing, surprised at herself that sleep could even approach and touch her when the hours were passing and she'd done nothing towards helping herself or Roderick Palmer, and the crashing and the hum and the final thud brought her to full consciousness again, frightened, trembling, her skin prickling with sweat.

She listened to voices calling and steps running up and down the stairs, along the landing and up and down again. Feet ran downstairs too. There was a voice talking – on the phone, Sarah was sure, though the words were only a murmur to her in her room – then feet went running down the stairs again.

Finally steps began to climb the stairs, slowly, heavily. She lay there in that prickling sweat, terrified, remembering a voice that had whispered to her from the wall – how long ago had it been? She couldn't even remember now, but she could hear the wall whispering those words, 'There's a nice straight staircase out there. It would be so easy if Palmer went up carrying a few magazines, perhaps, and fell on his way down again.'

She knew, quite certainly, that it had happened, that their other plan, of dealing with herself and Roderick Palmer together, had evaporated because of Esmay's interference, and the staircase had been chosen . . .

A silent scream tore pain in the back of her throat as she saw him coming. She had been so certain, so lost in the dreadful picture of him lying still and silent on the floor at the foot of the stairs, that there was something equally horrible in seeing him walk across the carpet towards her bed.

There was something different about him, she realised. The plump pink face seemed paler, the cheeks hollower and for the first time she thought of him as a man striding towards old age. His shoulders were humped and he kept rubbing at his hands as though frost were touching them.

He sat down heavily, not reaching as usual for his pipe, and just sat there in silence, not even looking at her, for several seconds. Then he said, 'Something dreadful happened, Sarah,' and she was reminded of the child saying, in fear and fright, that something dreadful was going to happen in that house.

Roderick Palmer straightened a little in his chair. His gaze met hers. 'I'm sorry, Sarah. Your nurse sent me to tell you. We knew you must have heard the row and nurse can't leave Mrs Laurence.'

Her stomach seemed to give a horrible lurch. For a minute she thought she was going to be actually sick. 'She fell down the staircase. The doctor's on his way. I'm afraid her leg is broken.'

She felt like laughing, and that was ridiculous, and terrible, too, she reminded herself. It wasn't a laughing matter. She tried to picture Esmay, with her usual hopping walk, encased in plaster, and couldn't, but it was a lot easier to try and do that than erase the horrible picture she'd had of an Esmay silent and still and in a coffin.

Roderick Palmer went on, 'She fell down most of the staircase and landed with her leg doubled under her. A terrible thing. Sarah, my dear, you mustn't worry.' His hand touched her shoulder again. 'Mrs Laurence will be fine again soon. Nurse called it a nice clean break, if such a thing could ever be called nice. A strange thing to say, really . . .' Sarah realised he was speaking on and on in an effort to relieve his own shock and dismay '. . . but I know the phrase means it should heal well. It won't be long before she's up and about again and raring to get hold of that dresser again. That was what she was after, Sarah. She was coming to lunch, you know, and to get you to give her the nod that she could have the dresser, and do you know, Sarah, she was lying there stunned and shocked and in pain and she said to us all, 'Don't you dare let that Gwenyth get hold of my dresser while I'm laid up.' Can you imagine that? Oh, I suppose it was shock of a sort, an attempt to steer her own mind away from what had happened to her, but it sounded so damn queer. She was lying there with her leg at a strange angle, and her face screwed up with the pain of it and talking about getting that dresser ahead of Gwenyth.'

His hands rubbed gently together again. 'It's a terrible business, and of course now I expect there'll be trouble for the child.'

Sarah hadn't been really listening to the monotonous voice. There had been only words of no importance. She had been concentrating on the one horrible, inescapable fact that Esmay was out of action, that tonight she wouldn't come up to this warm quiet room and sit there while Bragg was absent from the house. It was all she could think about. She couldn't even feel sympathy for Esmay's pain and shock. Her whole mind was filled with fear for herself, and for the man at her side.

His monotonous voice went on, 'I expect she'll be in serious trouble with that niece of yours. Sarah, you must try to make sure some way or other that that doesn't happen. She's a nice little kid . . .'

Sarah's thoughts came back from that whirlpool of self-centred fear and concentrated on what he was saying. It was something about Rose, she knew, and when she had focused on the words, sorted them out and looked at them she was remembering Rose's voice piping, 'He said I'd be handy in case there was an accident,' and rage took the place of some of the fear. Not all, but enough so that fear was stifled for the moment and she was thinking of someone apart from herself and Roderick Palmer.

She winked once, urgently. His voice stopped, then he nodded. 'Oh yes, I knew you would. We'll have to get Gwenyth in here and make her understand that the child isn't to get into trouble.'

But why was Rose to be blamed, Sarah wondered. He didn't say and after a while he went away again and left her to listen to voices and calls and tramping feet and slamming doors downstairs, and the sound of a car coming and going.

Finally the doctor came upstairs to her, firm hand touching her wrist. He looked down at her and said, 'Mrs Mississippi will be all right, don't worry,' and she thought in amusement, That's impossible! Mississippi, indeed! He does it on purpose. He doesn't forget any of our names. He likes to be thought a bit of a dill, a bit absent-minded, and all the time he's summing us up quite shrewdly . . .

She wondered what he was thinking as he looked down at her, if he could see straight through the barrier of her faded blue eyes and read her frantic thoughts. For a moment she thought he actually had, when he said, 'Those stairs of yours are murderous.' Then he added, 'That's just the type of stairway that should be forbidden. Straight and narrow-treaded and high, just asking for trouble. Especially with a child round the house.' He added, crossly, 'Your pulse is jumping. Stop worrying. You don't want Rose to get into bother over this, do you?' At her double blink he nodded. 'I'll see she doesn't. Stop fretting.'

Her eyes tried to ask how Rose could possibly be involved, but failed. She had to go on lying there, curiosity unsatisfied, hearing him walk away.

It was Bragg who told her. A strangely subdued Bragg, with darkened hair ruffled for once and her cheeks flushed, and little beads of sweat on her upper lip. For once, Sarah thought uncharitably, the woman looked almost human. She sounded human, too – the oozing voice was gone. It was muffled and husky.

She said slowly, 'They're like children, that pair, Mrs Laurence and Mrs Oatland junior, I mean. Just like children, and look what came of it!' She eyed Sarah almost accusingly as though it should have been put a stop to by Sarah herself. 'I caught her, you know, sneaking in. That was about ten o'clock. She tried to get on her high horse with me, but I wasn't having it. I told her you were asleep, and she couldn't call me a liar because you were and she didn't dare wake you for fear of what I've said to the doctor. I'd have made him keep her from the house and she knew it. But I'd hardly shooed her out of the place and headed her back to the stairs when Mrs Laurence came sneaking up. Oh well, sneaking's not the word, but coming up quietly, just the same. She had the grace to turn beet red when she saw me, and Mrs Oatland was on her like a flash, accusing her of going behind her back to get at you about the dresser.

'Going at it hammer and tongs, they were. So childish. I could have hit them both. I told them to go, and they did in the end, but Mrs Laurence had this lunch appointment here and Mrs Oatland said that she was coming along, too, to see, so she said, that Mrs Laurence put nothing over on the sly.

'Childish!' The word came out explosively. 'I put a stop to it myself. I told them one visitor at a time was enough and it was all planned for Mrs Laurence, and the doctor wouldn't allow Mrs Oatland to come too and start fighting and arguing in front of you. She was furious, of course. Not that I cared a fig for her temper and she had to give in.'

The Phipps pair would have heard all that, Sarah thought wearily. Listened inside their door at the row on the stairs and known that Esmay would be going up the stairs alone later on.

They must have realised, from that 'sneaking-in' that Bragg had spoken of, that both Gwenyth and Esmay had the key to the front door. Sarah couldn't remember now what reason there had been in the past for Esmay to have a key, but it had been given her some time after David's death.

I remember now, Sarah thought. It was because I was sorting through David's things and I never answered the bell, because I kept getting filthy, going through all that accumulation of papers and oddments in the rooms upstairs. I gave her the key so she could come in by herself.

It was odd to think that Esmay had remembered it, when Sarah herself had so easily forgotten, but she must have kept it easily accessible, and the Phippses had known, from that morning's quiet entrance, that Esmay would use the key again that lunchtime and be on the stairs alone.

What had they done to her? And how had Rose come to be blamed?

Two questions she wanted to ask desperately and as though knowing what was in her thoughts, Bragg went on heavily, 'Such a terrible thing to happen though, and the child wasn't really to blame. She dropped her yo-yo on the stairs, you see. Probably slipped out of her pocket, or else maybe she was playing there after seeing you – that's what Mr Phipps suggested. He was the one who gave her the wretched thing in the first place. Oh, it was a kind thought, but why didn't he think that the child might leave it lying around? He said she was playing on the stairs with it and evidently tired of it and left it, or else it dropped out of her pocket when she was going away.

'And then Mrs Laurence had to go and step on it when she was coming up.'

Rage was building up in Sarah, a cold, bitter rage and she didn't try to fight. It was rage against Murray Phipps and rage against Bragg, too, for being so easily taken in. Couldn't the woman see that Murray Phipps was the last person to be buying toys for a child?

Then her rage died in puzzlement at the realisation that Phipps couldn't have seen that the yo-yo was left on the stairs. Rose must have been careless, that was all – but she couldn't believe it was just an accident. It was too much of a coincidence that Esmay should be the one who had fallen and been put out of action.

Bragg said, 'The poor child's in tears, of course, and her mother's been at work. I tried to comfort her, and Mrs Phipps did too, but Mrs Oatland's down there now with a doom-is-coming look to the set of her face. They all want to see you. It's funny, my dear,' she said, her voice expressing complete surprise, 'how we all keep coming to you, and yet you can't solve anything for all our talking . . .' She shook her head. 'I'm worrying you, aren't I? We all do?'

Sarah's double wink was swift. Bragg's gaze was on her searchingly. 'I suppose . . .' she began at last, then hesitated, 'I suppose it's an interest for you. Bringing you into the swim of things. Is that how you feel?' At Sarah's agreement the younger woman said hesitantly, 'Then do you feel up to seeing Rose? She says you'd know she wasn't fibbing, though how she knows that I'm sure I don't know, but she insists it's not her yo-yo, which is plain silly. After all . . .' now she laughed '. . . can you see the rest of us playing with one? Oh well, will you see her or not, my dear?'

Sarah's agreement was given before the words were finished, but for all that she had to wait a long time before Rose finally came, pale-faced, silent, and stood beside the bed.

Sarah waited helplessly. She longed to reach out with hand and tongue and comfort, and couldn't. She couldn't do a thing till the child spoke, and Rose seemed reluctant to say a word. Only when Roderick Palmer joined them did her tight-lipped mouth unlock, 'It wasn't my yo-yo. It just wasn't. I hit mine. I hit it hard. Against those bannisters, and a big piece of red paint just came off it. I didn't care. I didn't want it.' Her voice quavered. 'I thought it was a silly thing. But he smiled and smiled and I pretended I liked it and I played with it while he stood there, but when he was gone, I forgot about it.'

'And it dropped out of your pocket later on, eh?' Roderick said. Rose rounded on him passionately, 'It didn't!' Her small fists were clenched, her thin face red with temper. 'The one Mrs Laurence fell on is different. It is! Mine had a big piece of red paint gone and that one hasn't. There were two. Mr Phipps must have kept the other.'

A queer little sound, part grunt, part laugh, came from Roderick. He said gently, 'I couldn't for the life of me imagine Murray indulging in a game with a yo-yo. Look, Rose, no one's going to toss you out of the house over this. That's what you're frightened about, isn't it? But it won't happen. Will it Sarah?'

He smiled at the child then, taking her hand. 'You see? Everything will be fine, so don't be a little chuck-head. You didn't want the yo-yo and you forgot it and it finished on the stairs. That's all there is to it.'

'It isn't!' Rose's voice was a near scream. She kept repeating the two words over and over till he gave her a brisk little shake and a stern command to be quiet. She was abruptly silent, then turned to Sarah, asking desperately, 'Do you think it's true, what he says? That . . .' Her voice trailed into silence then began again in delight, 'You see? She believes me. She said so.'

Sarah knew they were both staring at her in surprise, with delight on the part of the child and shock on Roderick's.

The man said slowly, 'But Sarah, that's ridiculous. Granted you want to stick up for Rose, there couldn't be two yo-yos – two red yo-yos, hanging around the stairs. Do you mean to tell me you think Murray bought two?'

Yes, she gave back defiantly, eagerly, but he only shook his head helplessly. 'I don't understand at all. Did Murray tell you perhaps, that he'd bought a present for Rose, and an extra yo-yo too?' At her negative he said again, 'Well, I just don't understand. You think there were two, right? But you don't know. Right?' He looked from Rose to Sarah. 'Where does that leave us, Rose?'

'With two yo-yos,' she answered smartly.

'And not much else. Sarah, there's a mystery here, isn't there? Is this the mystery you wanted to talk about last night?'

It wasn't, of course, but she had to keep him on the subject of Murray and Esmay's accident, so she agreed it was, and then realised it was the wrong thing, because now his voice was harsh and annoyed. 'But that's impossible, Sarah. Murray didn't buy the yo-yo till this morning. He went out first thing and came back with it just before he handed it to Rose. You're talking nonsense. You want to help Rose, of course, but can't you see, Sarah, that you're throwing the blame at Murray now?'

It was no good, Sarah realised bitterly. Without a voice to fight and argue with she was completely helpless. Roderick wasn't going to question any more on that tack. She'd annoyed him now and worried him, because Murray was his son-in-law. Naturally no blame must be thrown at Murray. Naturally . . .

She knew the child was waiting for something else to be done and said. Her sigh of disappointment was clearly audible when Roderick Palmer said at last, 'We'd best just forget the whole thing. After all, no one can really blame a child and as you're satisfied she can stay on here, Sarah, there's really no more to be said.'

Firmly he added, 'We'll talk about something else. Or rather, we'll still talk about Rose. Do you know, Sarah, that Rose was one of the first on the scene? She was in the kitchen up here helping Mrs Furlong, and she ran down like a flash and actually had the sense to stop Mrs Laurence from trying to move.

'So, you see, the doctor was right, wasn't he?' He was smiling again. 'Saying that he thought Rose would prove handy in case of an accident. Maybe you'll finish up as a nurse or . . .'

'No, he didn't.' Rose disagreed firmly. 'The doctor never said that. It was Mr Phipps.'

'Murray did?' For a long moment he thought that over, while Sarah waited and hoped, but then he shook his head. 'Murray keeps being a surprise to me, Sarah. He never seemed to enjoy kids' company you know and yet . . . well, look at the way he's taken an interest in Rose here, and he seems to understand her so well, too. It's an eye-opener, isn't it?'

Sarah might have laughed, if she'd been able, though it wasn't laughable. It was pathetic and terrible that in Roderick's hands now lay a clue to Esmay's accident, and he didn't realise it and probably never would, before his time for thinking of anything was running out and her own, too.

The remembrance of that drained away the last vestige of amusement from the situation. She heard only dimly Roderick speaking to the child again and then the swift patter of small steps across the carpet, then Roderick said, 'She'll be all right, Sarah, and it was best she went. She's getting over-excited about it all. Best to forget and refuse to discuss the whole thing any more, to my mind. Now look, I'll tell you something funny, but maybe you'll best never let on you've learned it. Your friend, Esmay, was parked in the broom closet.'

At her unwinking stare he chuckled. 'Talk about a couple of adults acting like kids. Did you know your friend and that niece of yours had a set-to this morning? Argey, bargey and ya-ya at one another till it made my sides sore. Both of them after first pick at your furniture, but I will say your friend Esmay is quite open about it all. Well, they had this fight, and your nurse told them to run away and off went Gwenyth in a terrible huff. Esmay pretended she was off, too. But she didn't go. She told me so down there in the hall. Whispered to me, "I stayed two hours in that wretched broom closet so Gwenyth wouldn't get a chance to sneak back without me knowing, and now look what's happened – she'll have all the time in the world for getting in ahead of me." Nearly crying over that, mind you, instead of her busted leg. Makes you laugh, doesn't it?'

It didn't and she told him so, because she was thinking that if Esmay had been in the cupboard she would be able to say if Rose had been on the stairs later, and if Murray Phipps had, too.

She was thinking of that, and nothing else, and was surprised at his dismay. 'Oh well, of course it wouldn't,' he said. 'I see now. You're angry of course, and you've a right to be. Two grown women carving up your possessions like that is enough to annoy anyone, I expect.' His shoulders heaved. 'But for the honest life of me, Sarah, I can't help laughing at the idea of that bird-like old creature stuck in the broom closet, with one eye to a crack to watch for Gwenyth.' Then he sobered. 'Sarah, you'll have to do something fast about this set-up. You'd best get your lawyers down and let them question you about what you want done all round.'

Her single wink was heartfelt, though she knew there'd be no time for seeing her lawyers, let alone having them patiently question her. She wished she could see what time it was, but her head wouldn't move so she could see the clock.

'I'll come back after lunch, Sarah,' he said. 'We can play the word game if you like, or . . .' He chuckled. 'That was a fast wink. Right then, we'll play the word game. What letter shall it be?' He ran through the alphabet rapidly and stopped in surprise at 'M'. 'Still back at that? Still mysteries, Sarah?' At her agreement he said, still surprised, even she thought, a little annoyed, 'All right, then, I'll come back and we'll try to sort it out.'

———

The child came back first, though. When she came in softly and settled beside the bed, she seemed smaller than ever to Sarah's anxious gaze, and the blue eyes, behind the blue-rimmed glasses, were swollen.

'You believed me, didn't you? Really and truly believed me?' she said with a husky desperation that went to Sarah's heart. At her swift agreement Rose sighed. 'I wish you could talk and say why you know I'm right, because now everything's so mixed up I'm not sure about it myself any more, and my mother is furious. She says I'm getting to be a horrible little liar and maybe I need a good boarding school to straighten me out, and the doctor said that what I really needed was an understanding father.' She added gloomily, 'That made my mother madder than ever.

'You see he came.' She edged closer to Sarah's side. 'My mother was home quite early really and wearing her headache face so I was awfully quiet and I didn't like to tell her what had happened, only the doctor came and said this was a nice kettle of fish, wasn't it, and she wanted to know what he was talking about, so then she knew.

'She told me I was the absolute limit and the doctor said, "Oh, no, accidents will happen" and she said they shouldn't, not accidents like that anyway, and I said that it wasn't an accident, because it wasn't my yo-yo at all, though I didn't know where mine had gone. They both got cross, so I told them about Mr Phipps giving it to me and me playing with it a bit while he stood there, just to be polite, you see, only I didn't want it at all.' She paused and took a deep breath. 'He kept smiling and smiling all the time he stood there, and I didn't like it much, so I said I had to go and help Mrs Furlong and thank you very much for the nice yo-yo and he said it was a pleasure, and I went upstairs, and I never came down again till Mrs Laurence fell. I didn't!'

She stopped again, then said forlornly, 'But they don't believe me at all. At least, the doctor says maybe I'm speaking the truth and the yo-yo could have slipped out of my pocket on my way up, but it didn't, because I was holding it in my hand all the way, because Mr Phipps was watching me go up you see, and I didn't like to just shove it out of sight.'

She was silent again, gazing blankly into space. Then she said quietly, slowly, as though it were quite incredible, 'But now it's my yo-yo after all. The one with the big bit of paint gone. I told them about that and the doctor pulled a yo-yo out of his pocket and swung it in front of us and said, "This is it, Rose, and it has a piece of paint gone."' She shook her head so violently that the short brown hair flopped limply round her head. 'It's all wrong, because I saw this yo-yo on the ground and I picked it up, you see, and it wasn't mine. I let it drop again and I never saw it again, but now that one's gone and mine's the one that was on the ground. The doctor says so. He's shown it to me.'

She said, 'My mother says I'm a horrible little liar, and the doctor said oh no, perhaps she's honestly making a mistake, honestly thought it wasn't her yo-yo at all, you know, and she said, "Oh there you go again, making excuses for wrong-doers," and they started arguing all over again, and my mother told him he was utterly impossible, and I was tired and my head ached and I wished they'd stop it, so I said that she'd told me he was someone I could admire and respect and the finest person she'd ever met and what about that?

'Then she got madder than ever, and the doctor laughed.

He laughed and laughed and laughed and said, just like me, "And what about that?" and my mother said would I go away please, right this minute, before she wrung my neck, so I went.

'Mrs Oatland . . .' the desperation was back in her voice '. . . can't you please say why you believed me? Why you're sure there were two yo-yos?' and then she shook her head helplessly at Sarah's silence.

'Mrs Oatland,' she began again after a long silence, 'do you think that Mr Phipps doesn't like Mr Palmer? I mean, I've thought and thought about what he said when he was playing with that mirror that silly way and his voice was funny. Oh, I can't explain that, you know, but I kept thinking that he didn't like Mr Palmer at all.' Her soft voice held wonder. 'It was like saying, "Oh, I hate you, I wish you were dead." Do you understand what I mean?'

After Sarah's agreement she said, 'I think he was being cruel to Mrs Phipps you see. He called her an old cow, you know. He did, honest. And she cried, too. Oh, not about being called an old cow, but when he was speaking about seeing Mr Palmer dead and . . .'

'Rose, what are you saying?'

Sarah had never before heard Bragg speak in that fashion, the oozing murmur of voice given way to an authoritative, angry demand. She saw the child's thin body jump, saw the scared look in the blue eyes and then Bragg was in her sight. 'Just what are you saying to Mrs Oatland? What's this about Mr Palmer being dead? Why, you must be a dreadful child – trying to frighten her – you're always lying, so far as I can make out and. . .'

'I wasn't! It was a silly sort of game Mr Phipps was playing and I heard it. He was looking into a mirror and pretending he could see the future and that he was seeing Mr Palmer all dead.' Her voice rose shrilly over Bragg's attempts to soothe her, till finally the woman was listening in complete and absorbed silence.

When Rose was quiet again, Bragg said slowly, 'I've never before heard anything like it.' Now the oozing gentleness was back, for Rose this time, 'Oh, but my dear, you mustn't fuss about it all. People are strange sometimes. It was a rather cruel type of joke.'

'Just the same,' she added to Sarah when Rose had been firmly dismissed, 'I think it's a bit much, don't you? You know, I've always thought the pair of them didn't get on very well, and you can't tell me a man who really liked his wife would start telling her he could see her father lying dead. Mrs Oatland, does Mr Palmer know about this?' Bragg nodded. 'I hope he doesn't hear. It was just a bit of spite, best forgotten, don't you think?' Astonished, she said, 'You don't think so? Why ever not? Good heavens, if Mr Palmer got to hear of it, my dear, he'd be far from pleased. It wouldn't do at all because Valma told me the old man is going to set them up in a hotel of their own very shortly. She added anxiously, 'So you can see that it's important he doesn't hear that silly story. He'd be angry about it and it might spoil . . .' She sighed. 'Oh, dear, I wish people wouldn't be so childish. First there's Mrs Laurence and your niece and now there's Mr Phipps, and frankly I'd never have thought he'd stoop to that sort of child-ish taunting at all.'

She sat in frowning thought for a moment before asking, 'Do you think Rose is telling the truth?' She shook her head at Sarah's response. 'It just beats me.'

That was what Roderick Palmer said, when he came back to keep his promise to her. She could tell, by the way he was walking across the carpet, that he was tired or worried or both. It showed in his face, too. He looked as he'd done when he'd come to tell her about Esmay, with the plump pinkness seem-ing to have shrunken and faded.

'It just beats me, Sarah,' he said heavily. 'I'm not going to beat about the bush. I was listening to you and Nurse talking. Val seemed so upset over lunch I was glad to be out of the place. I thought for a minute or two that she was going to have hysterics on us, though why she's so upset when the fuss is all over I can't make out.' He made a little gesture as though dismissing the matter. 'But that aside, I came up to see you and heard you and Nurse.'

'It was a shock, Sarah, a helluva shock, and I don't like it a little bit. So that was what the kiddie overheard, was it? Murray pretending to look in the mirror and seeing me dropping dead tomorrow night – oh no, wait on – it'd be tonight, wouldn't it? Well, it's a pretty thing to say, isn't it? And what was he angry about, I'd like to know, that he was gazing into mirrors that way and seeing his wishes come true, because that was what he was doing, wasn't he?' At Sarah's agreement he said, 'I can't make it out. He'd known by then about my offer to set them up in a hotel together, so where do I stand now? Does it mean he doesn't want the hotel at all?'

He eyed her consideringly. 'So you think that's it, and that's damn interesting. Sarah, how I wish you'd get your tongue back! You seem to know more of what's going on in this house than the rest of us put together. That's because we all come and chatter our heads off without anyone breaking in and cutting us short. He smiled faintly. 'And then, of course, there's that talking wall of yours giving you a bit more information and . . .' The smile died. 'Sarah, I wonder how much that wall has told you. You told me, didn't you, that you knew Val and Murray had been discussing what would happen when I was dead. Were they wishing the event along, Sarah. Now be honest.'

She was, cruelly, because she saw the last of light and gentleness go from his eyes. He said bleakly, 'So that's that. They want the whole of my money – now. Is that it?' He nodded again at her agreement, then said in bewilderment, 'Why can't they be satisfied with what I had to offer? But you can't answer that, so we're stumped again, except, now, I remember. You didn't agree with me, did you, when I said before that working together would fix their marriage? Didn't you agree that I was stupid, something like that, anyway? Sarah, have you known all along they wanted desperately to get out of their marriage?'

She was honest, again, hoping desperately that he'd keep on the same subject, start putting two and two together, but all he said was a heavy-voiced, 'So they're hoping instead I'll drop dead and let them off the hook completely. They seemed happy enough over my offer though, that's what I can't understand. Oh, I suppose it seemed better than nothing, that's all, but now I don't know what to do for the best. Maybe it'd be best to let them go their own way for a bit, tell them to separate and see how they like it.'

Dismayingly, he said shortly, 'Forget it, Sarah. It's not your problem and I shouldn't be worrying you over it.' His smile was so obviously forced it was pitiful. 'Now look, I promised we'd play the word game again, didn't I? And you wanted a word with 'M'. It's not mysteries again, surely?'

Sarah hesitated. They seemed to get nowhere with the word, but it seemed best to concentrate on it rather than let him turn to some other word that could be even further away from the subject of murder. After a too-long hesitation she deliberately gave three winks.

He stared at her in silence a moment. 'Not "yes", not "no", so what the heck is it? Maybe? Perhaps? So I'm right. Now let's see, where does that land us. "Perhaps a mystery"?' He rolled the words round on his tongue twice, then smiled triumphantly. 'You mean there's something you want to talk about that might be a mystery and might not. Well, fine, but what is it? You know, Sarah, you and I, with a bit of practice at this, could finish up on the boards as one of those mind-reading acts.

'Is it something in this house? Right, that's one thing we've settled.' His voice was growing enthusiastic. 'Something about the wall?' he ventured abruptly and crowed in delight at her agreement. 'Something you've heard through the wall?'

Joyously she agreed again, and his smile broadened. 'Keep

on, Sarah,' he said, 'we'll get it yet. Now we know you've heard something through the wall that's puzzling you and needs an explanation. Right? Good, now what is it? The wall . . .' He half turned, gazing at it, then his smile died. He said slowly, 'It must've been Val and Murray you heard. Right again, aren't I? So it's something they have to say that's puzzled you and . . . worried you? So it has.

'Let's take it carefully, Sarah. For a start, was it about me? It was. Another thing settled. We're doing fine. Was it to do with this business of Murray looking in the glass and hoping to see me throwing a fit? It was. There's one thing about you, Sarah, you can't pull punches. No soft soaping facts is there, when it's only "yes" or "no" you can answer. All right, don't worry, I can take it.

'Where are we so far? Murray and Val have been talking about me and wishing me dead and there's something about it all that needs explaining and is worrying you. You've said a lot, Sarah, without saying a word.'

Ask, she was silently begging, if Murray didn't do anything more than wish your death? Ask if he didn't plan it down to the last detail. She was sure he would ask that and then the whole horrible story would come out to its last final detail and he'd have to believe it, and then, incredibly, he said, 'Well, of course, I know now what it is. You felt I had to know about it, didn't you? Right. You couldn't stand the idea of me sitting around making plans in all ignorance and have them blow up in my face, could you? All right, I know about it now, and you mustn't worry any more.'

Anger filled her at the absurdity of it. She wanted to remind him that something was a mystery, something needed explaining. As though he guessed, he went on blandly, 'You're wondering, of course, how they could agree to going on with my plans when they're so obviously at loggerheads and just want to be free of each other, and free with my cash, into the bargain. But there's no real mystery, Sarah. It's actually like I said before, they've talked a whole heap, but when it gets down to bedrock they think there's a slight chance they can make a go of this hotel, together, so they're putting a smiling face on any disappointment they feel and they're going right along with my plans.

'You stop worrying about it, Sarah,' he urged her, 'and now for pete's sake, let's take another word and get down to something pleasant – the sort of things you like yourself. Sarah, do you like music?'

Anger still filled her, fought with despair and left her too limp to answer anything. He looked at her in swift concern and said, 'I've tired you. I keep forgetting you're really a sick woman, Sarah, that's the trouble. I think we all do now. You're so much on the button, for all your silence, but this day's been a big strain on you, hasn't it, with us all badgering you and telling you our troubles . . .' He shuffled to his feet and stood looking down at her. 'I'll go away again, Sarah. You get to sleep.'

Sleep, she thought resentfully, and rage came back, because, just through his refusal to go on asking questions – that really mattered – both of them might be sleeping for ever very shortly.

'Auntie!'

The one word had the ring of authority, the coldness of a determination not to be baulked. Reluctantly Sarah heard it and more reluctantly opened her eyes, dismayed by the sight of Gwenyth, rigidly upright, in the bedside chair.

It wasn't going to be the usual sort of visit, Sarah thought wearily. Gwenyth was seated for the first time. That meant there was a lot to be said, and she intended to say it without interference from anyone.

Resentfully Sarah wondered where Bragg was, why the wretched woman didn't come and save her patient from further badgering, but Gwenyth said, a trifle smugly, 'I had the doctor's permission to come and see you. To tell you how Esmay is. I've been down to the hospital to see her.'

It was the last thing Sarah would have expected. She had never imagined Gwenyth in the role of comforting the sick. The thought of it, and Esmay's reaction to it, was tantalising, but the explanation for the visit was given with the burst out, 'It was judgement on her. That's what I told her. Judgement.'

I bet you did, Sarah thought in amusement.

The voice was fraught with anger and impatience. 'You wouldn't believe it, Auntie, but she came here first thing this morning, to try and get you alone and make you give in to selling her some of your things – the best of them,' she added bitterly. 'I knew she'd try that, and I came myself, and though it wasn't my doing, we started arguing.' Now virtue smugged her voice. 'Nurse was quite right in making us both leave. At least, telling us to leave. She said we were disturbing you and frightening you as you would be able to hear us quite plainly. Naturally I left at once, but Mrs Laurence . . .' the voice choked on the name '. . . actually hid herself in the broom cupboard by the stairs. Hid there, for two solid hours. She claims it was because she knew I'd try to sneak back in before she could see you herself.'

Sarah was getting bored. She didn't want to listen to the saga of Esmay's sins, or to any more talk of the furniture. If she'd had a tongue she would have said crudely that Gwenyth might as well go home and sit and wait for the morning, when the lot of it would be hers in any case. Then abruptly she was fully awake, again, awake and alert and wondering and hopeful, because Gwenyth's voice was confiding, 'Auntie, there's something odd about that accident. Oh well, the word "odd" is wrong, I expect, but there's something "unpleasant", perhaps I mean. Oh, and not actually about the accident itself, you see . . .'

For heaven's sake, Sarah thought impatiently, does she know what she *does* mean?

Gwenyth went on, her voice sinking so low that Sarah barely caught the words. 'I told Esmay the child was taking things very badly and claiming it wasn't her yo-yo on the stairs, which was naturally all nonsense, and all of a sudden Esmay – really, Auntie, for someone who'd just broken her leg and had it set and put in plaster she's the most vocal creature I've ever struck – cried out, "But look here, that wretched infant wasn't on the stairs at all," which sounded a lot of nonsense.

'Then she pointed out that all of us – herself and Nurse and Mr Palmer and me were all on those stairs, moving around and arguing and that, and none of us so much as stepped on the wretched yo-yo, and then Esmay nicked into the broom cupboard and hid. You'd think she was proud of it, Auntie. She hasn't a scrap of shame about it! But she went in there and kept the door a little open so she could see if I came back – so she said. And she claims that the child wasn't on the stairs at all. Mrs Furlong came down and went up again just a little while after I'd gone and Nurse did the same and there wasn't anyone else except Mr Phipps. He went up and stayed up there talking to Nurse. Esmay could hear him. That was when she decided to come out. She said she thought she'd better, while he was up there, so there was no danger of him popping out his door if she came out later.

'She didn't want to be caught, though considering the way she seems proud of hiding there, I shouldn't have thought it would have worried her one scrap. But out she came and started up the stairs and . . . down she fell.

'So . . .' Her voice dropped again, and now Sarah could hear the words only brokenly. 'he must have . . . isn't that odd . . . his pocket . . . would you think? But fancy keeping quiet? Just shows, doesn't it? I call it mean letting a child . . . she's only a few months over eleven . . . not at all fair. I must say, it's mean.'

She drew back a little and her voice strengthened again so that the words came clearly. 'Esmay was furious about it. After all, it's obvious. If the wretched thing had been there on the stairs before, one of us or Nurse or Mrs Furlong would have crashed on it, so it just wasn't there at all, d'you see, Auntie? It had to be Mr Phipps himself who dropped it, when he went upstairs. Oh, I expect he was terribly upset and frightened enough not to admit to it, but letting a child take the blame isn't nice, is it?'

Sarah would have loved to have been able to say, No, but murder isn't nice, either, is it, Gwenyth? and watch the high colour fade and the rigid back bow under the shock.

She simply lay there, and ridiculously, could feel only a complacent triumph at the thought of the way Murray and Valma were having their plans twisted out of shape completely and utterly, without them knowing. They wouldn't know, she reflected, till it was too late and at that, all the complacent triumph was gone, because what was the use of them being caught and taken to prison, when it was too late for herself and Roderick Palmer?

Her world now was filled with fragmentary little pictures: Murray Phipps smiling eternally; a small red yo-yo, with a big patch of paint gone, lying on the stairs; Esmay huddled in a cupboard with one eye to a crack of open door; Esmay finding that old key to the house and sneaking in first thing in the morning; her own self, after David's death, going through the accumulation of rubbish David had hoarded; and Esmay coming up the stairs unheard, after using that key . . .

All the pictures shattered and broke, leaving a bright vacuum that was filled again with one other picture: Esmay laughing at Sarah's fright that day and presenting her with a parcel, telling her it was to keep her wits from going rusty. She'd been impatient when she'd unwrapped the Scrabble game, though she'd dutifully played with Esmay whenever the latter had come and brought out the box, but it had never really interested her. She'd never been a person who liked word games.

Now though, it was different. A word game had given her some communication with the world, and if she could only get hold of the Scrabble box – excitement and hope soared again – there were all those little wooden squares with letters that could be held up in front of her, and nodded to, so that a visitor could form a word she wanted to talk about, a word like 'murder'.

When Bragg came back Sarah was sure the woman would notice her excitement and seek the cause of it, but Bragg seemed distracted, though now she no longer talked of the coming evening and her theatre visit. She was silent for once, not even the usual soothing syrup of words trickling steadily over the useless human dough under her hands.

But when her patient was settled again to Bragg's satisfaction, the younger woman sat down heavily in the bedside chair, gazing into space, hands limp in her lap, as silent and motionless as Sarah herself. It wasn't till some noise sounded somewhere in the house that she started, life and alertness coming back to her blank gaze, and movement to her hands. One moved to smooth at the already smooth sheet under Sarah's chin, and her voice, determinedly gentle and bright again, asked, 'Is there anything else you want, Mrs Oatland?' When Sarah gave a single wink she looked disconcerted, even annoyed, and murmured, 'My, you're getting demanding these days, aren't you? You have poor Mr Palmer in quite a fuss trying to make out all you want and now . . . oh well, I'd better try this word game of his, I suppose. What letter is it you want?'

She was faster than Roderick and almost missed Sarah's wink at the letter 'S', and then she simply sat staring at Sarah, face blank, as though she were unable to think of even one word that began with the letter, then she began muttering, as though more to herself than Sarah, 'Soap and sausages, well, you couldn't eat those anyway, and there's sand and seat, which couldn't apply. There's sheets too, but I've just given you fresh ones, and there's ships, which would be plain non-sense. And there's . . .' Her gaze roamed slowly round the room and brightened. 'There's shepherdess too, isn't there? The ones that niece of yours was making all the fuss about a while back. Is it the shepherdess you want? Hidden away out of sight, maybe? No? Well then, is it one of your possessions, this thing beginning with "S"?'

Good Bragg, Sarah congratulated her silently. Wonderful Bragg. Now try again. Her eyes encouraged her as she gave agreement to the question.

Now Bragg was interested. Half smiling, she leaned forward and started reciting, her gaze on Sarah for some sign she was guessing right, 'Sofa and settee? – that's a lovely one in the downstairs lounge, dear – I'd love it myself. Set of china? Set of cutlery? Does set come into it at all? Oh, it doesn't – well, we can forget that, then. Now wait on, let's do it this way . . .' she leaned closer still, half laughing now '. . . you give me the second letter of the word. So it's "C",' she cried in delight at the quick wink at the third letter. 'But my dear, I can't think what that can be. Scotch? Well no, I didn't think it would be, and surely it's not scouring powder!' Her laugh rang out. 'Oh wait, give me the third letter. That's the best way. Here we go again.' Rapidly she began to recite the letters once more. 'Scr . .' she said triumphantly at the quick wink. 'Well, I don't know, that makes it worse, I can't think of a single thing, so you'll just have to give me the next letter.'

For a little there was silence. Bragg's lips moved, mouthing over the letters one by one, then she cried tiumphantly, 'Why, you're clever! It's Scrabble, isn't it? You want to play a game, but not chess like the doctor said. You want the Scrabble board?' She was already on her feet. 'You wait, I'll find it.' Then her expression fell. 'But there won't be much time tonight. I'm supposed to be going out.'

Slowly she sat down again. She said quietly, 'Mrs Oatland, I don't think I really want to go, but how can I refuse now? Just the same, I can't think the same of him, or Mrs Phipps either, because she must know, too, and I think they've been dreadfully unfair. Mind you, he was probably afraid of a real row, and maybe Mrs Laurence sueing him for damages, come to that, but . . . I thought better of them both. Of course it's easy to blame a child, and say to yourself, 'Oh a child will for-get about it and adults won't say anything to bring the subject up again,' but the point is she has to live with the feeling of guilt and the knowledge she's being blamed unjustly and that's not right at all.

'You see, Mrs Laurence rang up from the hospital. She wanted to speak to you really but, as I pointed out, the phone's not in here, and I couldn't shift you to it – that's something, my dear, we must get fixed, but now you can hear friends could phone and chatter to you even if they can't see your answers.' She drew a long breath. 'But she told me it was Phipps who dropped that yo-yo. He had to, because the child wasn't there to do it.

'You know, she worried me. About that, but something else, too. She told me to watch out, that next thing I'd be get-ting blamed for a mistake that one of the Phippses had made. "You leave Sarah to that woman and if there's a muddle she'll never admit it," is what Mrs Laurence said. Oh, don't you worry now, there's nothing to muddle really, but I've been remembering the way you said you didn't want Mrs Phipps in here and realising you know a lot of what's been going on in this place. You probably sum us all up much better than other people do, because you've so much time. You don't trust Valma Phipps at all, do you?'

She shook her head at the answer. 'It seems funny you felt like that, when I thought her a good friend and . . . oh well, leave it, my dear. She can't muddle anything tonight. There'll be nothing to muddle, I promise you, and now all the plans are made I can hardly refuse to go, but I shan't leave you to her again. I promise you that.'

Sarah, in mockery, wondered what she would say if her patient, with answering brightness, gave back, 'But there'll be no need, my dear. I shan't be here – after tonight.'

Sarah had never known anything so tiring as the hour that followed. She had been so sure that with the Scrabble board and letters in front of her she could get through to Bragg, make her understand that this evening she mustn't go out, make her understand that murder was planned in the house, but when the woman finally came back with the Scrabble board, she had only one thought in mind, that Sarah wanted to play the game. She spread out the board and kept talking, striving to find the best way of letting Sarah join in, and then finally her face clouded and her eyes dulled with disappointment and annoyance. She said tartly, 'But you're taking no interest at all,' and when Sarah gave no sign to that, she asked, 'But you said you wanted the Scrabble, didn't you?'

At Sarah's agreement, she said, 'Well, here it is. Don't you want to play? You don't! Why did you want it then?' she asked pettily, pushing it aside, looking down at the board in disappointment as Sarah lay unmoving.

Slowly her expression cleared. She started to laugh. She said, as she'd done before, 'Why, you clever thing! It's the letters you want, isn't it? It's the word game again. I can set out the letters in rows in front of you and point and you can give me a wink when I've reached the one you want? Just a version of what I was doing before – running through the alphabet for each letter, isn't it? All right then, we'll fix it that way. Now what letter do we start with?" Rapidly her finger went over the squares and stopped at 'M'. 'Oh, I know that one. It's mysteries, isn't it? Mr Palmer is still trying to think what you mean by that. All right, we'll run down the letters again. Why, it's "M" again. Now for the second letter.' Her hand moved swiftly. 'That's "U". Now for the third. That's "R".' She smiled in delight. 'Now take it again. Oh, we have a "D" this time. That's murd . . . goodness, it's not murder, is it?'

At Sarah's one single, triumphant wink, Bragg's mouth opened and stayed open in astonishment, while Sarah, keyed now to high excitement, was silently willing her to hurry up, to start running down the letters again to find another word. This time, Sarah was deciding, she would make the word 'Phipps', and surely Bragg would understand then that murder and mystery and Phipps were all connected and again and again one plump white finger would run over the little letters in front of them till the whole story was out.

Then Bragg was laughing. She was saying, 'Well, you are a one! Getting along nicely, aren't you? You'll have us all chasing up and down and all over the town soon. All right my dear, I know now, Mrs Furlong did tell me you were a great one for books. You must have missed them dreadfully of course. Well, first thing Monday I'll go to the library and get out some really good murder mysteries for you. Tomorrow I'll go through the books here, too and try to find something to keep you going.' One hand was ruthlessly spinning the little wooden letters towards their box again. 'And now I'll have to go and get dressed up. Mrs Phipps will be up later, but don't you fret, my dear, there'll be no muddling here tonight.'

Not muddling, Sarah reflected. Just murder. That's all there'll be tonight, you stupid, unheeding creature.

CHAPTER 13

Roderick came back before Bragg was gone, and Sarah knew, as soon as he entered her room, that worry still sat, like an ugly gnome on his shoulders, bowing them. He gave her a quick smile as he sat down and said, 'So you're getting bossy, Sarah, and I'm a bit of a fool. Funny thing, but I never thought of mystery books at all, and if I'd had to choose a book for you I'd have plumped for a nice cosy romance, which just shows how much I know about you. Oh well, I'll soon know all your likes and dislikes, now we've got the Scrabble board to talk with. That was a very good piece of thinking on your part, Sarah. Lord, the way your wits are ticking over, you'll be on the move again soon.

'But you know you had me in a real puzzle.' He wagged a reproving finger under her nose. 'I kept thinking of that word "mystery", and you saying there was one in the house – never thinking of course of mystery books you have lying round the place – and I puzzled and puzzled and started trying to tie all sorts of ends together till I had a really complicated knot. It just shows you how you can try and make toffee out of straw and glue. Now don't you laugh at me, because it's your doing, tying me up in puzzles that way, but I even started thinking of that business of Mrs Laurence's fall and little Rose claiming Murray had another yo-yo, and then that bit about him saying Rose would come in handy in case of an accident in the place – and good Lord – now don't you dare laugh, Sarah – but I got to thinking, What if Murray meant Rose would be handy to take the blame in case there was an accident round here? See how you'd got me in a flap? Oh, I admit it didn't make sense, but it was all your insistence on mysteries in the house, and Murray and that nonsense about the mirror, and I know this is a terrible thing to say, Sarah, but I got to thinking – dear heaven – he and Val would like me out of the way and what if that yo-yo was meant for me to trip over, with the child taking the blame for leaving it about?

'You see what a muddle I was getting into? Beats your blessed mystery books, doesn't it? I'm an old fool.' Then at Sarah's double wink, he smiled, 'You needn't try to tell me I'm not. I am and I know it, but I was worried about Val and Murray, the whole set-up, and then your talk of mysteries and Rose and her saying the yo-yo wasn't hers and all that . . .' His voice trailed off. He said, straightening, smiling again, 'I'll go and get that Scrabble box, Sarah, and then we'll have a bit of a talk till Val comes up to sit with you. She insists I have an early night, says I look tired out, and for once she's about right.' There was a faint wistfulness that jarred on Sarah. 'Nice sometimes to have someone fuss over one a bit, isn't it?' Then he laughed. 'But of course you get a bit too much fussing, don't you? Here's the box, Sarah. Now I'll spread out the letters for you. What do you want to talk about?'

It was no good any more clinging to the word 'murder', she reflected helplessly. 'Murder' and 'mystery' were both disposed of now, to everyone's satisfaction. She didn't know what word to use. Desperation and disappointment had already tired her unbearably. She could feel herself sliding down into the depths of hopelessness, where she would be content to let events take their course as quickly as possible. She tried to tell herself that that reflection was ridiculous, and one she should be ashamed of, but it was no good. Like Roderick, she was tired out and needed an early night . . .

A great wave of new shock rolled back to bring her up fighting again. She thought of those words, of Roderick speaking, of Val fussing over him and she knew what was going to happen. He'd be given a hot drink, dosed with sleeping tablets, and seen off to bed.

He'll never wake up, she told herself. Neither will I. Gas is going to flow through all this house. She was so certain of it that in her imagination she could almost smell the gas already; could almost feel it writhing invisibly through the corners and angles of her home, drifting up the stairs and turning the corner to her own room, to come close and touch her face.

She realised dimly that Roderick's stubby finger was pointing at the letters in front of her, but she didn't know what to do. The one word she had clung to – that important word 'murder' – had failed her, and there seemed no other. Then abruptly she winked.

'"Y",' he said eagerly, 'and next, Sarah?' and his finger went jabbing, till it stopped at 'O', and stayed there. 'Yo-yo, Sarah?' he asked and at her wink, his hand dropped from the board.

'I wonder why you want to talk about that?' He was looking at her puzzled, 'I'm not imagining things any more, if that's what's worrying you. I mean, that silly business of me imagining Murray could ever have tried his hand at getting rid of me just doesn't add up at all. Are you worried about Rose taking the blame?'

At her sharp wink he nodded, 'So that's it. You said before you thought there were two yo-yos. Are you still on that tack?' He shrugged at her agreement. 'But it's not possible – oh, you reckon it is?' Now surprise was in his face, and something else too that she couldn't grasp, but something that altered the very shape of his face, making it seem to droop sadly round the mouth. 'Sarah, tell me this, honestly – and no guesses – I want plain honesty. Do you know, for a dead certainty, that there were two yo-yos?'

The droop to his mouth seemed to grow at her answer. 'Then, Sarah, do you mean you think Murray was the one who dropped it?' He said shortly, 'That's nonsense,' but his eyes were bleak and frightened, she realised, and hope and triumph came welling back.

'Look here, Sarah, I can't leave it at that.' Now his voice was determined. 'Some way I have to get out of you what all this is about. So far I've got there were two yo-yos and you're sure Murray dropped the one that caused the accident. Well, that's settled, then. Now we head for something else. Did he do it deliberately? My God, Sarah, what are you saying?' Now the monotonous voice was harsh and as frightened as the eyes behind his dark, rimmed spectacles. 'Was it meant for me?'

She knew her answer bewildered him. He said slowly, 'It wasn't. But Sarah, that doesn't make sense at all. Why would a grown man drop a yo-yo on the stairway deliberately – for fun? Just to see someone take a tumble for the enjoyment he'd get out of it? No, you agree with me there at least. Of course he wouldn't. So why would he? Sarah, do you mean he intended your friend, Esmay, to take that tumble?'

He simply stared at her and said in that same harsh voice, 'That's ridiculous, Sarah. Murray doesn't even know the damn woman. Now look here . . .' He sat there, his hands pulling at one another till she could have screamed with impatience at him. Finally he said, 'So that's it, but . . . good God, Sarah, it's outrageous. I mean, you've got some good pieces, some fine pieces, actually, stuff I'd rather like to have myself if you wanted to sell, and granted Murray knows plenty of dealers and he's taken commissions from them in the past, but to send someone flying down the stairs just so he can have a free hand here to talk you into selling to some dealer he knows for the commission on it, it's . . .'

He sat there in silence, leaving her bewildered. She tried to make sense of his words, and couldn't. She seized at last on the word 'dealer', her mind scurrying round and round it, darting at it, darting away and trying to make something of its peculiarities before she really bit into it. When at last she did, the whole thing was so absurd she wanted to laugh and instead she cried, from sheer desperation.

The tears welled from her eyes and fell heedlessly down her cheeks, soaking into pillows and sheets while she reflected on the fact that Murray had evidently taken commissions from furniture dealers in the past. And now, with time running out for herself and Roderick, Roderick had made the mistake of thinking that Murray, in need of money, had got rid of Esmay so he'd have a free hand – so he and Valma would have – to coax her into selling to dealers he'd bring to the place.

You fool, the welling tears reproached, but all Roderick Palmer could see was the tears. He jumped up, aghast and the carefully laid out letters were scattered all over the bed as he called for Bragg, as he stood helplessly by the bed, repeating, 'I'm sorry, Sarah, I'm sorry. I'm really sorry. But it's impossible, you know. You must have been worried sick, but it's impossible. Lord, we're crazy, both of us, the things we can think about Murray. Me, thinking he could plan to get rid of me, and you thinking he could shoot your friend Esmay down the stairs just for a good slice of commission on your furniture. Lord, we're crazy to think such things.'

Then, very quietly, so that the hurrying Bragg didn't hear, he added, 'But Sarah, oh my God, there must be something really bad about Murray, something we've both seen, for us ever to think that way at all.'

Valma Phipps didn't bring her knitting. She came in quite silently and slipped into the bedside chair, almost without being noticed. Then she sat, gazing towards the window, face averted from Sarah.

So she has that much shame, Sarah reflected, but she wished the younger woman would speak and break the silence that seemed to be pressing intolerably on the house.

Bragg hadn't wanted to go. It had been so plain that Murray Phipps, coming upstairs to escort her down, had stood in the doorway of Sarah's room and asked reproachfully, 'Don't you want to come, Cornelia? The old lady won't come to any harm. It'll actually be a change for her to be left to someone else. Won't it, Mrs Oatland?' He had come to the bedside and bent over Sarah and smiled at her.

You look like a wax mannikin, she had told him silently, with slicked back hair and a permanent fixed smile, and probably if we saw inside you you'd have a little wax blob instead of a heart.

She and Valma had remained in silence, listening to the steps, Murray's light and almost silent, Bragg's heavy-footed even in light black pumps instead of her usual heavy hospital shoes. And the silence grew and grew, while the younger woman sat with the averted face.

Then at last – and Sarah knew that the strain had been as great for Valma as for herself and that now the younger woman must talk or scream or run – she said, 'You've been very clever. Too clever, and it's absurd to think that an old helpless woman like you can do so much. First you overhear us and then you wriggle and struggle and nearly tell everything, trying to talk of murder and mysteries, but you didn't manage it, did you, for all your smartness, and you needn't think, you know, that afterwards anyone is going to wonder, because they've written those words right off as nothing but you wanting some books read to you, and there'll be no hint of anything but accident anyway, so you needn't think anything will come out afterwards, because it won't, and even if it did it wouldn't do you any good, would it?'

She added, 'Roderick is lying down,' and was silent again.

After a little she began, as though she were carefully checking everything and trying to seek reassurance that all would go well. 'That Mrs Abcons is in her own flat, and there'll be no trouble from there, because the wall between her flat and the rest of the house deadens everything. We've tried it, you know, several times, and it's so, but of course you must know that for yourself because you put it there, didn't you? But she's there and the child won't come up here again. She's not allowed to. She's forbidden to come up here alone. She can only come up when Nurse or Mrs Furlong escorts her up to help in the kitchen or something, so you see she won't be hanging around either. So there's no one to interfere in any way at all.'

She said again, 'Roderick's lying down downstairs.'

She stood up abruptly. She said, surprisingly, confusing Sarah utterly, 'He'll be up again later, so I'm going to hide that wretched Scrabble board. You're too clever, and you can't be trusted, so I'm putting it right away, so you can't use it when he comes up.'

But he wasn't coming up, Sarah thought helplessly. He was going to have a hot drink and sleeping tablets and go to sleep down there in his room and never wake up again because the gas had overpowered him.

Then Valma said, further confusing Sarah, 'In a little while I'm going to have a migraine.'

Sarah felt wild hysteria rising in her. It sounded so absurd, as though the woman was discussing a cup of tea, or a shower bath.

Valma added, picking up the Scrabble box, 'I'll hide this, then I'll come back and then I must have a migraine,' and went from Sarah's sight, her steps soft and almost soundless on the carpet. In a little while she came back. She sounded breathless now. 'I had to think of a place that seemed reasonable,' she explained carefully, 'so that it wouldn't look as though it was hidden, just put out of the road for the moment. We can't have any more mistakes. There was nearly one about the yo-yo, you know.'

She sat down again. When she spoke, there was a tremble in her voice. Sarah, watching her, saw the nervous quiver at the corner of the pale mouth too and wished she had the use of her tongue, for two brief minutes. She was sure that given that she could have broken the woman into running, into screaming, into sheer panic, but secure in the knowledge that Sarah couldn't upbraid her, or scream, or argue, or do anything at all, Valma went on, trying, Sarah knew, to push aside that silence covering the house. 'It was simple, you know, to take the yo-yo out of Rose's pocket again and we never noticed, till after, that hers had a big piece of paint missing. We nearly slipped up, but Murray noticed it. In time.'

She said again, 'Roderick's lying down.'

Why this insistence on that point, Sarah wondered. She was utterly confused now. She couldn't make sense of what was happening. Roderick was lying down. She had expected that, but at any minute, apparently, Valma was going to get sick, and Roderick was going to come upstairs . . .

But, of course, she realised triumphantly, Valma was going to have her migraine and go down and say she could no longer sit with Sarah. Roderick would be roused, from half slumber, and sent upstairs to Sarah . . .

Roused, she remembered. He was lying down now. He'd come up and she knew he'd be half asleep, that he'd have had sleeping tablets.

She remembered something else – Rose saying that Phipps had talked to Bragg of the old man's pipe smoking, coupling it with his habit of taking sleeping tablets. Saying how bad it was.

She tried to connect it all up and failed. There was only the hazy certainty that Roderick would be half asleep when he arrived at her side again. He wouldn't be likely to want to play the word game again – or would he? He might, she reflected, in an effort to keep awake, so a tiny sliver of hope remained to be grasped at there.

For the rest, she didn't know. She could only remember Murray Phipps saying that she and Roderick had to be dealt with together, and tonight they'd be together, a helpless old woman and a man half asleep.

But it won't work, she told herself impatiently. It's impossible. Valma would smell the gas down there. Even if she's sick, she'd have to smell it and wake and get out or die herself. Or . . . when you had a migraine you were very ill, Sarah remembered. Would a woman in that condition, who might have taken some dope, too, remember, staggering out of a house full of gas, that there were two other people upstairs?

She wasn't going to, Sarah knew. Later on Valma would say she'd forgotten and had stumbled out of the house only to collapse completely, and when she'd come round . . .

But a thousand things could go wrong, Sarah reflected with that same impatience. Josie and Rose would smell the gas, too. The whole thing was impossible, and yet . . . tonight a helpless old woman and a man half asleep would be alone in her warm quiet room and Phipps had said they had to be disposed of, like so much unwanted refuse, together.

———

CHAPTER 14

Cornelia Bragg said, 'I'd like to ring the house before we go in.'

'Ring . . . the house?'

'It's not an unreasonable thing to do, is it?' she said tartly. She felt strangely uneasy. Part of it, she knew, was due to the new dress. It had been a sad mistake. It was too tight across her hips for one thing, and was going to be a mess of wrinkles after sitting for three hours in the theatre, so that she was going to look a freak. He wouldn't be likely to want to take her to coffee or supper afterwards, but she didn't care about that. A lot of her unease was due to the fact she'd seen him in a new light that afternoon. The business of the accident and Rose Abcons was still a nasty taste in her mouth. She knew it always would be. It was even difficult to keep her tongue quiet right now and not tell him that she knew.

She was uneasy about her old dear, too. She kept remembering Sarah's dislike of Valma Phipps, her fear of some muddling, some danger happening through Valma.

She thought, I shouldn't have come. All round, whichever way I look at it, it's going to be a miserable evening.

She said again, more tartly still, 'It's not an unreasonable thing to do, is it?'

She wished he'd stop smiling. It was getting on her nerves. He'd smiled through having his foot trodden on; through the taxi driver overcharging them; through being pushed and jostled in the theatre foyer; and he was going on smiling over his quite obvious annoyance with her request.

'I was only thinking,' he explained patiently, 'that if the old lady's gone to sleep the phone will wake her. In any case it's barely half an hour since we left, and Cornelia, we can't phone now! The show's going to start. Now come along.' He was bustling her along, though she tried to hold back. 'We'll phone at the first interval. Come along, come along now, we'll phone later,' he assured her smilingly.

The smile remained – a white blur of teeth in the dimness beside her – when the curtain went up on the first act.

'What are you brooding about, pet?'

Josie Abcons put down her book, looking across the room to the child curled up in the big basket chair. 'You're not reading that book at all. You're not doing anything but brood. Is it . . .' She hesitated, then went on carefully. 'Is it about that silly yo-yo?'

Rose uncurled her tall, skinny body. She said flatly, 'I was wondering if he's dead. In there. Dead. Like he said. That was what I was thinking about.'

'What, oh oh, Rose! That business of the mirror again? You're impossible! We told you it was a lot of silliness. I told you Mr Phipps was going out, so there could be no . . .'

'I don't like Mr Phipps. He says all sorts of things. He lied about that yo-yo.' Now her cheeks were flushed with temper and she was trembling in sheer rage. 'I hate him! I do, so there! And he said Mr Palmer was going to die just like he hoped it would really happen. He did, so there. I think . . . I don't care if you're cross . . . I think he put that yo-yo there himself, so Mr Palmer would fall down – all the way down – and break his neck and be dead, just like he saw in that mirror!'

Josie Abcons stood up. She said quietly, 'Rose, go straight to bed. This instant, please! You're not to speak another word till the morning. That's final.'

Roderick was very tired. He came in almost stumblingly, and his hair was ruffled. It should have made him look younger, but instead he looked older, just an old, tired man who was going to be no help at all.

He settled himself into the chair and said apologetically, 'Val's really off-colour, Sarah. She says she just wants to lie down and die. Her mother used to get this way with headaches, too. Best thing was to leave her alone. That's what Val says she wants, too, so I'll take over up here.' He yawned widely, 'Good lord, excuse that.' He promptly yawned again. 'Val was right about me being tired out, but I'm not too tired to take over up here, Sarah.

'Now look, where's that box of Scrabble? That will help keep me awake. You know, I did think perhaps I ought to get hold of Bragg and tell her to come back, but it seemed absurd.' Her rising hope plummeted again and he went on, 'It's only for a couple of hours anyway, and you'll probably drop off yourself. Anyway I didn't know the theatre. I asked Val and she didn't, either.'

He was searching round her room. His voice rose in pettish anoyance. 'Sarah, I can't find the box anywhere. Has it been taken out of the room?' He came back to the bedside. At her single wink he frowned, 'Well that was a silly thing to do, I must say. That'll be Nurse, I suppose. Always tidying up these nurses. They can't stand anything alien in a sick room. Just plain nonsense. Oh well, I've another idea. Look, I'll get a big piece of paper and write the letters on it. That's easier than yapping my way through the alphabet all the time. I won't be long.'

She lay there, waiting, trying to think what word to use to catch and hold his attention, then remembered the result of his last coming. They hadn't finished that talk at all before she'd dissolved into tears and Bragg had come and he'd gone away.

When he came back, triumphantly holding up the sheet of

scribbled-over paper for her to see, she let his finger touch the 'Y' before she winked. Instantly he frowned. He said quietly, 'Not yo-yo, Sarah?' At her agreement he shook his head. 'No, we're not going to talk about that any more. Oh, I'm not hiding my head in the sand. There's something wrong about Murray. I've always known that, but the rest, that's sheer imagination. We neither of us like him or trust him, and we've both too much damn time on our hands. That's our trouble, my dear. Too much time and too much imagination and too much dislike of a person can lead anyone astray.' He patted her shoulder. 'And then you've had murder and mysteries and your love of books in your head, too, and you've been practically writing a mystery story lying there in bed.

'But it won't do, Sarah. In fairness to Murray we've got to draw a line somewhere. So no more about that damn yo-yo. Think of another word, there's a good girl.'

I won't, she thought rebelliously, but she knew she must or else he'd put the sheet of paper aside and there'd be no communication at all. Anything was better than that, and better than him falling asleep.

Sleep, she thought, and realised that in her hands now was a chance to send a message. She waited impatiently while his finger travelled up and down, till he'd spelt out the words, 'Don't sleep.'

He stared at her in astonishment, then burst out laughing. 'I'm yawning my head off, aren't I? I'm sorry, Sarah, but you'll go off yourself soon.' He added slowly, 'I feel terrible, to tell the honest truth. If I knew where that nurse of yours was . . .' He stopped. 'One wink, Sarah? You know, do you? All right, then, spell it out and I'll try and get her back, though it doesn't seem very fair, does it?'

This was no time for fairness, she wanted to cry. Bragg had to come back and her eye went winking its signal as it followed his finger's travelling over the letters.

He stood up then, and yawned again. He said, 'All right,

Sarah, the Davos Theatre. I'll ring them and get the message through. Oh, my God.' He stumbled against the bed. 'I'm tired, my dear. I'm so damn tired I can hardly stand.'

And slowly, while she looked on in despair, he gently sat down again in the chair beside her, as gently rested back in it, as gently closed his eyes.

Incredibly, horribly, a snore filled the room.

———

CHAPTER 15

Gwenyth sat upright beside the bed. She said coldly, 'My mother used to say no lady lost her temper.'

Esmay gave back comfortably, 'I never wanted to be a lady. Always sounds to me of tight corsets and good works and giving the clergy seeded cake in the parlour. Now look here, Gwenyth, let me say my piece. You want some of Sarah's furniture, and so do I, and if I know anything both of us are going to lose it, so we'd better call a truce and get to work to beat this Phipps.

'Oh, do be quiet!' she added impatiently. 'I've a lot to say and my leg's on fire and I have more bruises than I have bones. You try falling downstairs and see what you feel like! Where was I, oh well, about this Phipps. Now look here, I told you before he must have dropped that blessed thing himself and now I'm sure he did it on purpose.

'Oh, for goodness sake! Shut your mouth, I can see your tonsils from here. I've been thinking a lot. Nothing else to do except think of my leg and bruises or think of Phipps and the yo-yo, so I thought, and the more I thought, the more I didn't like it. He was stickybeaking, you know, when we were having that spat on the stairs. He and his father-in-law – nice looking fellow that, but never mind – were standing there listening too, and I wouldn't mind betting Phipps knew where I headed when you left.

'So what if he did? I think he waited till lunch time, then

marched upstairs, knowing full well I'd take the chance of nicking out of my cupboard while the coast was clear, and pretending I'd just come in. He was talking away upstairs, stopping any of them coming down, don't you see, and taking the toss he'd prepared for me.

'Well, I took it,' she said bleakly. 'Oh, don't interrupt. Of course, you don't see, but when I thought about it all I couldn't see any reason for him wanting me out of the way. He wasn't my nephew after my millions and he hadn't put me in the family way – stop that idiotic cackling! They're the best possible reasons for throwing someone downstairs. Then you popped into my head and I thought, What if he's after the furniture like Gwenyth and myself, and that seemed nonsense because even an ego-ridden creature like that doesn't go round breaking people's legs just for furniture he could buy elsewhere, even if he had to pay a bit more cash for it.

'Cash, I thought, because that man has money-mad eyes. And you needn't smirk. He has. He's a real greedy type. I may have been married only once, Gwenyth but, believe me, I've known a lot of men and known them well and that Phipps is a greedy grasper. I thought to myself that furniture had other possibilities to someone after cash. If he acted as a dealer's agent he could net himself a nice fat commission on all that stuff of Sarah's.

'See what comes of having a good think? He's there in the house and his wife has been trying to make herself pleasant and with me out of the way they could easily – with Bragg co-opted to help and she likes them, the silly fool – have you pushed out into the cold and then they'd have a free hand.

'So I used my phone here to ring a dealer I know and just asked him if he'd ever heard the name Phipps round the dealer's room. I had the answer a while back and rang you to come here and see me. He's been a dealer's agent before, all right.

'Oh, stop pulling faces,' she snapped impatiently. 'It might sound ruthless, but you'd be surprised what a man like that'd do for money. Can you explain that yo-yo business any other way? I can't for the life of me imagine a man of that type playing with yo-yos. It's nonsense.

'So it's up to you. I'm stuck here, and they'll cut you out too if they get a chance. Best way is for us to call a truce and for you to go to Sarah and tell her we'd like to share things out without argument, then at least we'll be ahead of him.'

She jabbed a finger towards the silent Gwenyth. 'And you'd better hurry round. Tonight. That pair won't lose any time. He'll have a dealer round before you can pull that sour look off your face, and he'll have her lawyer round too and be getting her nod to the dealer taking over the furniture. He's not getting away with that, unless you're too much of a fool to step in. Are you?'

Gwenyth said slowly, 'I'm not a fool.'

One word, a touch, and he might have woken. Sarah reflected on that and thought how ridiculous it was they were so close together and yet she could do nothing at all to help either of them.

The snore was the worst part and that was absurd too, but it was such a human sound, such at odds with murder and death and disaster that it was truly horrible.

She wondered afterwards if Valma had been outside the door, just waiting for the sound, because suddenly she was there, in Sarah's sight and, oddly, she was holding Roderick's pipe.

Only then did Sarah realise that Roderick hadn't had it with him, and strangely, fear seemed to drift away, to be replaced by a strange interest in what was happening. She saw that the pipe was alight. She saw Valma bend and place it on the carpet, beside a magazine that was tossed down to fall with pages askew. At no time did the woman look either at Sarah or the sleeping man at the bedside.

Slowly she straightened. She said, breathlessly, 'There'll be smoke. Lots of smoke. It's smoke that kills. Not fire.

Murray showed me. In a book. Things smoulder and burn and they give off poisonous gases. Once that happens it's a minute, or two – just that – and no one can live.' Her voice rose shrilly. 'So you see you won't know a thing about it. Not a single thing. There'll be just smoke and then . . .'

She went running across the room. The door slammed and the house was silent again, till another snore ripped across the quietness, to echo and die.

Just as I'm going to die, Sarah thought with a strange disinterest. The whole thing, now it had happened, was so unreal she couldn't believe that in a little while a tongue of flame would lick from the pages of the magazine by the burning bowl of the pipe, to smoulder the carpet, to spread and reach out in fingers of flame all through her room, while Roderick slept on and she lay silent and helpless; that smoke would come and cloud all the possessions she knew so well, and sweep them all, possessions and Roderick and herself, into oblivion.

She tried to call out, and there was only a strange, ugly sound. Another snore, she thought and then realised it was in her own throat. Sound had come back, strange, useless sound that was no good at all, but she lay there, filling her throat with it, mingling the ugly sound with the sound of snoring, till the absurdity of it, the cruel irony of it, made her weep.

———

CHAPTER 16

'I'm not a fool.'

Gwenyth sat stiffly upright in the doctor's surgery. She repeated the words. 'Though Esmay Laurence seems to think I am. I said to myself, Perhaps this is delirium and I thought you would know.' She added honestly, 'I wanted advice. It seems absurd and, you see, Esmay Laurence must know if the child went up the stairs or not, and she's quite right about one of us having fallen on it if it was around on the stairs before. We were milling all over the stairs. It couldn't have been there then. So . . .'

'So . . .' John Holden cocked an eyebrow at her. 'So you think I'll now take over and prove it one way or the other?'

She flushed. She said, 'I'm not a fool. I wasn't going to rush round there and start repeating that . . . well, what she says, but if the child didn't drop that yo-yo then it looks as though he did, though I don't agree with Esmay when she says he wouldn't play with a yo-yo. Quite often I've been surprised by the things people use as toys. I've seen businessmen – men you'd call hard as nails – play with trains, and those funny beads they say are soothing to the nerves. Oh, he must be a dealer's agent. Esmay must be right there but, still, to let her fall . . . oh, I know, she's right that people do terrible things for a very little money sometimes, but what do you think?'

'I think I owe young Rose an apology,' he said slowly. 'I proved her a liar.'

She started to speak, but he wasn't paying attention, he was thinking of Rose's toy that had seemed, if Rose was to be believed, to be playing hide and seek with another yo-yo, one with its paint intact. He said, 'We'll go round there. I want to question Rose, and apologise to her. I want to see Mrs Oatland too. She might know something about this. It's a surprising, but very true fact, that she knows more of what goes on in her house than most of the walking, talking rest. Now come . . .'

But Gwenyth was settling herself comfortably in the chair. With sudden coyness she said, 'Now I'm here, there's something I want to talk to you about, doctor. After meals I seem to get a twinge . . .'

How slow it was, Sarah reflected. There was neither smoke nor flame yet, but she could smell the tobacco burning. It reminded her of David. He'd often smoked in this room, though she'd as often complained that the smell hung to the carpets and the furniture and the curtains and that one day he'd go to sleep with it lying on the arm of a chair and they'd have a fire . . .

His deep, earnest voice seemed there in the room with her, saying, 'If there's ever a fire near you, Sarah, roll yourself in the counterpane or anything heavy and smothering, and fall yourself on the flame if it's only a smallish thing. You'll put it out with no damage to yourself or anything else. Remember Sarah, roll yourself up and roll on the flame.'

She thought, There's a thick counterpane to this bed, I could roll right off this bed, all in my blankets and counterpane and smother the flame before it runs away with everything, including our lives . . . if only I could roll at all.

She said heavily to the smile, 'I'd best phone the house now,' and then, because she simply didn't care if she was polite to him or not now, she added, 'It's not much of a play, is it?'

'The first acts are often disappointing. *Why* did you want to phone the house? Did you leave the kettle on?'

The mockery was acid, and she recognised it, her eyes narrowing. He doesn't like me, she thought. A few hours ago the knowledge would have been disturbing and shattering. Now it made her wonder why he had ever asked her out in the first place.

She said, fumbling with her purse, 'I want to make sure the old dear is quite comfortable and happy.' Deliberately she added, 'She doesn't like Mrs Phippses.'

'Oh dear, but we must make allowances mustn't we, for illness and old age and . . .'

'She's sixty-one. That's not old.' She held up a five cent piece and went to rise. 'I'm off to phone to make sure. . .'

His hand drew her down again. 'Relax.' Now the mockery was gone. He sounded earnest and sincere. 'I wanted you to enjoy this evening without worry, but I told Val if anything happened, if anything was wrong, to ring the theatre here and let me know. I left our seat numbers at the box office.'

She stared at him, grateful, her dislike of him mellowing a little. 'I must say that was thoughtful. I should have done it myself. I must be slipping, mustn't I?' She put the five cent piece back into her purse, making an effort now to be sociable. 'I didn't think much of that first act, like I said, but I must say I'd like to see what happens to the old father . . .'

'You will, you will,' he said soothingly. 'Just relax and stop worrying.'

There was something different about his voice, strangely different. She didn't recognise, till the lights were out, what it was, and then her cheeks flushed hotly, burningly, under the darkness, because she knew his voice and manner had been a parody of her own in the sickroom.

Rose said, 'I don't care.' She stood straight, her chin up, hands linked behind her back to stop them trembling, and her eyes wide and defiant behind the shelter of glasses.

Josie Abcons said tiredly, 'You're the limit! Ever since we came to this place there's been nothing but trouble, and now to catch you spying in windows! You should have been in bed, too. I told you to go there and stay there.'

'You told me I wasn't to talk again till morning, either,' Rose tossed back, 'and now you're making me.'

'In just one . . . oh forget it! Tell me exactly what you were up to, and one more bit of sauce and you'll collect a slap on the bottom, so remember that.'

'I went to see . . . if he was dead.'

Josie stared at her in astonishment, anger gone under a flood of dismay and worry, because there was no defiance now, no amusement, nothing but a kind of dreary acceptance of a duty that had had to be carried out.

Rose went on rapidly, 'I kept thinking and thinking and I couldn't sleep and I had to see and I sneaked out and she was there. She's not up in Mrs Oatland's room at all, and it was queer. She was shivering and shivering. I could see her and all she was wearing was a slip and that was silly, because why didn't she have on a dress? And she was carrying the canary. Mr Palmer gave Mrs Phipps a canary. He brought it with him. It has a green cage and I heard him tell her every house ought to have a cat or a dog or a bird, and as he didn't think she'd be allowed the first two he got a canary, and Mr Phipps said, "Well, I suppose it won't eat us out of house and home" and he sounded real grudging about it, but Mrs Phipps made out it was sweet, and she loved it, and she made a terrible fuss over it, but she couldn't love it at all. Not really, because she was out there tonight, just in her slip, like I said, and she was carrying the canary in its cage, and she put it under the trees in the garden, then ran back inside again. And there're cats come into the garden at night.'

Josie was frowning. She ran her fingers through her short-cropped hair and said in despair, 'This place is crazy. Absolutely and utterly crazy, and the Phipps pair seem the craziest bit about it. Listen . . . oh no, wait . . . but yes. Rose, show me the canary.'

When they stood beside the covered cage, Josie stooped to lift the cover. The tiny bird gave a faint whistle, but stopped when the cover dropped again. Josie said slowly, 'It's . . . oh, I don't know. I thought it might have died, but this is a mad thing to do.'

'She said she loved it, but she doesn't.' Rose's voice accused her in the darkness. 'Why don't you go inside and ask her why she put it out here?'

'No. I shan't do anything of the sort. It's none of our business. Just the same I'm not leaving it here. You can carry it inside. In the morning we'll simply put it back.'

Rose said slowly, 'She was supposed to be sitting with Mrs Oatland while Nurse was out, but she's not. She's in . . .'

'Oh, for goodness sake, it's none of our business.' Josie stressed the words in her anxiety, then her voice dropped. 'Listen, pet, this disposes of your other problem. Mr Palmer's sitting with the old lady, do you see? They're up there, look.' She pointed. 'The light's on. They're up there playing the word game, so Mr Palmer's all right and Mrs Oatland's all right, and now the canary will be all right, too. Any more problems to be solved?' she asked dryly.

Rose nodded, 'Oh yes, why is she running around in her slip? That's silly, especially when she was shivering and . . .'

Josie put her hands to her ears. 'No, no, no,' she cried. 'The whole place can run around in their birthday suits for all I care. You just come inside and go to bed.'

Cornelia Bragg wasn't thinking of the play any more. It was dull and boring and the theatre was too hot for comfort. So were her corsets. She was acutely conscious of them digging into her midriff. She told herself bitterly it was like being in a cage, with the bars closing in tighter and tighter, to press into her flesh.

Like a cage, she thought, and memory showed her the

outside of the theatre, a steel grille and a girl behind it and a queue of people. She felt Murray Phipps's hand again on her arm and heard him say, 'Thank goodness we don't have to queue,' and felt herself steered again past the box office.

They hadn't gone near it, she realised sharply, so he'd lied when he'd said he'd told the box office their seat numbers in case she was needed.

She spoke quite loudly, so that several heads turned to stare and to hush her, but she didn't notice them. She repeated, louder still with shock, 'You never went near the box office! Why did you lie about it?'

It wasn't tobacco smoke now. Sarah was certain of it. There was a nose-tickling, unpleasant smell to it that spoke of burning dust, and threads of wool, of dyes and other things, that told her the carpet was beginning to smoulder.

Gwenyth asked, holding her breath on the answer, 'What do you think?' And the breath exploded. 'That you eat too much, swallow too much air and finally get a pain from too much everything. Tell me something, did you see that confounded yo-yo, after the accident?'

'Yes.'

'What did it look like? Did you pick it up?'

'Ye-es. It was just an ordinary thing. One you could buy at a chain store, I expect. A red one.'

'With a long chip out of the paint on one side?'

She hesitated, then shook her head. 'No. I picked it up and I remember I turned it over, but it was just an ordinary red yo-yo. I put it down again, out of the way. Why?'

He didn't answer. After a moment he said, 'There were two of them then. The one I found, after it was all over, was Rose's – she admitted that. She said all along the one she saw after the accident had no paint gone. You confirm that. Yet the one I found was Rose's, with the paint knocked off. So there were two of them.'

He stood up. He said violently, 'It's not safe for Josie and Rose to be in that damn place, do you realise that?'

She started to run after him as he made for the door. She babbled, 'What about my aunt? Why, the man's a criminal! What about my aunt, alone in that house with . . .'

He stopped, said, quite calmly, 'Do you know, I bet that old girl would be a match for anyone, even Phipps, and even in her condition.

Sarah knew it was the one hope left. Her throat was raw with effort and there were no words, only that horrible grunting that disgusted and shamed her, but it was coming louder and louder as the seconds ticked on and she forced it out to fill the room with ungainly, ugly sound.

And Roderick Palmer was stirring. She could see first a leg twitch and then a shoulder heave, then his chin lift a little, and his jaw slacken, his lips parting, and then dazedly his eyes opened, to close again, then re-open and finally focus on her, vaguely and then in astonishment and rising shock.

He said thickly, 'Sarah,' and his nose wrinkled, head lifting more and she knew he was smelling that horrible smouldering of the carpet.

Her throat strained and fought, and suddenly they were there, words formed from that awful grunting, straining and croaking through the room in a great shout, formed of memory and David's advice, 'Roll on it, roll on it!'

For just one minute wild hope and triumph was there and were as abruptly gone, before his gaze unfocused and his head drooped, the shoulder slumped and the leg twitched and sprawled into a new position, and there was nothing left, because her voice was gone, and her throat was completely silent again.

———

CHAPTER 17

He tried to catch at her arm, and caught her sleeve instead, but she didn't care that she was almost dragging him from his seat, or that she was falling over feet in the darkness and that voices of protest were raised all over them.

Anger held her and continued to hold her in the face of the usherette's flashing torch and soft remonstrance, and willy-nilly he was forced to follow her out into the foyer.

She saw with satisfaction that his smile was gone, and maliciously she thought how wise he had been to keep that eternal smile fixed there, because his mouth in repose was mean and ugly, altering the whole expression of his face.

She asked, 'Why did you lie to me? You never went near the box office at all, so they didn't know where to send a message – if one came.' And then as his hand touched her arm again she said flatly, 'Oh no, you're not keeping me here. That play's a lot of rubbish.' With a mere gesture to social politeness she said, 'It was kind of you to invite me, but I shouldn't have come. I know I bored you with the talk of the old dear, and you didn't want me fussing, but telling a lie like that is wrong. Wrong, do you understand? And no, I shan't go back inside. We might as well go home.' Again she made a bow to social politeness. 'I'm sorry if I spoilt your evening, but I shouldn't have come. I'm a nurse and now the old dear is on the mend she needs me more than ever.'

Now the smile was back. He said lightly, 'All right, I was

wrong, but I didn't want to go haring off after phones, that was all. Come and have coffee and something to eat at least before you go back.'

She said, 'I'd rather go back,' with a stubbornness he knew wasn't going to be thrust aside by anything.

His smile grew broader. He said, 'Just as you like, I'll get a taxi,' and, anger dying, she followed meekly where he led.

She was still meek and quiet as the taxi began to move. It wasn't for some time that she asked, 'Where on earth are we? This is opposite to . . .'

He laughed then. 'To a restaurant I know. Oh come on, Cornelia, don't be a spoil sport. This was my evening out as well as yours. I'd booked a table out here anyway. I wanted your advice about something, and I'm dashed if I'm going to tell you my troubles with old ladies listening and people popping in and out and walls talking.'

'Walls talking?' she echoed slowly.

The smile grew broader. 'A-ah, so you don't know. Your patient's been holding out on you, has she? Well I shan't tell you till we're in the middle of supper. Now, do we go?'

She didn't want to, but she wanted to know what he'd meant by a talking wall. Sulkily, determined to show her displeasure in spite of her curiosity, she settled back in her seat.

She wanted to know about the canary. That was Rose's main thought. She wanted to know a whole pile of other things, too, but the canary was at the top of the list. She told herself that Mrs Phipps was cruel and terrible to leave the tiny bird out in the darkness where cats would come in the small hours and try to claw it through the bars. Even if they couldn't reach it it would be frightened half to death, she knew. She wondered if Mrs Phipps had any idea of that or if – and the thought was absurd – the woman thought a canary was like a cat and had to be put out at night.

When Josie had left the bedroom, Rose simply slipped from bed again, swung herself on to the window sill of the wide picture window and jumped lightly to the ground on the other side. She didn't think about getting back. Getting out was enough for the moment, she considered, and soft-footed, in her pyjamas, she slipped round the side of the house.

Only one of the downstairs windows was lighted. She went to that and stared. The nylon net curtains let her see through clearly. It was obvious that Valma Phipps thought no one would come prowling round behind the high wall that circled the garden. She was sitting in a chair by the bed, quite still, wearing only a pink cotton slip, and her face was blankly gazing into the mirror.

For a moment Rose could only remember Murray Phipps looking into the mirror and speaking of the future, and she wondered if that blank-eyed face was seeing things there in the glass, then the woman moved, got up and went out of the room.

The windows were long ones that reached right to the ground and they weren't locked. Rose's small hands opened them and her thin body slipped inside. She couldn't hear a sound as she moved across the room and out of it and through the lounge towards the hall door, but there was light now from her left, towards the kitchen.

She knew she was going to get into trouble, but she didn't care. She wanted Mrs Oatland quite desperately. Mrs Oatland listened, and it was a listener she wanted, someone who'd listen carefully to the story of the canary and then answer questions about it.

Mrs Oatland would do all that, Rose was sure, and Valma Phipps wouldn't be there to interfere. There'd be only Mr Palmer and he listened, too.

She went up the stairs silently and then stopped, because the door facing her was closed. She went to it slowly and edged it open and then stopped, because there was a strange, horrible noise from inside. She nearly closed the door again, and then she smelt it – a strange smell that matched the horrible noise. Everything in the room, Rose thought, was suddenly horrible and she was frightened.

She shoved the door fully open, staring in and it was all her nightmares and fears come to life because she was sure Roderick Palmer was dead. He looked dead and there was smoke and a voice crying, 'Roll on it, roll on it!'

She wanted to run away and couldn't. There'd been such desperation in that dreadful cry that she couldn't go without answering it, but it had made no sense at all, then she saw the curl of smoke, the flicker of flame and it was instinct that had its origins in that throaty cry that drove her to the bed, to pull off the counterpane and throw it over the smouldering carpet and tiny flame and stamp on it, over and over, up and down.

She turned and was afraid all over again, because they were both dead. She was sure of it, and soft footsteps were coming up the stairs. She wanted to hide and absurdly, she fell to the floor and tried to crawl under the feather counterpane and then realised how stupid that was. She stood up again, dragging it with her and flashed to the wardrobe, opened it and tumbled in.

The keyhole was big and like a great shiny eye. She could see through it clearly. She could see Valma Phipps, still oddly dressed in that slip, come in and stand and stare and mutter and bend, with trembling hands, and a box of matches, over the carpet and the burned patch. Rose saw flame again and then the woman was gone.

The house seemed suddenly to come alive. There was that dreadful unvoiced cry from the room again, and the phone shrilling from the landing and the front door chiming from below. She shoved open the wardrobe door and ran. She didn't want Mrs Oatland now, or Roderick Palmer. She was sure they were dead and she was terrified. She ran down the stairs, still trailing the scorched counterpane, and threw open the front door.

She tumbled into the doctor's arms. Her voice babbled, 'That's why she took the canary out. She really and truly loves it. And she didn't want it to burn. But she did, them, she hates them, but not the canary. Don't you see that?'

All that day the wall talked to Sarah. Bragg had, first thing, drawn her bed to the window and Sarah was glad of it doubly, because from there she couldn't see the scorched patch on the carpet.

She lay there, quite content, not even regretting her lost voice. It had come when it was needed and it would come again, she was sure, and other things, too – the first faint stirrings of life through limbs and spine and body. They'd come back in time, she was certain now, and for the moment she was right in the stream of life and living, because the wall talked unceasingly. Though the whole house knew of it now, it was as though they'd decided on a conspiracy to draw her into everything that happened, because all day they talked and acted out their hours in the room below her.

Only one thing Sarah didn't know – what had happened to the Phipps pair. It was something she was glad she couldn't even ask, because she didn't want to remember them.

She had listened to Bragg, and Bragg had a different voice that morning for the police. It had been smug and complacent and just a little bit excited, as the wall had whispered, 'I was beginning to see exactly what he was like, you know, and it was the wall that did it. I was fed up with him and his blessed smiles and I kept thinking of him blaming poor Rose for that accident, and I was telling myself he was a nasty, cruel type and all of a sudden I remembered the way the old dear was upset when she'd been against that wall after they'd arrived, and she'd never been that way before, and I just leaned forward and asked him bluntly if he'd said things to upset her, just for the fun of it and I told him I wouldn't put it beyond him.

'His face gave him away and I just got up and left and went to the phone. He couldn't stop me that time. There were too many people round. Oh, of course I was too late to be of any use . . .' her tone had been dissatisfied then '. . . but when there was no answer, everyone being too busy then to answer it, I just grabbed a taxi and came back.'

Afterwards there had been Rose's small breathless voice speaking of the mirror and the future and saying, 'I thought he was dead, you know, like Mr Phipps saw in the mirror. He looked dead, and so did Mrs Oatland. I'd have run right away without doing anything, only a voice spoke, but I'd never have been there at all if it wasn't for that little canary. Maybe I'll be allowed to keep him and look after him, because we're going to stay.'

And Josie Abcons's voice, with some of the sharpness and stillness gone from it, so that it sounded younger and happier, broke in to say, 'The doctor's suggested I leave my job and become housekeeper and nurse help here and live here for board and lodging and a little cash. I'd like to, actually. I think she's marvellous, that old lady. Mrs Furlong doesn't want to stay on either.' Her voice had rippled with amusement. 'She says she won't work in a place with talking walls that babble of murder.'

Later still there had been the doctor's voice saying, 'Of course I'll be round here a lot, Josie, so you won't . . .' and her tart reply, 'It sounds as though I'll need to plant an apple tree – an apple a day, remember?'

'I'll send you one, if you really want it,' he had said quietly, and there'd been only silence, to be filled later on by Gwenyth's voice demanding, 'What are you whistling? You've been doing it all morning.'

It was Roderick Palmer's voice that answered. 'Just an old song. A bit before your time, possibly. It's about a girl who stood out among a million others.'

'For heaven's sake – with all that's been happening . . .'

'Haven't you eyes in your head, Gwenyth?' he asked, and his voice had been quite angry, 'Haven't you noticed there's a woman in a million round in this house? By the way,' he had added dryly, 'I wouldn't get too set on having that dresser if I were you.'

'You're all certain she's going to get better,' she began, and he broke in.

'She has to get better. I have to show her my own home, and my favourite towns and cities, and you needn't look as though you think I'm an old fool, Gwenyth Oatland.' His tone rebuked her, and the wall questioned loudly, hopefully, 'Am I an old fool now, Sarah?' And then she regretted her lost voice because there was no answer, not even a wink, even if he'd been there to see it, because her eyes were filling with tears at his soft question, 'Am I, my spunky girl in a million?'

THE END

Patricia Carlon was born in Wagga Wagga in 1927. She was educated at various schools in New South Wales before settling in Sydney. She continues to write, is a prize-winning cook, a keen gardener and lives surrounded by her cats.

She has written everything from articles, short stories and serials to short and long novels. Her work has been published in Australia and England under various names in daily papers, magazines and on radio. Much of her pseudonymous writing has been romantic fiction. Her most substantial work, however, encompasses crime and thriller novels, of which she has published at least fourteen. These were first published between 1961 and 1970 in England, mostly by Hodder and Stoughton in the King Crime series. Many have also been published in other European countries and her work has been translated into seven languages.

She was awarded Commonwealth Literary Fellowships in 1970 and 1973.

Her crime novels were not published in Australia, rejected in the sixties because publishers there, in her words, 'didn't want anything but police procedure stuff.'

The Whispering Wall is a suspense story peculiarly and definitely an original. As readers, we are continually teased by echoes, half-remembered murmurs from movies once seen, stories read and put aside, plays once enjoyed. It is a tribute to

Patricia Carlon that despite a number of similarities with other works in the genre this novel is unquestionably *hers*.

We are reminded of the opening sentence in H.P. Lovecraft's gothic horror extravaganza, *The Rats in the Walls*, 'The oak-panelled walls were alive with rats,' scuffling, busy but unseen. Behind Carlon's whispering wall are the murderous plottings of human rats who are seen as well as overheard. Indeed, they share the refinements of their schemes with one of the victims, supremely confident that they can never be reported or discovered.

On first reading we are reminded of Lucille Fletcher's famous radio play, *Sorry, Wrong Number*, about a bed-ridden hypochondriac who telephones her husband's office, overhears two men planning a murder, and slowly comes to the realisation that she is to be the victim. Unlike Fletcher's desperate, trembling woman, however, Carlon's Sarah Oatland is self-possessed, intelligent and convincing. The continuing conversation in her head is so intimate and detailed that we want to scream out in maddened frustration.

The murderous plotters in *The Whispering Wall* are tenants who have taken over part of Sarah's own house, bringing to mind Marie Belloc Lowndes's *The Lodger* (1913), which, as well as being the first treatment of Jack the Ripper in a novel, is still one of the best suspense thrillers ever written.

What makes Carlon's book either superior or equal to these classics is her skill at locating unexpected threats and terror in the ordinariness of a house's timetable and objects, in making everyone seem dangerous, even the innocent, and especially those who have Sarah's well-being at heart.

The idea for the book developed when with friends Patricia Carlon started telling ghost stories in her two-storeyed house in front of its sealed fireplace. She wondered what would happen if someone woke in the dead of the night and found 'the spooks' talking. This terrifying notion finds its echo in *The Whispering Wall* in Sarah's helplessness to control the goings-on in her own house in the face of an invasion by a cast of strangers: the vulgar and knowingly unsentimental Nurse Bragg; the has-been heart-throb, Palmer; the anxious and worn-out single mother, Mrs Abcons; the arrogant doctor; the greedy insensitive relative, Gwenyth, waiting for the chance to sell-up; and the real heroine of the book, Rose, the anaemic, confused but sharply precocious eleven-year-old. Carlon casts her as Sarah's voice, imperfectly heard but, in her innocence, doubly dangerous.

Among these familiar types is the ever-present sense of dislocation, the terrifying feeling that time and space are out of joint, that no matter at what time of day the story unfolds, the events are set in shadows.

In this claustrophobic tension, Patricia Carlon makes it all believable by attaching the reader to 'normal' life. Much depends on the house's interior (the furniture, the architecture); the domestic arrangements; the observations of character – Gwenyth's greed and snobbery, Rose's mother's possessiveness, Palmer's vanity, Bragg's slyness – and Carlon's colloquial speech: 'There she was, only as lively as a fish on a slab'; 'If you take the fairy pills you'll grow two extra ears'; 'I can think of someone who needs an extra pair of ears'.

This novel belongs to the tradition that sees the crime novel as a superior form to the romance and the conventional spy thriller. Its strength lies in the drama created by the clash between good and evil and in the satisfaction gained by witnessing innocence endure. At the back of it all is Patricia Carlon's ability to keep us intent on the page, fixed with expectancy.

PETER MOSS AND MICHAEL J. TOLLEY